FIRE FINCH

PRAISE FOR JT LAWRENCE'S
THE MEMORY OF WATER

"So riveting that I read it from cover to cover in a single sitting."

- LITEROGO

"I loved this literary approach to the crime novel ... Slade makes for a strangely enticing protagonist."

– BOOKED UP

"Visceral and dripping with voice."

— MICHELLE WALLACE

"This book is a dark journey into a bewildering maze of memories and experiences, some real, some imagined ... if you are willing to immerse yourself in a mind that is disintegrating right before your eyes, strap in and hang on."

— WP, Amazon reviewer

ALSO BY JT LAWRENCE

Why You Were Taken (2015)

Sticky Fingers (2016)

The Underachieving Ovary (2016)

Grey Magic (2016)

How We Found You (2017)

THE MEMORY OF WATER

JT LAWRENCE

FIRE FINCH
www.firefinchpress.com

The Memory of Water is a work of fiction.

Names, characters, places and incidents are the product of the author's imagination or are used fictitiously. Any resemblance to actual persons, living or dead, events, or locales is entirely coincidental.

2017 Paperback edition

ISBN-13: 978-0-620-74655-7

2nd Edition

Published in South Africa by Fire Finch Press, an imprint of Pulp Books.

www.jt-lawrence.com

Book design by Mandie Van der Merwe; adapted by author

In Memory of Laurence Cramer

THE MEMORY OF WATER

"So here we are again, with the cold-eyed, cold-hearted artist,

the one who has sacrificed himself for his art

and forfeited his human ability to feel, but this time there's a distinct

suggestion of a pact with the devil.

Not only the heart has gone, but the soul has been lost as well."

- Margaret Atwood, *Negotiating With The Dead.*

A MONUMENT TO LOST CAUSES

My little sister's body was blue when they pulled it out of the river. Such a small thing, she was. Usually the shock of it would make one disillusioned, confused, blurry. Not me. I was startled into detail. Shocked into being the most alive I had ever been. Her sleeping lungs made mine gasp for air. I was electrified by the green of the river reeds, strangled by the summer air; everything else out of that moment was washed away by the gurgle of the persuasive current.

The men were taller than trees, the men who helped. They had heard my high-pitched flailing but not in time.

Afterwards, the grey tree-man couldn't leave Emily lying on the ground. Cradled in his arms, her wet dress stuck, resolved, to her body. He tugged at it, as if to cover her, as if to shield her, but not in time. He was planted in such a determined way it seemed that he would never again move from that bit of land: a monument to lost causes. The other man sat on the bank, gulping, head wobbling on shaking knees. He had tried to revive her with a combination of violence and care, unsure how much the porcelain body could endure, desperate to get her drifting heart pumping. He went from savage breastbone-beating to gentle kisses and back again. Gasping, shuddering, all four of us dripped.

We waited for the screams in silence and dread.

PART I

"An idea that is not dangerous
is unworthy of being called an idea at all."

- *Oscar Wilde*

I.

At Least Someone

Is Having An Interesting Morning

In darkness: headpounding, stomachswimming, eyesitching.

I reach for the bottle of San Pellegrino I keep next to my bed. Someone has taken it.Bastard.

No, that's not right.

The neighbour's junker is grumbling. Jack Russell barking.

I left the bottle in the den last night, was using it to top up my whiskies. Amateur mistake. I raise my eyelids just enough to get a bright slice of white ceiling.

After a few shallow breaths I stand up and fall down. Starsinhead. Dizzy. Make it to the coffee machine and flick the red switch. It growls.

Scratch my stubble. Brainonfire.

The morning glare through the kitchen window is

ruthless. I close my eyes for a while to give them a bit of a rest. I need to piss and shower and eat something greasy. Breakfast at Salvation Café. A double Bloody Mary blitzed with raw egg and Tabasco.

Now warm, the coffee machine grinds, blasts and spits. The fridge is vacant apart from some old oil-blemished pizza boxes, crystallized balsamic syrup and a never-opened jar of mysteries picked up at the last organic market with Eve. I should never go to organic markets. And I should never have bought such a leviathan fridge. Peering into its airy innards makes me feel lonely. It never used to be this way. This appliance has seen its fair share of riches: countless bottles of Veuve Cliquot and glittering round tins of Russian Caviar, like gold coins for giants. Now it sits, sulking, vacant, desolate. My heart is an empty refrigerator.

The milk is beyond rescue and it swirls down the sink trap. I stir the coffee too hard, slopping it down the side of the mug, leaving an eclipse on the pale marble slab of the countertop. I'll clean it up later.

Like the walking dead, dripping hot mug in hand, I stagger to my writing desk in the den to survey the damage, taking care to not trip over the piles of books lying in the way. It doesn't look too bad at first glance. Doesn't look too bad at all till I see my murdered Moleskine lying like a dead animal on the edge of the bureau, creamy belly exposed, inky guts ripped out.

*

"*You* look like shit."

"Thanks. I look way better than I feel."

It's been a wreck of a morning so far and smiling hurts. I kiss her on the cheek and grab the chair in the shade, not too close, in the empty hope that she doesn't smell the stale whisky leaking from my pores. I put my phone on the table beside her bunch of keys: her silver apple keyring glints in the sun.

She is dressed up. I wonder if she is meeting someone after breakfast. Another man maybe, or a sponsor. Or maybe it's a shoot: apart from being an artist, she's a partner in a small film company. I am immediately jealous.

She lowers her very large sunglasses slightly and takes a look at my sorry state.

"Did you party too hard last night with what's-her-name?"

"Kind of," I grin. Ouch. "You could say that."

Eve sits back with her arms crossed. She always has her arms crossed. She's always disapproving in a hot librarian kind of way.

"So? How are things with her? What's her name again?"

The waitress arrives with menus too big to be practical. I struggle with mine and almost knock over my pre-ordered double-hot Bloody Mary.

"It's over. So it doesn't matter." I mumble, but she gets the gist.

"Why am I not surprised?" She sighs, closing her menu

and setting it down on the table. "What happened?"

"I broke it off last night."

"Another non-surprise then." She makes a show of yawning. Taps the table leg with her ballet flat. "Very boring, Slade."

This jabs me in the stomach. There are not many things I fear more than predictability. Being a bore: I find that terrifying. She knows this and indulges me with a half-smile, to show that she was half-kidding.

God, Eve is sexy in her tailored ivory suit and bare pink lips. Jackie O shades. Although she looks just as desirable in the paint-stained oversized men's collared shirts she works in. And her ponytail. I love her hair in a ponytail. What I wouldn't do to grab ... I realise I am daydreaming and try to remember what it was we were speaking about. I hide behind my Oakley's: this *babbelas* is making me feel a thousand years old.

Ponytails, lips, yawning: Ah, whatshername.

"Well, it wasn't working. I had to end it. She was no good."

A man from the adjacent table glances over, curious, then turns away before I can tell him to mind his own damn business.

"No good for your writing, you mean."

"Yes. Well, it's the same thing, isn't it? It's not like I can be okay without my writing."

It's all I have.

I didn't tell Eve I broke the news to the woman early in the evening so I could get home in time to work on a few notes. It didn't work: nothing came to me. In the end I – apparently - finished a bottle of whisky and tore up my notebook. Which is becoming a habit.

I ignore the flash of annoyance in Eve's eyes. She nibbles a nail.

"How did she take it?"

"Fine."

"Fine?"

"Not as heartbroken as the accountant, not as happy as the talk-show host. Somewhere in between. Pretty neutral, really. I think that's what I didn't like about her."

"Her grace? Equanimity? Even-temperedness? I can see how that could be very unappealing."

The waitress is back with a hopeful look on her face.

I clench my fist. "She didn't *give* me anything."

The man looks over again: I can feel his eyes on me. Who is he? A fan? A spy? An assassin? I glare at him and he immediately begins to inspect his sunny-side-up. Nosy fucker.

"I bet you didn't give her anything."

I look into the distance and adjust my scarf against the breeze. We order the Brie omelette and Caribbean sweet

French toast with maple syrup, berries and organic cream. A giant pot of Earl Grey.

What Eve didn't know was that karma had burnt me just that morning. The hangover wasn't the only thing nudging me to the edge. As I had lurched from my writing den to the front door and turned the key, I heard a car door slam shut outside and burn rubber. I remember thinking: at least someone is having an interesting morning. I'd made a distracted effort to close my dressing gown over my old Iron Maiden T-shirt and grey jocks, put on my sunglasses to mitigate the evil brightness of the Johannesburg sun, and opened the door. Nothing looked out of place but I'd had a strange feeling in my gut, which may or may not have had something to do with the previous night's Glenfiddich. A few cool, barefoot steps later I had the newspaper in one hand, coffee in the other, and felt a little better about life in general. Until I turned around.

It wasn't that bad. I mean, she could have thrown a Molotov cocktail through the window and burnt the place down altogether. She could have pulled an Al-Qaeda and detonated some sweet-smelling plastic explosive on the front lawn. She could have hired a Casspir – Mellow-Yellow - and mown the house down. That would have been worse. Instead she had graffiti'd 'SLADE HARRIS YOU CUNTING FUCK', all along the front wall in a particularly fetching shade of crimson. I still haven't decided if I enjoyed her creative license with the shoddy punctuation and the transmutation of the word 'cunt' into an adjective. Anyhow, it has a certain ring to it, and it's certainly not easy to forget. Full marks for punchiness. Standing there the cool morning air on my still bed-warm thighs and admiring her work had a kind of justice in it, I suppose, for I have hurt a lot of women and it seems time that one of them has become intent on punishing me. It is unfortunate, however, that this particular one happens to be a psychopath.

When I get back from breakfast with Eve I am still a little jumpy. I keep picturing Sally standing motionless outside my house, looking straight ahead, the epitome of calm apart from a single spray-paint-stained hand. A street version of Queen Macbeth. The idea unsettles me a bit, so I like it. Not because I'm fearless: the opposite is true. I spend the rest of the day avoiding walking past windows and don't open the door to anyone, not even the feather-duster man. I like it because having a beautiful, persistent, bunnyboiler ex could be very interesting.

And I am desperate for interesting.

2

Likefatherlikeson

A few days later I wake up with a grim sense of purpose. It's Emily's birthday. Born two years after me, she would have been thirty-six today. I can't really imagine it. She is frozen in my mind as she was on That Day – tangled hair, summer freckles and a milk-tooth smile – all but bursting with sunshine and promise. And here I am: limping towards forty with the bleakness that comes with age. Knowing the dull pain of the thought that I am past my prime. Some people peak at sixty, I know. It would be nice to look forward to something like that. Instead of what I have.

She probably would have done more with her life than I have with mine; had more meaning. Chances are she would have had a family with a faithful (read: tedious) husband and two little scurrilous sprogs. Dogs, too. She would definitely have had dogs. She would be like those yuppies I used to jog past in the morning with their golden labs and 4x4 strollers, who run right past people like me, who are more like the red-cheeked, defeated-looking fat man being pulled along by his huskies.

I arrive at my father's house in Belgravia with a bottle of Johnny Walker and some food supplies from Fournos. Every now and then I do a bit of grocery shopping for him. Like me, he is always more grateful for the whisky. Grumpy, but grateful. Likefatherlikeson. I do it out of guilt more than feelings of benevolence. I've never been particularly kind. I just feel the guilt weighing heavier and heavier the longer I put off seeing the old man; eventually I have to go just to salvage what sanity I have left. Shopping postpones the moment I actually have to start spending time with him, so it's usually a pretty drawn-out affair. There is always a new bottle of pickles to inspect, or a fresh artichoke to stroke. In *The Godfather* Don Corleone says that a man who doesn't spend time with his family can never be a real man. I guess I've never really been one.

I press the buzzer on the gate. It will take him a while to reach the front door so I wait, watching the paint peel. God, I wish he'd listen to sense and get the hell out of this place. It's so grotty. Probably not the safest neighbourhood, either.

I feel I am being watched so I look around a bit, feigning nonchalance, trying to not look like a paranoid white man. No one needs to know that I am a paranoid white man. Who isn't suspicious, in this country, where a healthy sense of paranoia keeps you alive? Stupid people, I guess, and people who have given up. I wind my watch.

The house takes up the entire block and is fenced off with dark, rotting planks. The gaps in it, like decaying teeth, serve as an invitation to opportunistic thieves. The front door is opposite a municipal park, full of drunken sun-sleepers and litter and lazy lovers with arses too big to sit comfortably on the knee-high gum poles of the wooden perimeter. In The Bad Old Days the grass was green and the playground full of bright new colours. Loiterers would be chased away (if you were black you were a loiterer, white – a visitor). I remember the taste of the painted metal of the jungle gym, I'm not sure why; I suppose kids try to taste everything. Metallic, cool and hard, with a softer, thick paint-skin.

I ring the bell again, just in case he didn't hear it the first time.

We used to be able to play there under the casual eye of my mother, who, more often than not, seemed far more interested in the depths of whichever paperback she happened to be reading, than in anything we were doing. She would shake out an old Transvaal Scottish tartan blanket, as if in preparation for a family picnic, then instruct us to have fun while she eyeballed her own version of make-believe. She'd flick her gaze up at us now and then for a headcount, not really seeing, but making sure we were still there.

I fell once, around the back of the house. There's a giant oak tree in the backyard. Staunch and towering, it will probably outlast all of my family's line.

I was climbing, probably showing off to Emily. The boasting made me feel cocky; overconfident. I don't remember why I fell, perhaps my foot slipped as I was scrambling, or my arm grabbed for a branch that wasn't there. But I do remember falling and what a strange feeling it was, actually being airborne. And then the *crunch* of backbone-on-land. Emily's scream. Little bubblegummer footsteps taking off to summon help. Not knowing what the warmstickyspreading feeling was on my back. I thought I should stand up, so that I wouldn't get into trouble. But I couldn't, so I stayed splayed in the shadow of the tree. Granny was first to run out, wiping her hands absent-mindedly on her ragged apron, her eyes trained on me. She never saw the need for hysterics. Decades of volunteering at the Red Cross, two dead husbands and a near-fatal car accident made her immune to dramatics in general. A Dutch immigrant with more common sense than you could shake a stick at. But she was running.

"Slade," she had said without alarm, "are you alright?"

"Yes," I said, or perhaps I nodded.

Yes, just fine. Except that I couldn't get up.

She used her cool, dry palms and swollen-knuckled fingers to feel for broken bones. Emily wailed in the background and was roughly hoisted, one-armed, onto Dad's hip.

"Can you stand?" Gran asked.

All eyes on me, I tried again, and it worked. I must have been numbed by the shock, earlier. I remember looking down on a smashed stack of tomato crates. You don't see them nowadays but they were made of rough-edged plywood strips held together with little nails. I had a blade of the wood wedged in my back, as if I were the victim of a half-hearted game of junior vampire slaying. A shallow wound, eager to bleed, but at least the sickening crunch hadn't been my spinal cord.

The lock of the door jiggles. Through the textured glass panels I see the large stooped figure that is my father. Stuck behind the black bars of the pedestrian gate, I watch his mottled silhouette fuss with the door until finally it opens, and he shuffles out on to the verandah, giving me an indignant look.

"Have you just arrived?" he demands, giving me no time to reply. "Why didn't you ring the bell?"

Does he think I'm an idiot? That I would just skulk here arbitrarily until he decides, on a whim, to open the door?

"I did, Dad," through clenched teeth.

"Well, are you sure? I didn't hear anything."

Don't lose your patience, Slade. You've got a good few hours to get through.

"Maybe it's broken. Here, let me ring it again."

I jab, with more violence than strictly necessary, at the button with my index finger.

"Can you hear it?"

"Of course I can't bloody hear it now. I'm standing outside!"

He is dressed in old tracksuit pants and a faded blue cardigan. There is a toothpaste stain on his shirtfront. His voice shakes with indignation. I would also be indignant, if I were him. If I'd had his life, his past.

"Come on, Dad," I say, "let's go inside. We'll sort this out later."

The interior of the house is a museum. Scratched wooden floors, faded Persian carpets, Vermeers staring down at you, their dusty eyes following your movement through the house. Cheap prints of *Girl with a Pearl Earring*, *The Milkmaid*, *The Astronomer*. Chandeliers with their original light switches.

In the children's rooms, huge oak built-in bunk beds as big as boats. Enough space for eight adults per room, never mind the children. In the bathroom, black and white floor tiles and a large, sloping bath on claws with enough of an angle to slide down if Gran's feeling mellow enough to let you splash around a bit. Emily being scolded for licking the pink soap which smelled so good. God, I wish he would just sell this place. Hanging onto it like a sentimental old fool. I sniff deeply and rub my temples. The memories are suffocating.

I dump the plastic packets of food on the maroon linoleum floor and hear something break. Typical. I don't want to get a rag and clean it up but I do. I carry the whole packet to the sink. He has laid out a box of water crackers and a tin of sardines for lunch. Sardines and vomit occupy the same little space in my brain, along with the smell of boiling tripe. My father is a millionaire but he eats oily fish out of a can as a treat. My grandparents took the whole post-war economic to heart, and my father seemed to inherit it. I would go as far as to say I think he actually *enjoyed* the recession. Just another justification for his white-knuckle-tight fists. I spend money like water. I think sardines are cat food. It's 2011 for God's sake. The war has been over for more than sixty years. It's the age of globalisation and consumerism. Spending money like water – where does that come from? It's not mine – it doesn't taste right in my mouth.

It was the stuffed olive jar that broke. Not too much damage done, everything else in the packet just needs a bit of a wipe. I pick an olive out of the broken glass and pop it into my mouth. I can't resist. I have the vague feeling that Francina is going to jump out from behind somewhere and scold me, which is what happens when I drink milk out of the bottle in my own kitchen. The olive is salty and I move it around in my mouth to feel its smooth, oily skin. I let my tongue trap it on the roof of my mouth, bruising it to release a little juice. Perhaps it'll be worth the shard of glass I may unknowingly swallow. It would be a pretty undignified way to leave this earth. I can see the newspaper headline: 'Famous Local Author Dies After Eating Stray Glass Shard'; or, worse: 'R.I.P. Slade Harris (Previously Famous Author).'

I know a guy who died choking on a piece of toast; I swear I'm not making this up. He was an alcoholic and crack addict most of his life and he lost everything he ever owned, including his wife and bewildered kids. He finally puts his life on track and chokes on a bloody piece of toast at the breakfast table. Maybe that's worse. Maybe, maybe not.

Dad shuffles in wearing his *stokies*. I can't believe how shabby he's looking. He is starting to smell like an old person. The sour scent of decay. What is it exactly? I try to work it out. Damp wool; un-flossed teeth; cat food; cheap aftershave. I give him an uncharacteristically generous smile. We have the same green eyes. His eyebrows are long and bushy, he has untrimmed nose and ear hair; I wonder how it feels for him to look at me and see this younger version of himself. It's probably a good thing I don't have kids. They would remind me of my decline and I'd resent the buggers. I'd probably have a lot more grey hair if I were a father. I went the safe route: I had books instead of kids.

He clears his throat noisily as if no one else is in the room. Living on your own makes you do things like that. You're used to being alone and lose the need to be polite with your bodily functions. I've lived alone for twenty-plus years now and, despite years of resisting it, feel my own slide into this hermit-like comfort. Open-mouthed throat-clearing at high volume is the least of it.

Dad opens the vintage fridge and takes two clinking bottles of beer out of the icebox. For however long either of us live I will always associate that sound with him. It's a friendly, comforting sound, like a wine-cork popping, or a gas ring being lit.

"There's a match on," he announces.

I knew. Of course I knew. Arsenal versus Chelsea. It's the perfect excuse to spend time together without talking. Especially without talking about Emily. Arsenal doesn't stand a chance.

"Really?" I ask, wide-eyed, "Who's playing?"

*

That night I go to a Mexican bar in Melville and get drunk. Family seems to have that effect on me. A lot of things seem to have that effect on me. The music is loud and upbeat and there is a huge portrait of Frieda Kahlo on the wall. I eat quesadillas that make my mouth burn with their fresh green chillies and I sip gold tequila: fighting fire with fire. 'One fire burns out another's burning' – I think that's Shakespeare:

Romeo and Juliet.

I went to Mexico once on a journo assignment. Wouldn't mind going back. Maybe a Cuba-to-Cancun cruise is what I need: a slow yacht, with warm sea air and crushed-ice cocktails; maybe lick a little coke off dark-skinned girls in metallic bikinis. God, I definitely need something. Sometimes I feel like I've done everything and that there's nothing new out there. Maybe I'm just a bit burnt out. I signal the bartender to top up my glass. He looks wary but does it anyway. What I need is a fresh, exciting experience, one which will bring the words back to my fingers. I need to think about it; perhaps when I am sober.

Feeling sentimental, I think back to Mr. Robinson, an English teacher I had in primary school. The only teacher with whom I ever really connected; an eccentric man who wore hats and had perennially ink-stained fingers. He never took any notice of me until I wrote an essay about our family dog, Maxwell, going missing. He was a vicious *brak* stray my parents had adopted when they were still young and idealistic. He tore up couches, swallowed shoes whole, and attacked trembling old ladies. By the time Emily and I started school he was corpsestiff with arthritis but he tried to bite us anyway with his black gummy jaws.

Mr. Robinson used to spout writing tips at us as if we were all aspiring Kafkas. It was about writing The Truth, he said. He quoted Hemingway: 'All you have to do is write one true sentence'. Then Merton: 'We make our selves real by telling the truth.' I was entranced. Money? For words? Words that had come so easily when I recounted Maxwell's short, crabby life, and the mystery of his disappearance. It turned out that my first muse was a dog.

Phuza-face glowing, eyes popping, Mr. Robinson taught me the oldest and most controversial writing lesson of all: to be able to write well – that is, convincingly enough to make your reader feel, *really* feel, your story – is entirely based on your experience of what you are writing about. Many experts have since rubbished this notion or seconded it, but I know that it is my truth. I have tried again and again to write purely from imagination but I am either stuck halfway through or end up so shamed by the prose I burn it (a delete button is sometimes not enough to purge yourself of truly horrible work). And so between Mr. Robinson and Vicious Maxwell (R.I.P.) I was able to learn my secret to great writing. And experience, as Oscar Wilde famously said, is one thing you can't get for nothing. As the tequila warms my throat under Frieda's monobrowed glare I wonder what my life would have been like if I had not been in class that day.

I wanted to write about the tree-climbing accident; I wanted to describe that feeling of weightlessness I had during the fall. But my mother was so angry with me I didn't dare ever bring it up again. She didn't speak to me for a week after the accident and when I offered her the shirt for washing, hard and stained with my old brown blood, she grabbed the skin on my cheek with her thumb and index finger and pinched it: a parrot-bite.

I never saw the shirt again.

I get up off my barstool without stumbling, pull some notes out of my wallet and slide them onto the well-worn, greasy counter, next to my dinner plate. Note to self: wallet feels a bit light.

Disgrace: 'spending money like water'. That's where I first read it; I wonder where he happened on it. 'No matter,' he says. An exhilaratingly desolate scene by Coetzee at his best, describing Lurie after the farm attack, when the dogs are shot and his daughter gang-raped. Alienated beyond the point of no return, Lurie sits in a sinking plastic chair surrounded by the smell of rotting apples and chicken feathers, feeling his will to live draining out of him like blood. Coetzee describes him as an empty fly-casing in a spider's web. The beauty. The bleakness.

I down what's left in my glass and leave.

Don't wait for experience to come to you;

go out after experience.

Experience is your material.'

- W. Somerset Maugham

3

SHE BROUGHT ME GRAPES

Just as I turn on the shower I hear my phone ring. I shirk it. If it's Eve, I'll call her back. If it's someone wanting money, I'm sure they'll be calling again.

I have the best showerhead in the world. It's the size of a prize-winning Camperdown cabbage and has fourteen different settings, all judiciously trademarked to halt copyright infringers in their soggy steps. I can choose anything from 'Waikiki Waterfall™' – a deep tissue massage which hurts like hell – to 'Rain Forest™'. It has lights that blink and change according to which setting you choose. The rain forest lights are the best for a hangover; dim with soothing flickers of green and yellow, although the misty water is a bit annoying if you want to have a good scrub. 'Monsoon™' is much better for that. Plus it reminds me of our Highveld thunderstorms, with its hot noisy jets and bright flashes. If I ever emigrate I'm taking this shower with me. Even the floor is perfect: it's tiled in some kind of natural stone that feels like suede underfoot. I'm trying the 'Desert Drizzle™' today. I like it. Despite the name, it reminds me of the eternally-saturated taupe skies of Berlin and leaves me suitably depressed. I love my shower. I tell everyone I know about it. I'll tell strangers, if they're interested and I find they usually are. I just think ShowerLux™ could have been a little more imaginative with their setting names. I would have more fun with 'Prison Hosedown™' and 'Tropical Tsunami™'.

I find myself rubbing my temples again. My brain is swollen on Jose Cuervo. I couldn't get my breakfast bagel down. I must stop drinking so much. A pickled brain is worthless to me.

I shower for a good twenty minutes, swapping from setting to setting, watching the lights change. The bathroom is steaming twilight. The dark fog swirls around me. I feel dizzy and then the lights go out.

I am woken by an hysterical black woman slapping me on the chest. I gasp and open my eyes. I seem to be splayed out on the bathroom floor. I touch my head and come away with bright red fingertips.

"Mister Harris! Mister Harris!" she screeches, as if someone is murdering her. She is on her knees beside me. There is a flurry of ebony arms in the air and high-pitched hysteria.

"What the …"

"Mister Harris!"

"Stop screaming, woman!"

Francina has always been a drama queen.

Oh my God, I'm naked.

Mid-screech, Francina recoils. I think she's just noticed the same thing.

"Mister Harris. You slip and fall! I find you here with water pouring and disco lights. I think you're dead."

"Okay, okay. Hand me a towel, won't you?"

"I think you're dead of heart problems like Ridge Forrester." She passes the towel and makes an exaggerated effort to look in the opposite direction as I fumble to stand. My limbs are marble. I shiver in wide tics.

"Bless you Jesus that I come in today!" she proclaims, arms akimbo. "You be dead without me, Mister Harris. And then I don't have no job. Bless you Jesus!"

Francina has the habit of blessing Jesus at every opportunity, as if he were a great sneezer. Sneezin' Jesus. She has also watched way too many reruns of *Gone With The Wind* and likes to model herself on Mammy.

"I don't think the situation was quite that dire, Francina," I say, not wanting to be reminded I owe her my life every Tuesday and Thursday for the rest of my life.

I've stopped bleeding but I have a handsome red slash on the side of my head. Using my shaving mirror I see that it's superficial and doesn't need stitches. In the hazy background the phone rings. Francina stands on the bath rug and looks at me, transfixed.

"I think I'll be alright now," I say, as a way of dismissal.

"Bless you Jesus," she whispers, and I am left alone.

Finally, dried and dressed, I put down some words. I can describe how it feels to be found, wet and naked, by a berserk domestic worker. I gingerly pat my wound. The pain is sharp and fleeting, like being cut by just the edge of a blade. My head is a little numb, my thoughts cloudy. Wrinkledskinbluelips. I can describe this. I can bring it to life in a way I would never have been able to do if it were yesterday. I've written a hundred words before I wonder what the hell I'm doing. I don't even have an idea for the new book but I have a scene of a sad man fainting in his overpriced shower. If my MacBook were a typewriter, I would yank out the page, crumple it up and slam it into the bin. Instead I drag the virtual document into my computer-world trashcan and feel empty inside.

Perhaps I'm being too harsh. Maybe it will lead to something. A knock on the head has led to all kinds of things in the past, most notably temporary amnesia in the soap operas Francina watches, where I'm guessing Ridge Forrester (R.I.P.) comes from. That could be the beginning of something. I open my Moleskine, crack the spine and pick up a pen. Man passes out in shower and when he wakes up, he doesn't know who or where he is. It could be interesting. Innumerable plots jostle in my head, the various confused, amnesiac protagonists elbowing each other and shouting to be heard. And then as soon as hope flickers, it is snuffed out. Amnesia is the lamest idea ever, by far the least original, hence its popularity in American soap operas where they can't have the CEO of the major fashion corporation die *again* ... unless you write it in a brilliantly innovative way, which has itself been done. Damn that genius Aranofsky. It's not often that I question my talent but today I feel I should be doing the coffee run for the writers of *Days of our Lives*.

I sigh and twirl my pen. Francina brings in a bottle of Italian mineral water and a sandwich on a side plate, then goes back for a paper serviette.

She must be feeling sorry for me – she is never usually this kind. It's ham and tomato on rye, with enough Dijon mustard to singe your sinuses. She must have done the grocery shopping. The cool heat travels up my nose and spikes my eyeballs. It feels good. Perhaps she thought I really was going to die. I suppose that's enough to make anyone feel generous for a day. Death definitely has a way of kicking you in the arse, forcing you to live.

If you survive it.

I spend the rest of the afternoon smashing my already-wounded head against the wall. I try free-association, reading the paper, reciting poetry, brainstorming, masturbating, listening to Lady Gaga, flipping a coin. It doesn't help. Poet Friedrich von Schiller had a habit of keeping nasty apples in his writing desk and sniffing them before starting his work. Auden preferred tea; Coleridge, opium. Kipling fantasized about having his own Indian 'ink-boy' to grind him fresh ink every day. I, on the other hand, would be happy with a burnt stick and a cave wall, as long as the words came. Writing has never been this hard.

I skydived once. I've been scared of heights ever since. It started well with a lovely lady-instructor, who went on to give me 'extra lessons' in my chalet the night before the jump. I was pretty blasé about it (the jump, I mean, not the sex. I was rather enthusiastic about the sex) and it sounds dull-witted, but it didn't actually occur to me that I would end up so very high in the sky. When the realisation struck and I decided that I couldn't possibly go through with it, I turned around to my lady-friend and told her. Either she didn't hear what I said, or she thought I was joking. She threw her head back, laughed, and pushed me out of the plane. In an instant I forgot everything she'd taught me, extramurally or otherwise, as I was caught up in sheer bowel-dissolving panic. I was so shocked by what was happening I didn't even have time to indulge in the whole life-flashing-before-my-eyes phenomenon, which I think I would have rather enjoyed. Luckily for me I was on a static line, so the cord I forgot to pull didn't kill me. My parachute lines were tangled, so I screamed and rocked from side to side which somehow loosened them. It seemed that Jesus (Bless You) was on my side and I remember a few moments of utter exhilaration as I took in everything around me: the topographical map beneath, the overwhelming amount of sky and, most of all, the silence. I have never since heard that startlingly clear complete absence of sound. I remember saying my name out loud as a way to assert my – meagre – existence. I was definitely having a moment. It was thrilling to the toes. I wondered why I had never done this before and swore it would be my new hobby. Which was when I saw the power lines. By then it was too late to do anything about it, even if I had remembered how to adjust my toggles to land.

I know it sounds like I knock myself out a lot but I don't, not really. I mean it's not a thing I'm known for. At a cocktail party you wouldn't introduce me as the accident-prone guy, or the bandaged/broken/concussion guy. I'm not the guy in slapsticks who falls into manholes and skis into trees. I don't even have a lot of scars. One fine line on my cheek from a scratch when I was a child. A small button on my back from the tomato-crate-stake. A silver gash on one of my fingers, hardly noticeable. Oh, and I don't have all of my teeth, not the original ones anyway. I can't tell the porcelain veneers from the real ones anymore. I've been bashed up a bit, that's true, but I'm just not that guy, despite all previous evidence presented to the contrary.

But I did have a concussion when I woke up in hospital the next day. Fractured ribs, smashed scapula and a collarbone broken in three places. A sprained ankle that took the longest time to heal. That's how I met Eve. She came to me like an angel in the night: a beddable Florence Nightingale. Sifiso had sent her with the latest artwork for a book cover that needed 'urgent' approval. How urgent can something possibly be? I had just looked Death in the eyes for God's sake.

Despite being exceptionally cheerful on all the morphine they were pumping into me, I disliked the artwork and told her so. As I was trying to check her out through the dark clouds of pain, the conversation went a little like this:

(SFX: convincing hospital equipment bleeping in the background, squeaking rubber soles of nurses on linoleum, et cetera.)

Eve (looking hot): "So this is where we are at the moment. Obviously it's still quite rough, a work in progress which needs crafting, but Sifiso wanted to make sure you bought into the concept before we refine it any further."

(Shuffling of papers and then: awkward pause.)

Me: "What? Is that it?"

(Everyone in the room pauses to look over at us.)

Eve: "Yes."

(Everyone in the hospital stops what they are doing to hear what comes next.)

Me: "Two months of work and I get this?"

Eve: silence. (Still looking hot. Red cheeks. Blushing. She must like me. I must show off.)

Me: "It's dogshit. I hate it." (Actually it wasn't that bad.)

Eve: "Oh … Okay. Maybe if you could you be more precise with …"

Me: "Precise? Sure. I wouldn't use it to wipe my arse. I think the artist should be stripped."

Yep, I'm that powerful.

Did I just say stripped?

Me: "Whipped, I mean. Whipped."

I make vague cuckoo gestures at my head to communicate the large amount of drugs circulating in my battered brain.

Eve crosses her arms. I am hooked.

Eve: "What I meant was, could you be more precise about what you don't like about it?"

The black clouds are getting thicker. I am riding on pink-purple pain-laced delirium.

Me: "The writing is post-modern, for God's sake. Avant-garde! It needs more chaos! More shaking up! Tell Sifiso I never want to use this piss-ant artist again. He has the talent of an … an … *aardvark*; and he clearly hasn't read my book."

I hammed it up a bit because Eve was particularly attractive and I thought she might end up thinking I was more important than I really was. Also, I was very high.

Despite being happily married – if there is such a thing, but that is a conversation for another day – Sifiso only hires gorgeous Girl Fridays. They are his own Playboy Bunnies in the little mansion that is his mind. Eve seemed to be the most delicious so far. I wanted to grandstand a little, fluff my tail feathers, show this pretty lady who The Big Guy was.

Eve (smiling): "That's a shame."

Me (caught off guard by her blazing smile): "Why's that?" I see rainbows. Lots of little rainbows emanating from her skin. Mmm, pretty.

Eve: "Because I was really looking forward to working with you." (Exit Eve.)

Me (under my breath): "Crap."

Then, on second thoughts: "Can I get some more morphine?"

Sifiso called me later that day to let me know how annoyed he was. He had spent weeks trying to persuade Eve to agree to do a cover for us. She was then an up-and-coming artist who was receiving great press for her latest exhibition and not keen to do anything too commercial.

Sifiso has a short temper and shouts a lot. He's short and shouty. Or perhaps shouty because he's short. He likes putting a lot of emphasis on the keywords in his admonitions; he especially loves shouting over the phone. Usually editors are quite nice to their writers, but not mine.

"She's an ARTIST!" he screamed down the phone. "A REAL artist! Not like the two-bit Corel Draw designers we usually get! I finally pull someone fantastic to do it as a FAVOUR and you tell her you'd like to WHIP her? What was THAT about?"

"I didn't quite say ..."

"You didn't know it would OFFEND her? Telling her she looked like an wild pig and that she should be BURNED at the STAKE?"

"Now, I don't think I quite said that ..." I mumbled, hoping to God that I hadn't. "But you need to shoulder a bit of the blame here, man. I mean what were you thinking?"

"What was *I* thinking?" he shouted.

Despite my shattered collarbone I was doing lots of forehead-holding and frowning.

Nasty silence from Sifiso.

"I was out of my head with the drugs! I was seeing in goddamn Technicolor! No wonder I was saying bizarre things. What did you expect? Besides, what on earth were you doing sending the artist on a run? Are things that bad?"

"*Eish*," he said.

"Don't speak Zulu to me. What the hell does that mean?"

"Slade," he sighs, "I am Xhosa." All I can hear is clicking.

"And?" I shout.

"And I had the courier all set up but Eve's such a great fan of your work, she asked if she could take it in person, so she could meet you."

"Oh," I said. Crap.

So Sifiso sent Eve flowers and I called to apologise. I outright lied to her and said that I didn't really remember much but, apparently, I had been rude to her and I was very sorry, would she please reconsider the contract she had shredded, burned and posted back to Sifiso. She laughed a lot and I knew from that moment that I liked her. She told me the contract was in fact still in fine form and sitting on her desk, and she would be happy to work on a new cover with us. It seemed Eve, unlike Sifiso and me, was a Grown-Up.

I'm sure she knows I'm in love with her but she's never been that into me. She is my Unattainable. Daisy Buchanan to my Gatsby. Rosebud to my Kane. Even though I live in hope, I know I will never have her. When I have sex with other women I am mostly fantasizing about Eve. Her petite frame; her generous tits; her cheekbones; her distracted glance; her creative mind; her short-nailed fingers. I am rougher when I think of her, and usually don't last long enough. I forget myself.

She cares about me, I know that. Even after I was such a prick to her in the hospital that day, she continued to visit to see how I was doing. That's probably when it happened. When I fell in love with her. Psychobabblers will tell you I'm obsessed with Eve because of my unresolved Oedipus complex, exacerbated by my mother leaving me at such a vulnerable age.

She brought me grapes, for God's sake. What did she expect?

4

SHAKING OFF SNOW

AFTER A LONG WALK HOME

"Harris, where have you BEEN?" shouts Sifiso into my ear.

"I've been around. What's up?" I think that maybe, if I'm really casual about everything, I will be able to diffuse his anger. I hold the phone away from my ear just in case.

"What's UP? I'll tell you what's UP!" he yells. Oh boy.

"What's UP is THIS: you've been AVOIDING my calls! Now why would you want to do THAT?"

I wind my watch.

"Are you angry about something, man? Want to talk about it?"

"You don't have time to TALK, my friend! That's unless you have been so quiet because you've been finishing the NOVEL you've owed me since FEBRUARY."

Eish. I didn't realise it had been that long.

Ha. Who am I kidding? Every month since February has slid by like barbed wire on naked flesh.

"Sorry. I wasn't avoiding you on purpose. Things have just been a bit slow around here. I'm battling with the ending."

More like, I'm battling with the opening sentence, but he doesn't need to know that. This seems to calm him down a little. He sighs, martyr-like, down the line.

"Look, Harris, I KNOW you don't need the extra pressure from me but it's my JOB, you know? I need to get that finished manuscript from you. Everyone here is breathing down my NECK." I visualise the veins in his neck almost popping out of the skin.

"Yes."

There is a welcome respite as he takes some time to gather himself.

"People are SAYING THINGS, Harris."

I harrumph at that. As if anyone would dare. I have more talent than this whole fucking city combined. I don't give a flying shit-arse what they're saying.

"What are they saying?"

"I don't want to upset you. I don't want you to think about it. I want you to concentrate on finishing the MANUSCRIPT. That's ALL I want you to think about."

"What are they saying?" I ask again, an edge to my voice.

"They're imbeciles. They don't know what they're talking

about."

"Sifiso …"

"They're saying you've lost it. You're dried up. BILTONG. You're finished."

"Oh." Expected, but it still stings.

"They say you only had three books in you and now you're empty. *Finito.*"

"Okay, I get the message."

"Kaput."

"Sifiso …"

"Toosuccessfultoofast. That it's over. IS it over, Harris?"

"Of course not. This one has just been a little slow. Tolstoy took ten years to write *War and Peace*, for God's Sake. Sometimes you can't rush these things."

I think I hear him stifle a chuckle.

"THAT'S what I TOLD them! And then I flipped them the birdie."

"Good."

"I told them to pick a finger!"

"Thanks, Sifiso."

"But it's still my ARSE on the line, my reputation, Harris, so for fuck's sake just FINISH IT!"

There's no way I can write after such a grilling so I decide to go for a walk around the neighbourhood, get some air. The air is fresh and the roads quiet. I suppose most people are at work. Thank Christ I don't have to sit in a smelly open-plan nine-to-five. Or have those humiliating office parties where you invariably end up vomiting punch into the accountant's dustbin, or shagging the half-conscious intern over the photocopy machine. Or have a manager of sorts, someone with receding hair and a *boep* who dresses in chinos and walks around in a loud tie with a mug in his hand, bestowing pie charts and spiky performance reports. The horror!

I walk past a little black cat that looks at me with dubious yellow eyes, sleek body poised, ready to dart. Skinny and elegant except for her short legs. Munchkins, I think they're called. Dwarf-cats. Perhaps if I weren't so selfish I would get a pet. Pets are good. Pets are normal. You can't spiral into the darkness when you have a dog to walk, a cat to feed. I've never really had my own, apart from Maxwell, who didn't really count. He had fleas that were more entertaining than him. And I've never really liked cats much. Too damn self-assured. And a little scary. They have this way of just appearing out of nowhere. Witches' familiars. Munchkin and I stare each other down. She's pretty. Despite myself, I want to touch her, so I take a tentative step forward. She's up and through the fence before my trainer touches the ground. I won't take it personally: I know thoroughbreds are skittish. I'm tempted to tell Starling & Co. to take a running jump with their three-book deal but then think of the advance money I have spent. Which is all of it. Despite the generous royalty cheques I get, I'm in a little debt. I'm a bit over my head with life in general. There's no need to panic, really. If I've written a bestseller before – three times before – then I can do it again. It will come, I sigh to myself, when the time is right. Bless you Jesus. I keep walking.

I'll never forget my first book launch. Sifiso was there from the beginning, a fresher face, a flatter gut, and hungry. Just as I was. He was a junior editor when he worked on my first book, *Mercenary*. He had rescued it from the slush pile at Starling & Co. and it became the book that launched his career, although you'll never catch him admitting to it. For the last decade we've shared an erratic bond that started with that scrawny manuscript. The book was about a woman who would do anything for money. I painted her as a cold bitch with just enough redeeming qualities to make the reader curious about what happens in the next chapter.

I didn't plan the novel at all.

The launch party was at the Grace Hotel in Rosebank, when it was still Something. My father came in an old suit and highly polished, scuffed shoes. I was so excited that evening, it seemed to pass in an hour, and at three in the morning Sifiso and I found ourselves stretched out on wide leather settees, the last to leave. He had the company credit card and we were drinking the last of many bottles of some Cap Classique and guffawing over our sudden success. He ended up giving me a lift home, not because of how drunk I was but because when we finally found my precious brand new Jaguar XKR in the parking lot, the tyres had been slashed and the doors keyed. The car itself seemed distressed and looked at me with blame in its headlights. Sifiso had been upset by this: he didn't understand why someone would deliberately drive a butcher knife into the handsome oily rubber of my Falken tyres, especially on such an important night. I acted as bewildered as he looked, even though I of course knew exactly who had inflicted the damage. The knowledge rang as clear as an alarm bell in my head.

I intentionally date women I think will yield the most interesting experiences. Warning signs on first dates, sending sensible men running in the opposite direction, guarantee I'm hooked. I like to think of them as sub-plots. Some sub-plots you should develop, others, not. Fay Weldon said that she was good with relationships, they just weren't very good with her. But she doesn't regret anything because it is all good copy.

There was Melany, who told me on our first encounter that she had father-issues (read: liked to get spanked). She taught me a lot about psychoanalysis and the Elektra complex. I used her for a short story. It was good. Eventually the relationship fizzled out: I could only stand to be called 'daddy' so many times before it became awkward. Then there was Vanessa. She was a sweet, pretty little thing, a most unlikely fan of S&M, or rather, M. She was a great character study for me: opened up a whole new world. She would take me to bizarre underground clubs and ask me to tie her up, which I did with pleasure. She had a walk-in cupboard of erotic outfits I had to write about the minute I laid eyes on it. It was like a costume department of a pornographic vampire film set. And the costumes weren't just for her. I liked the whips and studs and hot black latex but I drew a neat line at the gimp suit. I didn't mind the stuff that gave her a little pain without too much damage, but I wouldn't do anything that drew blood. She was disappointed but, as Clint Eastwood says, a man's got to know his limitations. The sex itself was mediocre. It was the only relationship I have ever left thinking that I hadn't hurt her enough.

Bella, on the other hand, was a different story. She was so clingy, so desperate that no matter how badly I treated her, she always came back for more. I didn't mean to cause her pain: I am a bastard but I do have some warmth in my veins; I had to sting her histrionic heart for her own good. She told me she loved me within a week of meeting me, tried to move in the week after that and, when that didn't work, tried to introduce me to her high-flier parents. I was cruel: I threw her clothes and bottle of Dior out of the window while it was raining and laughed out loud when she knelt in front of me, romcom-style, black spiders of mascara on her slipping down her cheeks, begging me to love her. I laughed. Not out of malevolence: the situation was ridiculous and I had a hard time taking her seriously. She would have fits of hysteria, tantrums where she would flail into my arms, stopping only when I crushed her against my chest, like a long-haired Fabio in some pulp romance.

And then of course there was Sally Ellis. When I met her in a cigar lounge in Sandton one evening, I knew I had to write about her. The warning signs were all there. A tall, beautiful, redhead (the red hair should have tipped me off but I was, for a while, in her thrall) who seemed mentally stable, intelligent, independent, had fantastic taste in shoes, and a villain in the sack. It was just asking for trouble. The initial month passed with me wanting more of her – a first – so we kept it going for a while longer. We had fun, made each other laugh, got on so well that I began to worry that I liked her company too much.

One night, when the relationship was still half-shiny, after too much to drink, I told her about Emily. No details, obviously, it just came up that I used to have a little sister. I had never told anyone even that. An almost-honest moment and – I should have known better – way too honest for me. Afterwards there was too much emotion in the air, it became hard to breathe. I began to think of reasons I didn't like her, but she didn't need much help from me. Her claws had already begun to show. It was as if she had been pretending to be someone else – which she was very good at – but every now and then her mask would slip. In hindsight I guess we were playing a similar game. It took me over two months to get her into bed, but the conquest was about more than sex. I crept into her life and absorbed everything I could. I found her complete lack of warmth fascinating. Behind the mask she was a cruel woman, she treated people abysmally. I had feelings for her. She would humiliate cashiers, chastise waiters at full volume and screech at beggars at intersections to get their grime away from her car. In the beginning the sex was incredible, but that also slipped and towards the end she was aloof and distant. I think I actually used the words "fucking [Sally] was like mounting the abominable snowman, but not as much fun". Not my most poetic line of prose but you get the picture.

She stopped seeing other people and, I guess, she wanted me to do the same but I have a philosophical objection to monogamy. I just don't think it's natural. If you consider all the adultery in the world you have to either believe that man is inherently bad, or that monogamy is just not sustainable. I think that monogamy is a concept created by our forefathers for our own good: a bit like the Koran, or the Bible. The point of printing those wordy epistles was to make the world a better place. Monogamy, as a principle, would mean fewer illegitimate children and venereal disease, with more solid family units to make everyone feel safe. Most countries wouldn't elect a president who fucks a different woman (or man) every week, preferring to go instead with Happily Married. I guess that makes our country an anomaly, unless you accept polygamy with benefits as a solid family unit. Clinton was thrown out for enjoying the most famous blowjob in history: our guy not only has five wives, but feels the need to shag his groupies on the side. Monogamy, like communism, appears to work only in theory.

I tried to explain this to Sally but she was a little slow on the uptake. Bit by bit I began to realise that one of her (many) personality flaws was jealousy: not the subtle, flattering variety but more the certifiable kind. I joked with her, quoting Hanif Kureishi, asking why people who are good at families have to be smug and assume it's the only way to live, instead of being blamed for being bad at promiscuity. She didn't find it funny. I did. She asked me what the hell I knew about family; that's when it started going very much downhill. I, being very good at promiscuity, used to send her flying into acid rages. Her true character came out in exchanges with other people when she would snap, bite and break people's necks (metaphorically speaking), like some kind of easy-on-the-eye Tyrannosaurus. It was magic material. I got more words down during that relationship than I ever had before. Once the fighting started in earnest and I had leached absolutely everything I could from her, I didn't hang around for long. It felt like our elaborate dance was over.

I turned out the manuscript in record time.

I remember feeling relieved, elated. I had this stupid smile.

I took her to the most public restaurant I could think of to break up with her, an expensive oyster bar in the Square. By then I didn't even find her attractive anymore. Those cruel green eyes, thin lips, flat chest, insipid skin. It was like shaking off snow after a long walk home. After helping myself to another glass of chardonnay from the bottle and finishing her naked pink prawn starter, I had to stop myself from skipping out of there. It was my first successful novel. But, I thought as I looked at my wounded Jag, it came at a price.

The threats started a week before the release, when the good reviews hit the press, culminating in the unfortunate tyre-slashing episode. I may have let it slip while we were dating that I would use my first advance cheque as a deposit on the car of my dreams. She knew the car, freshly driven out of the dealership, was my Achilles heel, and forced her cold kitchen knife right through the fantasy. Tyres mutilated, she Picasso'd the doors with her car keys; the gun-metal grey paint never looked the same. Sifiso advised me to lay a charge against her but I couldn't. I had no proof that it was her and I felt that I did, in a way, deserve it. I had more than enough money to fix it, and to buy the whole indoor soccer club beers the night Frank and I christened her PsychoSally.

She has mostly left me alone since then and only leaves threatening messages on my cell when she has had a particularly bad day, or sees something that reminds her of me, perhaps a steaming turd, or a particularly angry, infected boil, so I am surprised at the venom in this latest attack. Perhaps there is a sequel to *Mercenary*? A deranged ex is very fertile ground for a story. Little sparks of beginning-thoughts start glinting in my mind until I sit down with a pen and my new notebook. Then they disappear: snuffed out by the pesky winds of self-preservation.

I hope that Francina knows what to do about the writing on the wall. I guess the whole neighbourhood now knows where I live, which isn't great for privacy. Already paranoid, I will now have to deal with Gawkers.

I moved to this neighbourhood in northern Jozi because I felt people here were rich enough to mind their own business. The Parks: small lock-up-and-go stands on beautiful tree-lined avenues. The kind of suburb that reminds you that Johannesburg is an urban forest. I knew I didn't need a heated swimming pool, jacuzzi or sauna, nor did I need the cottage with the sky-lit studio. I definitely didn't need the huge porcelain-tiled kitchen but I must admit that I do like the gadgets (electric and gas plates, giant Smeg fridge, Juicerator, Smoothie-maker, ice-maker, ice-crusher, mini blow-torch, glass toaster with matching panini press, seven-tiered steam machine, wine-cooler, cappuccino-maker …) and God knows I don't need the other five rooms. But I do love the north-facing one – which I like to call the den – with its double-volume pressed ceilings and the way the light floods in there in the mornings. It is by far the most enchanting working space I have ever had; the two novels I wrote following *Mercenary* enjoyed their gestation in there. I guess, in a way, I have PsychoSally to thank for it. By the same token I could also thank her for the ridiculous, hefty bond repayment I have to make every month, which will probably contribute to the heart attack I will eventually have, causing me to fall (panini press in hand) into the bubbling jacuzzi and, therefore, to my eventual demise, securing her the best revenge without so much as the knowledge of it.

It's not that I don't know I sabotage my life. I'm completely aware of the fact I could lead a pretty normal life if I didn't purposefully fuck everything up so much. But what would I do with a petite housewife in Abercrombie & Fitch and two little thugs for children? What would I write about if I spent all day drinking freshly-pressed beetroot juice laced with vodka and taking the Weimeranas and/or ungrateful kids to the park, seeing the same Smug Marrieds for dinner every Friday night? Perhaps I'd have a demanding silk-smothered mistress, one who makes me lick her stilettos and promise not to leave my wife. Or a stripper prostitute in a scabby hotel room once a week, in a vain attempt to inject some form of dirty excitement into my sad little life. I doubt it would be very entertaining by anyone's standards. Yet this alternative way of living, the one I have chosen and designed with such care, is catching up with me. I feel myself being sucked into the widening gyre. *Things Fall Apart.*

Sometimes I wonder if I even have the right to exist. If I am my own invention, isn't it the same as saying that I am zero to the power of zero? Tapping this foot, tossing this paper ball into the air. Bret Easton Ellis says in his *Lunar Park* that if one gives one's life to fiction once, it becomes a character. A shadow of the real thing. No, less than that: a shadow of a shadow.

5

MAYBE EVERYONE ELSE WAS RIGHT

Francina lets herself in, as she always does, and stomps her way into the kitchen to make cappuccinos for us. It must be Tuesday or Thursday. By the time I join her she has my paper open on the kitchen table and is halfway through it. Her feet aren't up on the table but you get the feeling they are.

"You're out of rusks," she mumbles, licking a finger to turn the page. It is clear that an article has captured her imagination.

"There are some in the larder," I say, not knowing how I know this.

"No, Mister Harris, I mean the good ones from Woollies. The pecan nut ones."

My flat white is strong and hot with lots of foam. The kitchen is already clean – it's been Francinarised. I wouldn't cope with a life without Francina. She cooks, cleans, washes, dusts, irons and polishes like a Stepford Wife, without the creepy hairstyle. She wears the best get-up of anyone I know.

She's sixty in the shade but she is always trying something new. Long, preppy socks wrapped around her chunky legs one day, head-to-toe primary-coloured traditional garb the next. Today she has on a yellow raincoat (there's not a cloud in the sky) and the biggest golden hoop earrings I may have ever seen. She says she spends her (generous) wages on unit trusts but I reckon she likes to buoy the economy with it too.

Also, she makes good snacks.

Francina tears herself away from the newspaper just long enough to look me up and down and furrow her brows.

"You going to wear that shirt, Mister Harris?"

"Is there a problem with this shirt?"

She shrugs and goes back to her reading.

I go to the bedroom to change.

I arrive at Eve's place at one o'clock. She hates it when people are late, finds it disrespectful, so I always try my best to be on time. Ironic, as I'm usually the one that keeps women waiting. She has been a little cool towards me since our breakfast last week, so I thought I'd invite her out to lunch and attempt to charm her with my beguiling ways. I think she's still annoyed with me: she said she didn't have time, so I offered a quick one at her place. She thought I meant lunch.

She opens the door wearing one of her work shirts and an old pair of jeans. She smells of oil paint and Chanel.

"Ouch," she says, eyebrows raised, then points to the laceration on the side of my head. "Did you get into a fight?"

I follow her through the apartment and into her studio, watching her hips sway in front of me. Christ, it's hard being near her sometimes. Especially knowing there's a bed in the next room. Not that my juvenile fantasies of her ever really include a bed. Mostly it's up against a wall, or in the front seat of the Jag, or the heated pool, or on my kitchen table. But now I can imagine doing it here in the studio, getting covered in paint and …

"So what do you think?" she smiles at me. I feel like a puppy that's been caught chewing a Manolo.

"Huh?"

"It's for the bank. The triptych I told you about."

Eve's studio is always covered top to bottom in paintings and sculptures, so you have to pay attention if you want to look like you're not an idiot. There are new drawings of dolls – girls and men and animals – all over the walls. The triptych is easy to spot because it's shining wet. And it's the biggest painting in the room. It is of a nude stretched voluptuously across the three panels. Very dark. Erotic.

"God," I say.

"Do you hate it?" she asks with big eyes.

"No, I think it's exquisite."

She smiles like a little girl and takes my hand.

"Now you know why I am so busy. I need to finish it by next week."

"Nothing like a deadline to kick you up the arse," I say, not smiling at the irony.

She leads me into the studio's kitchenette and we begin unpacking the lunch I have brought.

"How's yours?" she asks.

"Firm but soft to the touch."

I can't believe I said that. I'm a complete imbecile. Eve is gracious and gives me a skew smile.

"I meant your deadline."

She fills the kettle, switches it on and I start to build our sandwiches. Eve is a tea zealot. I keep quiet while I wait for something to say.

"Have you come up with anything good? For your book, I mean."

I groan and pretend to be overly interested in the olive ciabatta I am sawing.

I don't want Eve knowing how desperate I really feel. Anyway, I am bad at this, this intimate dialogue. I have always felt silly saying I am having a bad time. It's self-indulgent. It makes me think of bald kids with leukaemia and makes me feel like even more of a dick, standing here, making a faux-Mediterranean lunch in my nine-hundred-rand-sneakers.

"All writers struggle at some point, even the greats," she says, as she pauses to lick balsamic syrup off her finger.

"Especially the greats. You're just spoiled because all your other stories came to you so easily." She pours two cups of what looks like urine into old mismatched mugs.

"It just … it feels different, this time."

"It'll come. I believe in you."

We take the Brie, kiwi and watercress sandwiches through to her makeshift office in the corner, where there are two fold-up chairs and a table. The walls are covered in illustrations and photos and the room is like an artwork in itself.

"Sifiso's all over me like a venereal disease."

Venereal disease? Why would I say that in front of Eve? Now she's going to associate me with herpes, chlamydia, gonorrhoea. God.

"Yes, well, he's especially good at that," she laughs and tilts her head. "So what are we going to do to get you over this … whatever it is?"

"I have to do something huge. Something that will eclipse all the others. I just need to figure out what that is."

Eve makes a face to show me she's thinking.

"Run a marathon?"

"Done it, and regretted it profoundly. Ended up at the half-way mark in a pub somewhere obscure with no way to get home."

"Take ecstasy, acid, tik?"

"Yawn. Centuries ago."

"Date a … er, I don't know. A transsexual?"

"You know Palahniuk joined a sex-addiction support group? He attended a whole lot of meetings to try to understand what it was about. So that he could write with compassion. So that he knew he was writing the truth."

"So what are you saying? That you're not the only crazy writer in the world?"

"Maybe not the only one."

"How about moving to another country?"

"Gee, thanks."

"I mean temporarily, to get a new story."

"Done it. A few times. But Marrakech '98: unbelievable. That's where the camel story comes from. Obviously. And then of course there was Bangkok." Where I ended up staying a little longer than I had planned.

I don't like talking about Bangkok.

A Thousand Camels, despite the unfortunate name, was one of my most successful short stories. It probably paid for my shower.

A Thousand Camels (digested)

by Slade Harris

A dashing British pilot ardently pursues one of the terrific-looking cabin crew (think Paris Hilton, but with a personality) who has overly-shiny golden blonde hair straight out of a Pantene ad. She plays hard to get because she knows he is married but gives into his advances. (Impossibly romantic scenarios of their courtship in all the beautiful cities in the world and lots of hot, slightly bizarre, hotel sex follow). So far it's a steamy Mills & Boon romance. This is where the story starts, when the relationship is stripped of its glossy plastic wrapper. The stewardess becomes jealous of the time the pilot spends with his wife and kids (no surprises there). Her bitterness starts eating away at her perfect complexion and she diets compulsively. She screams at him when they spend time together. The pilot, who started off banging a perfect cherubic goddess, now has to put up with a spotty, skinny banshee who's closed for business. He has a feeling that his wife is suspicious ("Another overnighter? Who with?") so he decides to break it off with Paris. Paris has other plans. While they are in Marrakech she tells him that if he doesn't leave his family to be with her, she will go to his wife and tell her everything. She reminds him that she has photos from their more adventurous days. He gives in to her blackmail and assures her that he will break it to his wife when he gets home. The next day they go walking in the market, smiling and bargaining, holding hands, when all of a sudden her hand is no longer in his. He looks around but can't see her anywhere and raises the alarm. It appears that Paris has been kidnapped (the stewardesses are warned before the stopover in Marrakech and Egypt to not go out alone, especially in crowded places, especially if they are blonde, because of the frequent rate of kidnapping in these areas). Late that night in a seedy bar, the pilot has the need to unburden himself to the bartender (this is the bartender I met, who told me the story – entertaining guy – I ended up spending many a night drinking sweet wine and eating schmutzullas *at his bar). So he tells the bartender how clever he is: he managed to sell his overbearing mistress to a local tout who offered him a thousand camels for her. So not only did he manage to rid himself of his little problem without bloodying his hands (not immediately, anyway) but he also made a lot of money. Ha ha (dusting of hands), ain't life grand? Another whisky please. And one for you.*

What he doesn't know, of course, is that the night before the pilot visited the bartender, Paris was confiding in the very same guy. She told him that a week ago she had given her best friend, an air stewardess she worked with (pretty brunette by the name of Jo), two 'parcels' to post in case of something happening to her. Each were identical in contents: the aforementioned dirty photos, a copy of a dated, scribbled erotic note, with a voice-recorded message of Paris saying that she was sorry for the pain that she had caused. One was to be sent to the pilot's wife and the other to the police. Ha! said the bartender. Ha ha! Wasn't that just the funniest thing? It had made his evening, he said. There was now the chance that the bastard pilot he was looking straight in the eyes would see the inside of a Marrakech jail cell, Paris would probably be rescued and all would be well in the world. Ha ha! That's what made him love life, he said, the way things kind of work themselves out. I told him I thought it was a fantastic tale and would definitely do something with it. He poured me a drink and said that wasn't the end of the story. I started wondering if he was pulling my leg with the whole thing. He assured me he wasn't. Then he tells me that the pilot was a bit unsteady on his feet so he called a 'friend' to come and collect him and, who else showed up but a doting little ear-kisser called Jo?

The End

True story! According to my friend the bartender, anyway. So sometimes speaking to people pays off. Look at Yann Martell. *The Life Of Pi* was Martell telling us the story of what that old codger in the tearoom in India told him. Hungry and broke, Martell wanders into a packed café and has to share a table with this old guy, who rolls into action, saying that he'll tell Martell a story that will make him believe in God. And hey presto! Suffice to say he probably isn't poor any more.

I must say, the pressure to speak to every obscure person I meet does pinch my balls. Most obscure people, in fact, have nothing to say at all. By that I mean they have a lot of words, but not a lot to actually say. The pain is exacerbated by the fact that I'm not really a people's person. I mean, I don't even really like people, in general. I find most of them a little dull and feel my finite life ticking away, when Mrs. Someone from Somewhere starts telling me what she thinks of the proponents of local trade razing the underprivileged foreign markets which depend on our currency, I have been known to throw my head back and yawn in otherwise polite conversation. You'd think that would put a sock in it but you'd be surprised at how many people don't get the hint.

"Bungee jumping?" volunteers Eve, sipping her tea.

"Skydiving trumps bungee jumping."

"Especially if you end up snapping your collarbone," she smiles. We look at each other for a while.

"You bought me grapes," I say. I can hear my heart beating.

Eve giggles. "What?"

I swallow, wipe my lips with a knuckle.

"You bought me grapes when I was in hospital."

"It's sad that you remember that," she laughs, teasing me. I play along. I laugh. I take another bite out of my sandwich. The truth is out: I am sad.

Eve is tender with me and asks if I am okay.

"I'll be okay," I say, playing it down, thinking of the bald kids. I absent-mindedly wind my wristwatch. It's like a nervous tic. Eve knows me too well. She dusts the crumbs off her fingers and comes to sit on the table near my chair. She puts her hand on my watch and looks into my eyes.

"You are going to be okay," she says.

The watch was a gift from Eve when I finished my last book. It's platinum. I find it is both a gift and a curse. A gift, because every time I look at it, I get warm twinge in my chest, thinking of Eve. A curse because it tick-tocks. Time itself is a gift-curse. Time says: 'Look here! Here is a precious moment to do something with!' Then as soon as you try to grasp the moment, it's gone. And you haven't done anything. And while you're thinking about that, there is another moment, and then it too is gone. Cruel, like an eternal game of pass-the-parcel.

After seeing Eve I am melancholic. I seem to be melancholic more and more these days. I actively push pictures of my shuffling, slippered father out of my head. I decide to go for an evening walk to clear my head, shake some endorphins into my bloodstream.

A quick confession: I feel dirtyguilty that while Eve was outside on the phone to someone I excused myself to go to the bathroom and instead, I crept into her bedroom. I didn't mean to do it but as I passed I caught a glimpse of her bed through the half-closed door and took a step inside. And then another step. Then before I know it I was stroking her headboard and smelling her pillow like a spooky stalker. I had picked up her perfume and was about to spray it before I came to my senses and fled the room. I worry that this is the onset of unpredictable bad behaviour. I am not a man who loses control. My whole life is based on control.

I kick a stone. I can control the stone.

I see the Munchkin again. She is sitting upright with her chest out and her paws elegantly positioned in front of her, like a Negro sphinx. She seems hardly bothered that I'm almost in her personal space so I inch closer and reach out to stroke her and again, she runs away.

My cloudy mood deepens into a thing of despair. I am empty. I feel like I'm being sucked into an existential vacuum. Usually when I hear the word 'existential' my eyes roll into the back of my head. Meaning Schmeaning, Life is here for Living. But today I feel like I may be missing out on something. That stomach-heavy idea you get on dark nights that maybe everyone else was right.

As I am falling off to sleep that night I hear a car purr to a stop outside my house. My eyes fly open. Oh God, I think, it's Psychosally with that Molotov Cocktail. I lie in corpse position: paralysed. I hear light footsteps outside. I wait for an explosion, or automatic gunfire, or the ragged revving of a chainsaw. I breathe as quietly as I can. Just when I think I'm being over-suspicious I am jolted out of bed by a racket of glass shattering. I cry out. The car drives away. I run towards the noise: I need to find the bomb before it blows up and takes my house with it. I stumble in the dark, trampling the broken glass, hyperventilating, till I find the missile. I pick it up and am about to hurl it out when I realise it's a rock.

"We are like the spider.

We weave our life and then move along in it.

We are like the dreamer who dreams and then

lives in the dream.

This is true for the whole universe."

- *Upanishads*

6

AN ISLAND TO RUBY WATER

Mood today: Much Improved. I've had a fantastic idea. Instead of moping around in my bandaged feet and infinite loneliness I'm going to throw a party. It will be the thing of legends. Think Malletier, think Hugh Hefner, think of the champagne-guzzlers in *The Great Gatsby*. I'll have the best caterers, buy the best booze. We'll be gorging ourselves on Beluga and Kristal, oysters and Veuve, abalone and Campari cocktails. I'll order two hundred fresh oranges, and someone to squeeze them. I'll invite the paparazzi, to keep them off my back about the new novel. Sifiso, too, of course, ha! He'll never know what's hit him. I'll get a DJ – God knows this house is big enough for one. I've never really had a proper housewarming so I sort of owe it to the place. These perfect wooden floors have never been danced on! This lounge has never had the sablesticky pleasure of a chocolate fountain! My couch has never had … oh wait, it has.

Okay … so … guest list … Eve. Sifiso and his wife. Uhhh. Frank From Football. Do the hired help count?

Me. Do I count?

Oh, I can invite Francina. She's always up for a bit of a jive. She'll bring a few mates. It will also make me look a bit more PC, having a few friends 'of colour'. They will probably also be the only ones who, strictly speaking, can dance. Note to self: remember to put chicken on the menu. I can invite the neighbours to stop them from calling the police at three in the morning when there's a naked drunk bloke singing on their front lawn, setting off the sprinklers. It's happened before. I developed a nasty chest cough afterwards.

But clearly that won't be enough if I want this party to be of gargantuan proportions. This is probably when liking people comes in handy.

I toy with a few different party concepts before deciding on 'Moonshine'. I had 'Poirot' (murder mystery party: cheesy), 'Memoirs of a Geisha' (with attending Geishas and naked Japanese nymphs wrapped in cling film and sashimi: done, done, done), 'Naked Lunch' (fig leaves for all: but reckoned Francina had been through enough without subjecting her to Mugwumps and the Interzone), and 'Monty Python's Flying Circus' (cheerful midgets, tightrope-walkers and fire-eaters would be fun, but it's just not literary enough), and in the end I settled for something a bit more conservative, for the simple reason that I realised in a flash of wonder and light (yes, I was in the shower) that I *am* actually Jay Gatsby. A few decades late and the wrong nationality, as am decidedly un-American, but I am the man who made Fitzgerald famous. Not quite as gay (I don't wear white suits and panama hats but I do admit to having episodes where I throw silk shirts around the room like a psychotic ballerina). And of course there's Daisy.

I sigh at the evidence: I have an unreachable star.

It's tempting to go as far as to say that I've modelled myself on Gatsby, but I know it's not true. I was unhinging my life years before I even picked up a battered copy. Mostly it's about being a figment of my own imagination. Meet Slade Harris, the tragic protagonist of his own life.

I have no friends and yet I am throwing an extravagant party. I have ordered 200 oranges (why 200? what am I going to do with the left over 196?) and have all but forsaken my family. As I write I create my life and the reverse is also true.

Like Gatsby, I'm a fraud. My whole life has been engineered, contrived. So much so that I don't really know who I am or who I was or who I'm meant to be. In moments of melancholy I see visions of myself floating upside down in my pool, an island to ruby water. There are worse ways to go, I assure myself, there are worse ways to go.

7

CONDEMNED TO BEING A SILHOUETTE

The band is testing their equipment and the bar is overstocked. I had someone scrub the graffiti off the front wall but there is still a faint scar. Hopefully no one will be able to make out what it says in the evening light. I cleaned up the broken glass and taped clear plastic sheeting to where the window used to be. I make last minute checks, smiling woodenly at the caterers, feeling ridiculous in a tux, wishing someone would arrive. Looking at the sky, hoping the weather will hold out. Winding my watch. I've always been insecure about parties. No matter how many people RSVP I still end up with pre-party jitters, thinking no one will come. Or worse, two people will come and see through the wormhole what a sham my life is, then leave without bothering to finish their pink gin and tonics, tripping out of the front door because their eyes have rolled so far back into their heads. My cell rings and I'm sure it's the first of many, calling to say that something better has come up and they won't be able to make it anymore. I should just tell the caterers to leave and take their beef *satays* with them. The bartender can leave but I'll keep the bar, for tonight. Maybe longer.

It turns out to be Dad.

"Slade," he says. He sounds strange. Skew.

"Hi Dad. How are you?"

"I'm … I'm having a bad time today, son."

I look at my watch. The party was supposed to start ten minutes ago and there's a not guest in sight. The DJ is going to despise me when I tell him to pack up his kit.

"Really?"

Silence. Is it a bad line? I don't have time for this.

"Dad? Really? Why?"

Oh God, I think he's crying. I really can't deal with this now. I smash my glass of bubbly and wonder if I should drop the call.

"Dad?"

Clearing of throat and a near-silent sniff. I can't deal with a breakdown from Dad, not on top of mine. A bloodline of broken-down men. It makes me think of road kill on a highway.

"I know I'm an old fool …"

Jesus Christ! I motion impatiently to the bartender to top me up.

"… but I've been thinking today …"

I cut him off. "Look, Dad, this really isn't a good time."

"Oh," he says, confused: I have stated the obvious.

The doorbell rings. The rent-a-butler will see the guest in. Hopefully it will be a guest, and not the feather-duster man. Although a feather-duster man would count, wouldn't he?

"I mean, I've just got a lot to deal with right now. Sorry. I'll call you in the morning."

"Of course. I understand." He tries to resolve the wobble in his voice.

"Chat to you tomorrow, then. Take care."

Frank From Football is here in a zoot suit, with a grin as wide as an oasis.

I hit the red button and throw my cell phone into the nearest bush.

Bless you Jesus.

A couple of hours later I inhale my fifth line of coke off the dressing room table's mirror in one of the spare rooms. I bought enough for whoever is interested and have had the waiters spread the code word. A giggling couple stumble in, kissing, then realising their mistake, stagger out again. The sixth line is smooth. I wipe my nose, check for residue. I hate the crassness of people who powder their noses in public.

The kick is cool, high, and instant.

I walk through my house and down into the garden, passing about a hundred people without recognising one. Everyone seems to be having a good time. Plumes and sequins seem to be scattered in every room of the house, and there are already people swimming in the bright turquoise nightlight of the pool.

"HARRIS," booms Sifiso, "great PARTY!"

He slaps me on the back the way a man after five whiskies does, as if I have done something impressive. Little does he know. His wife stands next to him, matching his height. Her name slips through my fingers. I over-smile in compensation. I went to their wedding, for God's sake.

"Having a good time?" I ask with a manic grimace. She nods and looks into my eyes as if trying to find something. A secret, or a shred of sanity.

"Where did you find the GO-GO GIRLS?" Sifiso demands, gesturing in the general direction of the attractive waitresses serving body shots.

"They're ex-girlfriends," I joke.

Sifiso's wife smiles politely. I feel like an arse. I am an arse.

"I'm off to get a refill," I say, "can I get you two anything?"

"No, brother, you've done ENOUGH!" says Sifiso. I look at him with a frown. Another slap on the back, which leaves me slightly winded.

"You can't hide the secret anymore, Harris," he winks.

I still don't know what he's talking about. Then: uh oh.

"It's OBVIOUS to EVERYONE!" he yells, his ice pirouetting in his glass. "You've FINISHED the book! And you know it's GOOD! Why else would you be having this amazing PARTY?"

People around us turn to face us, hands in prayer position, as if expecting an impromptu announcement from me. I laugh, awkward, and touch my glass to Sifiso's, then turn and walk as fast as I can to the bar.

Frank is there, faithful, drinking a Heineken and chatting up the bar lady.

"Hi Frank, enjoying the party?"

"Hey buddy," he smiles, "yeah."

We shake hands.

Frank always has a lot of intonation in his voice. He savours saying his words. So 'buddy' isn't made of two short, sharp, monotonous syllables when Frank says it, it's more like buuuyrrr-di Then his Yankee 'yeah' is a 'Yeah!'

I order a double single malt.

"So which one of these pretty women is your lady friend?"

Puurrdy women, lay-di friend.

"Oh, I'm not seeing anyone right now."

Frank roars in happy disbelief.

"You're kidding me, right? I've never known you to not have a lady friend."

"I suppose I'm in between relationships, then," I say.

"Ah!" Frank says, "so you've got a chick on your radar."

"Kind of," I say, knowing it's not strictly speaking true. Frank comes up with the strangest expressions. Sometimes talking to him is like interpreting some kind of military code. His smile is conspiratorial and he nods.

"That's cool, man. That's cool." He takes a sip of beer. "How's life otherwise?"

I'm just about to nod and say 'Terrific!' because I'm the host of this great party. I've had plenty of the good stuff and if anyone should be cheerful, it's me. That's the kind of things hosts are supposed to say. And I'm sure that Frank doesn't want a slice of my sorrow.

"I'm going through a pretty hard time, to be honest," I say, smiling so that he doesn't feel the weight of it. Thinking again of those damn bald kids. Why is it that lately, despite my dread of talking about my personal problems, I seem to be doing a lot of it? It's as if the words just hop out of my mouth.

"That sucks, man. Is that crazy chick back? PsychoSally?" There is light in his eyes.

"Er, yes, but funnily enough that's not the problem."

"Is it your soldier?"

"Excuse me?"

"You know, man, your pistol, your ammo."

"Oh, no, my pistol's just fine ... last time I checked."

"'Cos that kind of stuff happens to a lot of dudes, you know, nothing to be ashamed of. Some handguns jam, some fire blanks. That's just what happens, you know."

He gives me a slow nod, as if to encourage a confession.

"It doesn't make you any less of a m——"

"Frank, it's not the goddamn pistol."

He narrows his eyes in contemplation, suggesting those are the only things in life that can give you trouble, women and handguns. God, if only.

"Look, it's nothing, really," I say, "just battling a bit with the next novel. I'm a bit ... stuck."

Frank ponders this. Drinks beer, nods, ponders.

"It'll come to you, buddy."

It's more than that, though, I want to say, it runs a lot deeper than that. Instead I smile and take a long sip of my drink. I shake myself. Maybe he's right. Either way, this party was supposed to be about just letting go and having some fun, so I put on my party face.

I told everyone I invited to bring as many friends as they liked, which seems to have worked because my property is hot and heavy with the writhing bodies of strangers and stragglers. I dance for a while with a skinny blonde in a flapper dress who acts as though she is the star in her own movie, then move on to an energetic brunette with a feather headband. Gradually, for the first time in a long time, I start feeling good. I am looser: the lead in my stomach is melting, my feet don't sting anymore. This party was A Good Idea. Out of the corner of my eye I see Eve. She is watching me with a smirk on her face, like an indulgent mother. Despite her obvious condescension my heart lifts when I see her. I squeeze my current partner's forearm and leave the dance floor to go to Eve.

"Eve, thanks for coming," I say, hugging her.

"This is quite some ... party." There is a hint of distaste in her voice. I wonder if this is all just too much for her. Too much extravagance, too much indulgence. Or maybe it's worry: she knows I can't afford it.

"Have you seen the chocolate fountain?" I ask.

She nods and laughs.

"There were some girls, twins, practically swimming in it, on my way in."

"Were they naked?" I ask.

"No," she says.

"Oh well," I shrug, taking her hand, "let's get you a drink then."

I order a glass of champagne for Eve and another double for myself. I realise that I have been waiting all night for her to arrive. I wonder if I have actually had this party for her. My whiskybrain is thinking that this may be the night I am brave enough to make a move. The thought makes me cold and hot at the same time. Oh my God, I want this woman. I have wanted her for ten years.

She looks a little uncomfortable. I wonder if my face has betrayed me.

"Can we talk?" she asks. "I don't want to take you away from your party—"

"Of course! Of course we can." I look around the festivities and don't see a quiet corner anywhere.

I lead her inside and unlock the door to my den, locking it again from the inside. I move some books around to make space and then motion for her to sit down on the chaise. I take the leather ottoman, close enough to smell her hair. Through the glass doors we can see the party in the garden.

"What's up? Are you okay?" I ask.

"Yes, I'm fine. I'm worried about *you.*"

"Me?"

What? Why? Look at what a great time I'm having!

"I'm fine! I'm great! Don't worry about me," I laugh.

Is this why she wanted to drag me away from the party? To have a heart-to-heart? To piss on my parade? I'm not in the mood. I want to go and flirt and laugh and dance.

"I mean, sure, I'm going through a bit of a rough patch ..."

"A bit of a rough patch? Slade ..."

"Aren't you being a bit melodramatic?" I chuckle, knowing she won't fall for it.

"Sifiso just told me that you've spent your advance on the new book and you've already asked for more."

"Sifiso should shut the hell up. I owe a lot on my credit cards. Doesn't everyone? Post-recession. It's practically *de rigueur.*"

"But you haven't even started the book. Don't you think that's a little irresponsible?"

Ker-rist. Could she be any more overbearing? I am torn between pushing her away and ripping open her top.

"Eve, I get royalty cheques all the time. There's nothing a little royalty sum can't take care of."

"Really?" she asks, as if she knows something I don't. "What about your bond? You told me yourself that you're behind on your payments."

"They call every now and then to see how I'm doing. Offer to take me out for lunch."

"Are you not even a little worried?"

"It'll sort itself out, it always does."

"Look, I can lend you money. Just let me know how much you need."

The ape-man in me feels insulted.

"Eve, the problem isn't money. I don't care about it. And if

I did, I could get some. The real problem is inspiration. I need an idea. Can you lend me an idea?"

She looks at me as if I've just spoken in tongues.

"I'm going to ask you a question and you have to be honest with me." The look on her face is intense and the rest of the room fades away.

"Okay."

"Are you doing this on purpose?" she asks.

"What?"

"I mean, are you planning to write a book about a man who loses everything? Who gets his house taken away from him and has to live on the streets? Because if you are, then fine. Just let me know so that I don't worry so much about you."

"No," I reply, "but it's not a bad idea."

She wants to smile.

"I wouldn't put it past you."

"At least then I'd have something to write about. Instead of this."

"Still nothing?"

"I've written over a hundred beginnings. None of them have anything remotely redeeming about them. I've tried on my machine and on paper. I've even started sleeping with my Moleskine in case anything comes to me in the middle of the night."

This is torture. Admitting it to the woman I most care about in the world is like being run over by a train. I need her to see me as talented, successful, wealthy; instead, she sees this: this failure of a man. This rice husk, this fly casing. This shadow of a shadow.

"Look, Slade, I'm worried. It seems that you're not getting better. I mean I keep thinking that you'll have a breakthrough but it doesn't seem to be happening. Have you thought of maybe taking a break from writing? Doing something else for a while? Maybe get a job to pay the bills?"

"A break from writing? There is no such thing. That's like saying take a break from breathing. Putting myself in a coma. I can't."

"But I see how depressed you are. Your eyes are ... empty. You're not yourself. It's like I'm looking ... looking at a silhouette of you."

"Well, maybe that's part of my journey."

"I think at the very least, you should consider seeing someone."

"Unless it's someone who'll write my book for me, I don't see the point."

"So what are you going to do? Wallow in your writer's block till some kind of miracle happens? Do you think a story will drop down from the sky?"

"That's the way it usually happens, yes."

"But it's not happening, is it?" she demands.

I know she's right. It's practically beyond hope. I'm lost for words, lost for everything. Desiccated.

"I have a theory for you," Eve says, her eyes glittering, "but you're not going to like it."

I put my glass down, look up at her, waiting for a revelation.

"Here's the thing," she says, soft and gentle, like a nurse with bad news, "I think you're stuck because you're not giving enough, not putting enough of yourself out there."

I feel the warm beginnings of anger but I wait for her to explain.

"You're a taker. And you've been taking for a long time. And I think that you can only take so much from the universe before it closes shop."

I laugh bitterly. There is a sad old man attached to my back.

She is infuriating, and she smells too good. Like sex and cookies.

"Look, Eve, I appreciate the concern. I really do. I am a taker. I'm not denying it. I have to take in order to write."

I stand up and Eve follows suit.

"It's about more than that, Slade," her voice is rising, trying to get through.

"It's about how you use people and then throw them away. You leach everything you can and then you crush them and trash them."

In my imagination I have the vision of myself downing a beer, squashing the tin on my forehead and then throwing it backwards, over my head, a perfect landing in the bin. I don't cover my mouth to burp. In reality, I sway and look at Eve with weary eyes.

"I understand that you have issues with women; that it's very difficult for you, especially with what happened with your mother."

I grab her wrist to stop her words from splattering on the walls and carpet.

"Don't bring my mother into this," I whisper, close to her ear. "This is not about her."

It's a lie: it's always been about her. Everything has always been about her. And Emily.

"I just think that there are some things that you have to start facing!" she yells, "Otherwise how else are you going to get better?"

"I don't need to get better!" I yell back. "I need to be this! The person I am."

"Damn it. Slade, there are people who care about you! Who hurt when you hurt yourself! Why are you so fucking self-destructive?"

"It's not about being self-destructive. It's about living and living requires taking risks. My writing demands it of me."

"Ha! Like almost ending up in a wheelchair after deciding to jump out of a plane? And almost dying in Nigeria?"

I wave my hand at her to signal she's exaggerating.

"And Bangkok? You were in hospital for two months, Slade. No one even knew what had happened to you, or where you were."

"None of that was my fault! You know damn well that I was on assignments. Would you have had me turn down some of the most important writing assignments of my life?"

"Like driving your car over a bridge?"

It had always been a sore point. I wish I had never told her about it.

"I planned that very carefully, nothing could have gone wrong."

"It was suicidal, Slade. Everything could have gone wrong, you're just lucky it didn't!"

"Am I?" That was the bitter old man speaking.

Despite the evidence to the contrary, I'm not suicidal. If anything, these stunts make me feel more alive. Maybe Eve will never understand that.

Heat rushes inside of me. Part rage, part lust, my body is magnetised by Eve's. I step closer to her, too close, forcing her to take a step back.

"You treat your life experiences like … like notches in your bedpost! I just think … that if you had more meaning in your life …"

As I advance she takes another step back. I've had enough. I fling open the double doors that lead into the garden as a sign for her to leave.

I have to shout over the noise for her to hear me.

"Maybe I think that meaning is overrated. As far as taking risks is concerned – perhaps you should try it sometime. You, sequestered in your cocoon of a studio. You're hardly, as you say, 'putting yourself out there'."

Eve is trembling. She moves towards me. We are standing so close now I can feel the warmth radiating off her body and my senses are singing.

"It's a gift, Slade," she breathes, "my art, your writing. If you misuse it, it will abandon you."

The moment has come. There will never be a moment like this again. It feels like the world is holding its breath. I am electrified. Despite the violence of my feelings I am gentle when I grasp the back of her head and kiss her.

Not a second of hesitation passes before she slaps me. The revellers nearest to us turn to look. Eve whirls away and, in her haste to retreat, misses a step down, trips and falls onto the wet grass on her hands and knees. A hush falls over the crowd. She takes a moment before trying to stand up. Someone goes over to help her. I'm too angry for sympathy, condemned to being a silhouette. A voice in my head repeats 'it's over' again and again until I want to cleave my head open to release the pressure of the words.

I see a waitress out of the corner of my eye and click my fingers for a refill.

The rest of the night is a blur with missing snatches. I rebel against chaste, caring, maddening Eve by drinking enough to fell a large horse and behave as astonishingly badly as I know I can get away with. Ordinary people expect the more famous of us to be a bit strange, go a bit far, be a bit outrageous. What would Warhol be without his paranoia, Hunter S. Thompson without his Quaaludes, Johnny Cash without his philandering? We Somebodies are not expected to walk the line.

I remember skinny-dipping at midnight with some of the guests, including Frank from Football and the bar lady with the black fingernails and great tits. I steal watery touches of the pretty brunette I met on the dance floor and kiss her wet skin. I pin her up against the side of the pool with her legs around my waist and we make out like teenagers while I furtively stroke her clit. I can tell she wants me to fuck her, so I switch off the pool light for the five minutes it takes. I cover her mouth with one hand and pull her towards me with the other. I am so pent up from the encounter with Eve that I have an explosive orgasm. The girl giggles and purrs and I get out of the water.

Cut to Sifiso slapping me on the back again, smiling like a charcoal Cheshire cat and smoking a cigar. Cut to seeing the twins at the chocolate fountain and suggesting we take it into the bedroom. Cut to watching Francina dance to Abba. Cut to when the last stragglers and I are at the bar, watching the sunrise and drinking screwdrivers with freshly-squeezed orange juice. A waiter brings in egg and bacon rolls with HP sauce and hot chips drenched in vinegar. I meet a guy from Texas who speaks like a cowboy and a tall fish-eyed woman, dressed head-to-toe in black, who chain-smokes like Bette Davis. We talk about things that seem important at 5am: plastic surgery, designer sneakers, upcycling, the petrol price, Malema, Gadaffi, chicken roasted on a beer can, and no one wonders why the others are standing in a stranger's garden, drinking drinks they no longer need speaking to people they will never see again. No one wonders why this seems like a better idea than going home or what that says about the people doing it.

Cut to me realising the party is over, giving the faux butler the responsibility of ushering the last hangers-on out the door, and going to my bedroom where I hope to find the chocolate twins but actually find a cold, empty bed.

8

DIVINE DICTATION

There is a pleasure and pain in writing that is, ironically, difficult to put into words. When you are struggling to tap into the force it can feel like you will never get there again, that the muse has abandoned you, for bad behaviour, or just for kicks (muses have distorted senses of humour) and, if this happens enough, you can end up throwing your laptop out of the window and swearing off writing for life. And then one day – when far away from pen and paper, on the M1 highway or at a dinner party – something will come to you which you know is good, you know is original and fresh and important. You end up in the emergency lane, hazard lights flashing, ransacking the cubby-hole for something, anything, to write with, or the guest bathroom, scratching down sentences on double ply with borrowed eyeliner while other guests knock down the door. Divine dictation. The feeling that comes with it, intimate and sexy, pen on paper like lips on skin, a heat that starts in your pelvis and travels upwards, outwards, not so much a bolt as a current. You are turned on: physically, psychologically, spiritually. Nothing beats this feeling. Well, very few things beat this feeling.

I haven't had it in a while. I keep hoping that my muse will rescue me, lift me out of this pit of desperation. I try to have faith but when you show up to the page every day for over a year and get nothing, you start to feel a little bereft. I've tried to fake it, tried to force it, but that never gets me past a couple of hundred bad words. I gaze at copies of my published work and wonder where the hell all those sentences came from. And what a schmuck I was, taking it all for granted. The Catastrophe of Success, as Tennessee puts it, embalmed by fame … and then, nothing. The cold abyss.

This blankness, this snowstorm, this nothingness makes me reckless. I start thinking I should do more, travel more, taste more, try more, fuck more. I am cast adrift in pages and pages of white paper and I realise that I will do whatever it takes to get me writing again.

9

TENTACLES OF DEPRESSION

AROUND MY HEART

I won't bore the page with details of my hangover. All I'll say is that on a scale of one to ten it's a robust nine. The only other time I have ever had a bigger headache is when I had undiagnosed, untreated malaria in Lagos and spent a few delirious days sweating in my seedy hotel room, until a maid started screaming that I was dead and they arranged for me to be taken to a hospital. I was touched that she took it so much to heart but later found out that she was a deeply superstitious person and thought that I had a *juju* on me (Nigerian curses are contagious) and so was yelling for her own life, not mine. The worst parts of malaria were the crazy nighttimes, when I never really knew where I was and my dreams just became more and more surreal. At first I thought the symptoms were the side-effects of the malaria meds; then I suspected food poisoning; then that I had been abducted and locked in this pokey room with its resident cockroaches. Now there are cockroaches and then there are Lagos Cockroaches: the size of your thumb and built like army tanks. Pesticideresistant-waterresistant-fireresistantheelofyourshoeresistant. In the beginning it freaked me out, turning on the hotel light and seeing these ungodly things scatter for shelter, so quickly, wondering if they are imagined. Lying on the stained bed in the darkness, the bugs became less bashful and eventually came out to play. I remember – whether imagined or not – how they felt on my exposed skin, how their hard thoraxes shone in the moonlight, how their needle-like feelers felt in my ears, my nostrils. And the noise they made: scratchycrickety. At times when I thought I was coming out of the stupor I wondered if I had conjured them up but they swiftly asserted their existence: in the minibar fridge, crawling out of the porcelain basin plughole to surprise me while I was brushing my teeth and, once, a crushed corpse in my underwear. I almost jumped out of the window.

Lagos is a noisy city – especially at night. It comes alive with a raw, pulsing energy, like Rio's ugly sister with colourful litter and ringing gunshots and humidity that smacks you in the face. An old English professor of mine who has a reputation for his persistent puns and poignant turns of phrase refers to Nigeria as the Armpit of Africa. I've never known an entire country to be described so aptly in only three words.

So while my head feels like Hiroshima and my lacerated feet are stinging, I know that in theory it could be far, far worse. That's something I have going for me: a bank of really bad experiences – which sounds awful but in reality is great, because I can always compare my current state of affairs with some of my worst and come out feeling like Lucky Jim. Maybe that's why God made childbirth so painful, so that when your life is wrecked by children you know it could be worse. I keep the idea of my mother at bay. It could always be worse. I throw back two Disprins and a bottle of water. I'm sure they'll dissolve in my stomach.

I'm sorry I didn't get to enjoy the twins. Every time I think about them I get a pleasant twinge in my pants. I've tried a lot of things with girls (and the occasional guy) and have had more than my fair share of *ménage à trois*, my first going back as far as high school (which turned out to be a disaster, as you can imagine, no matter how much I closed my eyes and thought of the theory of Pythagoras). I still remember the girl, her face pinched with the shock of what had just happened. I guess the twin fantasy will remain just that, for now.

It is only when I walk through the house and see the devastation that it hits me, hard in the bottom of my stomach. Eve. Sucker punch.

The lounge floor is muddied with chocolate. The chandelier hangs askew.

I think she is lost to me forever. I'm not sure friends recover from that kind of fight. Especially after – I smack my tender forehead – God, I tried to kiss her. What the fucking fuck was I thinking? The shame makes me sweat.

I should call to apologise but I'd rather pull out my own toenails.

There are smashed flutes and tumblers and splinters of glass throughout the house, as well as the obligatory red wine stains (Flokati rug in foyer, wooden floor and deck chaise) and cigarette burns (sitting room Persian).

Maybe it's best to cut our ties altogether. She wants me to be someone I'm not and I want her very badly, just as she is. Besides, she seems to have become morally superior, and morally superior people are like piles.

The air outside is hot and dry. I retrieve my phone from the bush. I can see beer bottles at the bottom of the pool. Who knows what else is in there. I'll have to have the pool drained. Otherwise I can imagine, mid-swim, mid-lark, stepping hard on the stem of a broken martini glass, the sharp point being driven through the thick sole-skin and muscle, embedding itself deep in the soft tissue, like the needle of an angry urchin. I would have to pull myself out and end up bleeding to death on the bright green grass of the slope, only to be discovered by the caterers coming to pick up the last of their bains-marie. Or worse: a clucking Francina.

Not-so-celebrated Author Impaled on Designer Cocktail Glass.

God, the humiliation.

I could make it work, though. Just before my final breath I could hurl myself back into the swimming pool and float for my mock Gatsbyesque ending.

Maybe Eve and I were just caught up in the passion of the moment. Maybe there is something to be salvaged. But what is the point when I know that I can never have her? Who wants a friend who looks like Eve? It's like being given a Maserati on blocks.

In Peter Godwin's memoir 'When A Crocodile Eats The Sun' he expounds the theory that people love harder in Africa.

He writes that in Africa, death is never far away – 'Death has a seat at every table – and urgent winds whisper *memento mori*: You too shall die. You feel perishable, temporary, transient. You feel mortal.'. Maybe that's why, he says, you seem to live more vividly in Africa. The 'drama of life [here] is amplified by its constant proximity to death.'.

People love harder on this continent where things can be taken from you in a single violent fingerontrigger or flickofablade. I wonder if this goes a small way to explain why my feelings for Eve are so intense. God, I love her. She riles me with her horny body and virtuous lips. What will I do without her? My inky cloak descends upon me.

I look around, my arms drop to my sides and I feel the now-familiar tentacles of depression wrapping around my heart.

Just before I drop to my knees a spectacular idea startles me. I feel as though I have been stung.

It hits me between the eyes as clean and sharp as an archer's arrow.

My whole body gasps.

It's The Answer. To Everything.

The only other thought: that there is no other way.

I will have to kill Eve.

"The advantage of emotions is that they lead us astray."

- Oscar Wilde

10

EVE'S GRACEFUL DEMISE

I have to plan her murder. I am pinned to that fate like a crucified man to his olive tree.

In my mind's eye there is the dry and desolate landscape of my life; planted in the middle is Eve's murder, startling in its clarity and brilliance. I fight the idea for a while but it's like losing a mental arm-wrestle, millimetre by millimetre. God knows I love her, have always loved her but, for the sake of my own survival, I need to do this. Destinies have to be met. Sacrifices have to be made.

This is what will save my career. And with my career – everything else. I know it. Already I feel the hot excitement in my fingers. I am nothing without writing. It is my life force.

And my writing, like a certain bloodthirsty plant, needs to be fed.

I begin the planning tentatively, tasting it, rolling it around in my mouth. As it picks up momentum I find myself tantalised. There are so many ways to kill someone I am almost overwhelmed. Worried that I will become rabid and crazed like a family pet after tasting human blood, I take a step back and realise that this has to be approached in a cold and logical way: without the psychological chaos of bloodlust. Hitler was, after all, a vegetarian.

I take a cold shower (Inuit Deluge™), shave, dress in sensible clothes, and unplug my cappuccino machine. Caffeine has no place in this no-nonsense man's bloodstream. No sir, not today. Even the Juicerator is shunned: who knows what effect all that fructose can have on a sober man. If I had a tie, I would wear it now. But I don't. So I make up for it by wearing tan loafers I never knew I had. I begin to wish that I had a dictaphone to speak into, in a clipped American accent, like Agent Cooper in *Twin Peaks*. I pretend to have one anyway and, after pressing the imaginary red button in the palm of my hand, I say "Diane, remind me to buy a tie the next time I'm in town. An appropriate one, with stripes. You'll be pleased to know that for now, I have other things to worry about. I received the doughnuts you sent me, the ones with holes. Thank you. Diane, I need to go, I have a murder to plan." Stop.

On the kitchen table I set out reams of white paper, pens and pencils. I crack my knuckles and do a few wrist rotations and breathing exercises before I sit down. I need to be cool and collected. I need to be methodical. I wish my stomach wouldn't flutter so. I try to keep my mind even.

Where do I start?

In my limited experience of murder and speaking very generally, there seem to be three different ways of dying and eight different causes (please accept my apologies for my oversimplification; deconstructing death: it is necessary for me to get my head around this). Scribbled on the paper before me I have:

The Three Ways of Dying:

Accident

Suicide

Murder

The Eight Instruments of Death:

Weapon

Illness

Weather

Car

Fire

Water

Toxins (including venom, poison and drugs)

Asphyxiation

Now you could put these lists side by side and play joining the columns and come up with perhaps (I'm no mathematician) *A Billion Ways To Die.*

Id est, draw a line from Suicide to Weapon and you get hanging, a shotgun to the head, or taking the Panini Press into the jacuzzi with you. It's a bit like playing Cluedo. A line from Suicide to Illness will give you a heart attack via anorexia nervosa, or dying from Pneumonia after having sex without a condom. The list seems infinite. Then of course there are other broad categories such as homicide, patricide, matricide, infanticide. Cross Murder with Water and you get women driven by demons who drown their babies. Or Murder with Weapon: fathers who gun down their entire families, or lonely school kids in trench coats who don't like Mondays and take revenge the best way they know how. I try it out by resurrecting a few top-of-mind deaths I can think of, and all of them fit neatly somewhere on my list.

Steve Biko: Murder, Weapon

Leigh Matthews: Murder, Weapon

Sylvia Plath: Suicide, Asphyxiation

Helen Martins: Suicide, Poison

Ingrid Jonker: Suicide, Water

James Dean: Accident, Car

Ernest Hemingway: Suicide, Weapon

Michael Jackson: Accident, Drugs

Of course, some peculiar ways of dying are also revealed playing this fatal game of join-the-dots. Cross Murder and Weather: that could be interesting. Suicide and Freak Accident? Weapon and Illness: it's a story waiting to be told.

It goes without saying that there are a lot of violent deaths in South Africa: a legacy of our fractured history. You won't catch me bemoaning our crime rate at a dinner party (yawn!)

but I'm not in denial either. It's no secret that we have the highest rape stats in the world. It's said that women born in SA have a greater chance of being raped than learning how to read. And those are only the reported attacks. Sure, the old joke goes that 99% of statistics are bullshit, but where there is smoke ... Or in this case, where there is blood, there will most likely be bodies.

So it would make sense to dress up the murder as an attempted hijacking. In a country where there are thirty-nine violent hijackings a day it would simply disappear. I am sure a lot of assassins use this cloak. South Africa could become a veritable knock-off travel destination for aggrieved spouses. Honeymoon Hits. Perhaps it is already. Hired guns and better halves are not to be put off by Dewani. But a bullet in Gugulethu doesn't feel right, not for Eve. She is worthy of more.

All projects require a title, so I will name this 'Eve's Graceful Demise'. I write it in black koki in large letters. It takes up a whole sheet of paper.

It could be bloody (there is a satisfying symbolism in blood) but it shouldn't be too messy. Of course there shouldn't be any pain involved at all; I'll be strict about that. But it should be passionate. She is, after all, my unrequited love. We can play the 'If I can't have her then no one will' card.

A hit man (Mr. 'Jones' from Fochville: R12K a hit, R20K for two – almost makes you want to knock off another person just for the discount, like those three-for-two golf socks at the cash point you know you don't need but you end up buying anyway) will probably be the safest option as far as not being caught is concerned but it doesn't feel personal enough. No, I should be able to look her in the eyes as they close. I need to have courage. It should be a clear murder and should not be able to be construed as an accident. Henceforth I cross out the following on the list: hitting head on slippery bathtub; fingers mistakenly placed in electric socket; rotten oysters). It needs to be authentic. An overdose is tempting (mainlining heroin after drinking a bottle of Kristal might be the most delightful way to exit this world) but will most likely be construed as suicide.

Maybe something highly original, that no one else would think of. Could I create the circumstances for a freak accident? Flood? Earthquake? Lightning? African killer bee attack? I could be creative and have her die from eating rhubarb leaves (too old-fashioned) or moonflower seeds (too obscure), or give her a rare tropical disease (not practical. Also: contagious.). Or, I could distract her on a bird-watching trip in the Waterberg and push her off the edge of a cliff, but that seems a little underhanded.

A fire! A fire is very glamorous. Of course she would be dead beforehand, I wouldn't make her suffocate or burn, it would just be a way to get rid of her body. If we were at the coast I could put her on a boat and explode it. In South America I could sell her organs and leave her empty carcass in a refrigerated truck. If we were in Greenland I could drive an icicle through her heart and never have to worry about the cops finding the murder weapon. Then there's the old Roald Dahl favourite: braining someone with a frozen leg of lamb, roasting it with some carrots and spuds and serving it to the cops who come to investigate. There is, of course, the method used famously by the Turkish nobility who served chopped-up tiger whiskers to their enemies. The legend has it that the barbs on the whiskers stick in your intestines and cause you to leisurely bleed to death.

I also cross the following off the list: death by nicotine or Mr Muscle Window injection; hit-and-run; ricin-laced umbrella stab; silver body paint; gas leak; butterfly punch; arsenic-in-soup; puffer fish in the shower; strangulation; pillow-smothering. I find pillow-smothering such an interesting one. It's a pillow, for Christ's sake. Pillows are clean and soft and are associated with dreams and comfort and sex. In my opinion only Very Bad People would turn that into a murder weapon. A gunshot is so quick and can take place with half an intention. Pillow smothering requires a full two minutes of heavy-handedness and a sense of commitment I just don't think I have.

After hours of throwing a paper ball against the wall I realise that the answer may not be in my brain and that I need some outside help.

II

Don't Act Creepy, or,

Pink Strychnine

On the way to the library I feel fit. I haven't felt this good in seasons. I feel so good that I stop at the carwash to have the Jag given the platinum treatment. What it really needs is a good service, a new tail light and a bit of a panel beating but I haven't been able to afford that for a while. The sorrowful glances which come my way for having a dirty, dinged sports car is enough to drive anyone off the edge. Even taxi drivers shake their heads at me. But today money is no object for my beautiful baby. As long as they don't cut up the credit card. It occurs to me that I am spending money I don't have on a car I don't own. Ah, credit is a beautiful thing! I watch the attendant swipe the card and wait. Three, two, one – and yes! – the payment goes through. I turn the key and the nice carwash man waves me off. He may as well be waving a chequered flag. I pop the car into first, rev a little to warm her up, and accelerate in a wide arc onto the main road.

God, Jo'burg is beautiful in summer. Everything is so green. I can't help feeling optimistic. I love going to the library. Especially nowadays when no one really needs a library because of Kindle and Google. It's like having a huge revolving bookcase all to oneself. I walk up the corkscrew staircase with a bounce in my step.

My mother introduced me to libraries. It was 'our thing': books and reading. Emily would use her books to make stables for her fragrant pastelplastic ponies while Mom and I smirked at her.

If we had been good children during the day, she would let us climb into bed with her and read to us. One child on either side, with the book balanced on the incline of her warm, slanted thighs. I would edge nearer and nearer as the story progressed so that my whole body was in contact with hers. She would fidget and tell me to move over. 'Claustrophobic' was one of the first words I learnt. I craved proximity to her as if I had some kind of prescience of her leaving us. As if I knew that one day she would just vanish, and take colour with her.

But I still have those memories; she couldn't take those away, those golden hours. I still have *Alice in Wonderland*, *The Wizard of Oz*, *Charlie and the Chocolate Factory*. Sometimes I wonder if I truly did love books as much as I remember, or if I was so desperate for her attention that I just grabbed on to the only thing that she would – with reluctance – offer me. In true Oedipal fashion I guess I had a love/hate relationship with my mother's world of fiction. It erratically offered me the bliss of library trips and bedtime stories, but more often it took our mother away from us.

At first I didn't understand the lucky logic of libraries. Books for free? As often as you wanted? It defied all I had learnt in my five years of being. Amazed at my appetite for words, my mother coerced some friends into registering for library cards and then handing them over to us, so that we could borrow thirty books at a time. She would wink at me if the librarian seemed sniffy, then we'd giggle to our 'getaway car', clutching our precious plunder.

First I case the joint. Familiarise myself with the categories and layout. Then I move closer: grazing book spines with my fingers as I go. I seize any title I think will come in handy and when the load becomes too heavy, carry them over to the most private reading table I can find. There are whole books dedicated to anthrax and letter bombs. The selection process having gone well, I make myself comfortable and start taking notes.

I pore over books with titles like *Alchemy of Bones, An Almost Perfect Murder, Arsenic Under the Elms, Getting Away With Murder, In The Wake Of The Butcher, The Encyclopaedia of Murder, In Cold Blood,* and *Assassin!*

I discover concepts like seppuku (Japanese ritual disembowelment, hara-kiri style). I discover the difference between hydrazine and chloroform.

When I've finally read all I can about bloody and bloodless ways to shuffle off this mortal coil, I decide to take the rest of the books home. The bug-eyed librarian glowers at me as she sweeps the barcode reader over the five books I've chosen. Her mouth is a small pink pucker. A cat's bum. I think of my mother winking. I smile at her, which only seems to alarm her further, and skip out of there.

After two days of obsessive note-taking and more visits to

the library I feel I have absorbed every relevant thing I can from the written word. Now it's time to move on to popular culture. I go to my local DVD store and pick up a stack of murder mysteries, true-crime documentaries and enough microwave popcorn to stuff a horse. I pay very careful attention. I try to identify the mistakes the killer makes before the detective does. Sometimes I end up watching a scene over and over.

Nurse Daisy De Melker was caught only after poisoning her third victim. Before that she killed her previous husbands by sneaking strychnine into their daily fare. In those days pink strychnine was in fashion, which turned the bones of her prey pink. They hanged Daisy after finding evidence of arsenic in the thermos she prepared for her son the day he died.

'Son of Sam' mailman killer, David Berkowitz, despite being trained in Vietnam guerrilla warfare, made the mistake of parking his cream-coloured Ford Galaxy in the area where he shot those who were to be his last victims. In the car they found a loaded submachine gun and one of his infamous letters to the police. The lesson here is if you get away with too much, you get sloppy. Don't get sloppy.

Over the years, Belle Sorensen Gunness (also known as the Black Widow) killed as many men as she could persuade to marry her and cashed in on the insurance. She also killed her ranch hands and some of her children. Her sister blamed Belle's first husband who, in public, kicked the pregnant Belle in her stomach, resulting in her losing the baby.

Moses Sithole, South Africa's most reviled serial killer, murdered over forty people, before making the mistake of using his real name on an application form to lure a victim. The court verdict took three hours and Sithole was sentenced to over two thousand years in jail.

Coral Eugene Watts used to drown women in baths to keep their spirits from escaping. Herman Mudgett lured people to his hundred-room torture castle where he would throw them down an elevator shaft and later dissect the bodies. He sold the reconstructed skeletal models to medical schools. Charles Manson loved the Beatles and made his spaced-out groupies call him Jesus Christ. Former boy-scout Richard Angelo injected his patients with Pavulon and then 'saved their lives'. Sometimes the latter didn't happen. Aileen Wournos, famous for killing at least seven men, was finally tracked down at a biker bar called The Last Resort.

Who were the killers that weren't caught? Jack The Ripper, the bag-headed Zodiac killer, the Cleveland Torso murderer. And whoever killed Bubbles Schroeder.

I learn that in order to get away with murder there are some ground rules. Have a simple plan. Don't have a motive. Have an alibi. Don't boast. Don't act creepy. Socialise as usual. Obey all other laws, especially on the road. Don't leave DNA. Don't keep the murder weapon. Get rid of the body: no body + no weapon = no murder.

Slowly, deliciouslyachinglyslowly, the plan comes to me, like chapters in a book. I write everything down. It's not a novel yet, it's not even the beginning of the novel. It's the work I have to commit to paper before I write the first sentence. I don't have a plot yet, or even a premise, but I have a good feeling about this. There is a thrill in my fingers. I think this will lead to my best one yet.

My cliché: I feel alive again.

*

I arrange to see my GP, ostensibly for my annual check-up but really so I can ask him questions. (His name is Doctor Olaf, I kid you not). Also, I thought it would be the clever thing to do after passing out in the shower for no particular reason.

The conversation goes something like this:

(SFX: rustling of papers as crazy-looking doctor speed-reads five pages of blood test results.)

Doc: "I'm happy with your cholesterol but you need to watch your blood pressure. You know what I always say about blood pressure."

Me: "It's the most important number."

His face lights up. He has the energy of the eccentric professor in *Back To The Future.* His office is cluttered with promotional medical paraphernalia, as if he has promised to keep every freebie he has ever been sent. There is a stopped clock on the wall: an advert for a wrinkle cream.

Doc: "Yes! It can strip years off your life, you know."

As if I don't feel old enough.

Dr Olaf delights in facts. The more he can fit into the

limited time we see each other, the better. I am fascinated by a gaudy model on the tangle that is his desk: a man's severed torso holding internal organs. Pink lungs, green liver, yellow spleen. I have the inexplicable urge to touch them.

"Now, if you pass out again, you have to come back here for more tests."

That seems like reasonable advice. He lifts his arms above his head and stretches.

"Everything else is good. Maybe don't drink so much."

That's what he says every year, even though when he asks me, I always divide how much I really drink by a third. I don't take his wrist-slapping too seriously: he has a year-round tan and always smells like cigarettes.

"So, Doc, I need to ask you something. It's kind of private."

"Your blood tests are fine! Whatever you think you picked up, you didn't," he winks.

"It's not really about me, it's a rhetorical question."

"Ah. Your 'friend' has got a rash? Warts? Erectile dysfunction?"

I wish he'd keep his voice down.

"It's a strange question."

"Oh, believe me son, I've heard them all. They keep my job interesting! The stranger the better!"

"It's for my new novel," I say, savouring the sound of my

words.

Doc doesn't care; he is waiting for me to get on with the question.

"If you stab someone, in the heart, how long will it take for that person to die? Would it be quick?"

Now he is excited. Time to flex his medical brain. He does a two-step then begins talking with overt hand gestures.

"It would depend on a great deal of factors. If the knife is small it might only puncture the heart; if it's blunt it might get stuck in the ribs and intercostals. A large, sharp knife would obviously inflict the most damage. And the knife should be removed afterwards, so that the heart can collapse. That would be the quickest and least painful way, if you choose the heart. If you choose something else, for example the throat, it would be even quicker."

I can't slit throats – too brutal. I'm not a barbarian. Next he'll be telling me to scalp her.

"So you're picturing, like, a samurai sword?" I ask. Not very practical.

"If you feel the need to be aesthetic," he says dryly. "Otherwise, a kitchen knife will do."

I'm grateful to Doctor Olaf for his advice, but the whole experience left me feeling a little empty. No murderer would ask his doctor how to kill his victim. I feel I've cheated. So for the pharmaceutical side of the affair I decide to go underground. My drug dealer usually delivers (isn't that great? Door-to-door Diazepam! He's really business-savvy. If he had a credit card facility I would nominate him for entrepreneur of the year. What's also great about him is he takes real pride in his work) but I need my purchase this time around to be a bit more ghetto. Plus, I don't think my dealer is any way interested in what I am looking for. He prefers designer drugs with their appropriate prices. Also, he has added vitamin supplements to his offering, which I find disturbing.

I drive to Hillbrow, stop in a nice-looking suburb on the way and draw a thousand Rand. I don't even bother to look at the slip the machine spits out at me. Once on Louis Botha I slow down and look around. I ask the potential hijacker at the robot if he knows where I can score. He just shakes his head at me and there's a strange look in his eyes. He either wholeheartedly disapproves of drug taking or he thinks I'm undercover.

I ask a few more people but it's hard to not look suspicious. I'm in a Jag convertible in Hillbrow, for God's sake. Besides, everyone looks suspicious. It was a lot easier to score when I was a student. Not that I had to come to Hillbrow for a banky. I only moved on to harder stuff when I needed to, for a short story I wrote in my early twenties.

I pull in at the notorious petrol station and ask the attendant. He doesn't seem to speak a great deal of English. He just shouts in the general direction of the building and a few faces look up out of the dim interior. He puts the petrol pump nozzle in my fuel tank but doesn't turn it on. Another guy in greasy blue overalls ambles out to my window for a chat.

"Nice ride," he smiles. He's laid back, like a Rasta, but

without the trappings.

"I need GHB. Just enough for one night. But it has to be GHB, untraceable, nothing else. No mixed shit. And I don't want roofies."

"*Angazi.*" He shakes his head and sucks his lips. "I got roofies. More kick. Much better."

I can tell why this guy's a drug dealer and not a brain surgeon.

"I don't want roofies. You can trace it. I need GHB."

I'm starting to think this is a bad idea. Strictly speaking I don't even need to be here. You can make your own damn GHB, if you know how. If you have an iPhone and know how to spell Google. But the fear gnawing at my stomach is the reason I came, this dull paranoia, this feeling: you can't get this by sitting on your Chesterfield in the 'burbs.

It's hot. The tattiness of this place and the smell of petrol is getting up my nose.

"Well?" I'm trying to act cool but I can hear tick-tock before some ego in a cop car pulls up. I wind my watch.

"Drive around, I'll see you now," says the lipsucker.

"What?"

The other attendant chips in. He turns out to be able to speak very good English. They seem amused at my presence.

"Drive around the block, then come back here. Park in the carwash."

He takes back his nozzle, closes my petrol cap and pats the back window, leaving a nice set of fingerprints on the glass. It seems that these guys have lost their healthy sense of fear a long time ago.

I cruise around the block feeling like an idiot in my flashy car. This neighbourhood is Dodge City. The roads are full of potholes and the uneven pavements teem with weeds and junk. There are no road names. I should have parked somewhere and caught a taxi in. Doctor Olaf wouldn't be happy: I can feel my blood pressure spiking. There is a certain relief in pulling into the cool shade of the car wash, until someone switches the damn thing on and the old rollers scratch the shit out of my duco.

We take care of business without much going wrong. They hand me three pink powdery pills in a used Ziploc and grossly overcharge me for it. My dealer would tell me that it serves me right, buying from the competition.

Eve hasn't called and I'm thankful for that. It would be awkward. I wouldn't be comfortable seeing her. Looking at her thin, pale neck, so easy to strangle, or sitting across from her, thinking of the blood moving in her veins. And her beating heart.

12

WHO HAS TIME TO READ

IN THIS RAT RACE?

OR, WHITE CANARY

"Hey buddy, let me buy you a beer."

It's Wednesday night at our indoor soccer club and we've just been beaten two-nil by a bunch of hillbillies. Middle-aged punks who bring their pregnant teenage mistresses to watch the game. The *poppies* sit around *skinnering* and clap half-heartedly while downing Alcopops and smoking petite packs of Camels with neon-painted nails. Frank played well but I wasn't concentrating and let a few balls through.

"What an awesome party we had, huh?"

Last Saturday seems a decade ago.

"Dude, you throw the best parties. That waitress was a minx. She gave me her number."

"Have you called her?" I ask.

"Nah."

Frank has commitment issues.

"Hey, did you nail that short chick?" he asks.

I squint and have to think before I answer.

"The one in the pool?"

"*Ja.* The one with the tits." He jiggles imaginary melons on his chest in case I misunderstand the question.

We reach the bar, which is too bright, and Frank drops the melons and orders two pints of Windhoek draught from a bartender who looks like a Hell's Angel.

"No, I didn't."

"Pussy."

Meaty, tattooed arms pass us tall glasses of the good stuff. Frank tells the biker to keep the change.

We find a table at the back, away from the jubilant hicks, and sit down. The top is stained and sticky. Three beers later, we're bonding over some third-grade pork scratchings we bought from the bar.

"So what was up with you and Eve, man? She looked seriously pissed off."

Usually I wouldn't have too much to say about it but it's been an exhilarating week and I need to tell someone. Also, Frank calls me buddy so I guess he's the closest thing I have to a mate. We met when he joined our team. He's hardly my intellectual equal, but he laughs a lot, which I like. If the conversation ever turns to books or reading he likes to feign constipation and quote Mario Puzo: "Who has time to read in this rat race?"

I shouldn't say anything. It would be crazy to tell anybody. It could get to the wrong person and I would be locked up. I would lock me up. Besides, everyone knows it's Jinx City if you reveal the premise of your novel before you've started it. Like roasting chickens before they hatch.

Frank is waiting. I can't tell him.

Loose lips sink ships.

"It's a long story," I drawl.

"Is she your piece of action?"

"I'm working on it." I picture a white canary being sent down the mineshaft.

"That's funny."

"Why?"

"Ah, nothing. I just thought she might have been gay or something."

"Gay? Are you crazy?"

"I'd had a lot to drink by then, so don't listen to me. They were probably kissing hello or something. Her and a brunette. I have an overactive imagination in that department, you know. Lesbians. What can I say? They're hot."

I love how Frank compartmentalises everything; his intra-psychic synapses must be so neat. Life is about sport (mostly English football), beer, birds (hot or not) and guns (in the biological sense as well as the ones with real bullets). Life is simple for Frank, which is probably why he smiles and nods a lot. The music is turned up and the hillbillies start to *sokkie*.

"The thing with Eve is complicated."

"Dude, she's a woman. Enough said."

I'm feeling warm and fuzzy. I'm going to tell Frank.

"Look, Frank, usually I wouldn't tell anyone, it's considered bad luck, but I'm in the mood and I don't see the harm in you knowing."

Frank sits up.

"What is it?"

"I'm going to murder Eve."

Frank looks like a puppy that has just been kicked. He looks around anxiously to see if anyone had heard me.

"Dude, are you fucking mental?" he whispers, "Are you fucking off your tree? What if someone hears you? You can't talk like that, man, even if you're kidding. It's like joking that you've got a bomb on the plane. It's just not cricket."

"First, I'm going to sneak sedative into her tea. It does its thing quickly and then is broken down completely, not leaving a trace. This is to relax her, make her feel really good."

Frank shields his eyes and looks away as if pretending not to be in this conversation at all.

"Then, while she's in the bath with her eyes closed, I'm going to slide a porcelain knife into her heart. She won't even feel it. I'll watch her bleed out then clean her up. Carry her like a bride to her car, and drive her into the river. At first I thought fire but now I think the river is far more romantic."

Frank now looks like someone who has just made it to the toilet in time. His features melt into a dumb smile. He bangs his forehead on the table.

"It's for your book," he says in wonder.

"Of course it's for my book, Frank. Jesus. You thought I meant that I was actually going to murder someone? Eve? Fucking Christ! She's one of my best friends."

"Only for a second," he laughs, his face still showing relief.

"What kind of idiot would sit and describe exactly how he was going to kill someone in a public place like this?"

His wiring may be a bit shorter than I originally guessed.

"I don't know." He laughs in a high pitch. He may be a little hysterical. "I was wondering."

"Jesus."

He gulps down a good portion of his draught.

"So you've finally cracked an idea. Congratulations. Let's have one more beer to celebrate, I'm buying. You can tell me all the gory details."

"You write. That's the hard bit that nobody sees.

You write on the good days and you write on the lousy days. Like a shark, you have to keep moving forward or you die."

Neil Gaiman

13

MIND MAP

I spend the next day creating a mind map of the murder. I have time sequences built around Eve's routines, drawings of her house plan, inside and out, a key taped to the address. I have pictures of her, too. There is a map of the river. I include the pink pills in their packet in my collage; it adds another dimension, like one of her mixed media artworks. I wonder what she would think of it.

The murder weapon is a work of beauty, if I do say so myself. It was a gift from my mother a few years ago, which, I guess, has a peculiar kind of irony. The good thing about it is there will be no record of purchase and I have never seen anything like it in this country. It practically doesn't exist. Gifts from mom are always a surprise on two fronts. Firstly, because she tends to forget birthdays and Christmas and just sends things on an ad hoc basis. Secondly, the things she sends are puzzling. When I turned thirteen I unwrapped a second-hand bicycle pump. It sounds interesting and eccentric but there was never so much as a note included to help me understand the obscure presents. So I've always felt like I just didn't *get* them.

The knife is porcelain, Japanese, with an intricate carved handle. Sharper even than those they demonstrate on the shopping channel, where they inexplicably slice open tins and garden hoses. So sharp that I almost lost a finger trying to make *gazpacho* one day and thus relegated it to a drawer in the kitchen I hardly ever open.

Francina had to drive me to the hospital that day. Me, trying to stem the flow of blood so as to not a) die and b) stain the champagne suede interior of my Jag, with Francina trying to work out the difference between the accelerator and the brake. We arrived and parked at the hospital in starts and jerks of the V8. Francina, flaunting the key ring to other bruised, beaten and bleeding patients, wouldn't stop beaming for the hour we spent in the emergency waiting room (it was only then she confided she couldn't drive). Eight stitches and a reattached index phalange later, I let her drive us home again.

I haven't seen Francina since the party a week ago. She's usually very good at calling me if she can't make it to work, but I haven't heard anything and Thursday was her second no-show. So I'm a little worried but I'm sure there's a good reason. Like a fashion emergency. The house is still a war zone of sharp objects and party stains.

I'm quite glad to have the privacy anyway. My mind map takes up the entire kitchen table and the last thing I need is Francina in a tutu, mid-vacuum, popping bubble gum, trying to figure it out.

I have some small mementoes of Eve I don't stick to the map. A picnic serviette marked with her pale lip-gloss, a tortoiseshell hairclip, a Polaroid of us at a fancy dress party.

Despite my general good spirits there are fleeting moments of sadness that I don't have Eve anymore. We were, at stages, incredibly close. At times I have felt that I would do anything for her. The thing that drew us together, I think, is that we're both pretty much loners. Both had a nasty childhood, both find our salvation in our art.

"Deceiving others.

That is what the world calls a romance."

- *Oscar Wilde*

14

Unfortunately, Corpses Don't Bruise

Sifiso picks up on the first ring.

"CONGRATULATIONS! I knew you could do it! When can I see it? The suits are going to be so RELIEVED!"

"Sifiso, I …"

"I TOLD them you still had it in you. To be honest, I had my BALLS on the line."

Before I can stop it, the image of Sifiso's black hairy balls is firmly imprinted in my front temporal lobe. In my head, I gag.

"So, I don't have the *actual* manuscript yet …"

Silence on the other side.

"I've cracked something that I know will work. It'll be my best yet."

Still nothing.

"So I didn't want you to worry. That's why I called. Er …

Hello?"

A sigh reaches me.

"Look, Harris, you must tell me if you need anything. ANYTHING. Whatever will help you FINISH this thing."

"That's kind."

"It's got nothing to do with being KIND."

"Got any muses in your artillery? Preferably blonde with great tits?"

I'm only kidding. Ha ha.

"Sifiso, I'm only …"

The line goes dead.

So this is the plan I have finally decided on:

I break into the house before Eve gets home from work to do the prep work. I say 'break in' but really, we have each other's house keys for mutual house-sitting so I'm just going to let myself in. In my mind I have come up with a cunning plan that involves stealing her keys for half an hour, having copies made and replacing them before she notices. I would do it for real except that she's not speaking to me, so it would be complicated.

At 4pm I'll park my Jag a street down at the local shops where there are lots of cars and walk the kilometre to her building with my backpack. Once inside I'll pour the GHB powder into the kettle and wait for her to come home. After drinking her Oolong she'll feel light, uninhibited and disorientated. Because it's still early and she won't want to go to bed, maybe she'll decide to have a bath. If she doesn't I'll step out of her bedroom cupboard and run one for her, help her into it. By that stage she won't think it's unusual that I'm there. When she's in I'll kneel down at the side with her and hold her hand. Tell her she's beautiful and I will always love her. Kiss her lightly on the forehead and the lips, like putting a child to bed. I need to be up close. And when she's completely relaxed and has her eyes closed, I will unwrap the knife I have brought and stick it through her ribs and into her heart. Her eyes will flutter open, she'll look at me, wanting to know what has happened, why she has this heaviness in her chest, why she feels her colour is fading. Then I'll pull it out and she'll close her eyes again and it will be over. She will bleed then. Bright red bathwater against the porcelain of her skin. The gentlest murder ever committed.

Or rather, not committed, as I have to keep reminding myself.

I'll dry her with a soft towel and dress her in clean clothes, cutting them over her chest where she has this new slit in her body, so initially it'll look like something from the car, like the steering column, has punctured her. I'll lay her out on her perfectly made bed and wait until 3am when there's little chance of running into anyone while I carry the body to her car. Enjoy the quiet drive to the river. Once we're there I'll put her on my lap while I drive as fast as I can over the bridge and slam into the water below. This is one thing I've done before so I know how to get out of it. I know how quickly the water rushes at you and holds you in, wanting you to stay. I know the pressure exerted on the car from the heavy water outside makes it almost impossible to open a door. Jams the windows. I must remember to not panic when I realise I can't move, can't get away, that I have to take off my safety belt.

Then I will touch Eve's skin for the last time and swim away.

I'll have a car waiting in the trees nearby, with dry clothes in the boot. Drive the hour back to the parking lot at the shops while listening to Depeche Mode and swap cars. Leave the keys with the café owner as organised with the car hire company, with my fake driver's license (an international driving permit for only fifteen pounds from www.fakepermit.co.uk). I uploaded a jpeg of my ID photo and the card was in my letterbox within days. It's convincing enough and comes with a very attractive hologram design. Apparently my credit card statement will read 'Greeting Cards Galore (PTY) LTD.', in the same way as when you've been to the strip club and your statement reads 'T# Restaurant' instead of Teazers (I'm not quite sure who this is supposed to fool).

Once I put my key in the front door of my house I think I'm home free. But that's the thing. I mean if I really were to go through with it, there would be hitches and mistakes, all the better for the story.

Perhaps when I let myself into her apartment, she's already there. Maybe her car is at the garage for an aircon re-gas, so I surmise that she's not home but then end up walking bang into her, in the kitchen. I say I was going to surprise her and she looks around for champagne and roses. Instead, she finds ground-up sedative and a murder weapon wrapped in a fluffy towel.

Or else the GHB doesn't work: the scumbags have sold me dyed aspirin or speed and, when I step out of the bedroom cupboard she gets the fright of her life and shoots me between the eyes with the 9mm Beretta I never knew she had. Then she'll feel awful, so awful for shooting her friend in the head: she'll cry and groan and throw herself over me. Dial for an ambulance, scream into the phone.

Until she discovers the contents of the backpack and then she'll jump away from the bag and my prostrate body, as if from a wolf spider, cancel the emergency services, wait for me to bleed out, call the police. She'll sit on the edge of her bed, blood-splattered, gun hanging from limp hand, and look at me with a lost expression. The confusion will lead to exhilaration when she realises she has just cheated death and her heart will pump away.

Or I could be carrying her to the car when I walk around a corner and straight into a drunk resident trying to get his key in the door. He'd look at the body and know she's dead. He would recognise her pale face as the neighbour he's always trying to screw. He'd smile and pretend that he can't see shit because he's so drunk, perhaps make a sleazy joke, but as soon as he steps into his apartment he'll slam the door closed, triple lock it, and call the cops.

So I would have to kill him too, the drunken lamb. Punch him in the face, as he's scrambling to get that stubborn key in the door, and then slit his throat. Take them both hurtling off the bridge. And then of course the multitudinous things that can go wrong in the car underwater are just too much to go into, so let's not even begin. But when they find his throat slit they'll know it's murder, so the whole plan has to change anyway. The car will have to crash and explode to destroy the evidence.

Or I could dump him somewhere altogether different and make it look like he was just a drunk stumbling into trouble. I'd take his wallet and watch and leave his credit card for a travelling bum to find.

Or I could drag him into his apartment as soon as I've knocked him out and make it look like Eve killed him in self-defence. Put her fingerprints on a glass of wine. Rough her up a bit, tear her panties. Unfortunately corpses don't bruise. Still, a bit hard to swallow.

So many scenarios to choose from, my writing hand is itching. Without even touching my Moleskine I dive straight onto my laptop. The phone rings a few times in the background but I block it out. I'm writing so fast that I can hear the sound of my fingers hitting the keys in a strange kind of disembodied way, as if my thoughts are just being deposited right onto the screen in front of me. Divine Dictation. I write for hours and hours without even realising it. The sun is setting and the last thing I had to eat was a rusk with this morning's first flat white. I'm excited down to my lower intestines. My lungs are filling with air, my blood is rushing.

Christ, I love this feeling.

I feel like I could go all night but I don't want my prose to tire. I force myself to shut down the machine and I order in chicken *tikka* for dinner. I'm not hungry but I want to feed my body so that this energy keeps coming.

When I turn in for the night I know that I won't be able to sleep. I try to read Zadie Smith's *White Teeth* but, much as I appreciate her writing, I can't concentrate on the story. In the first chapter corduroyed Archie Jones is in the process of gassing himself in his Cavalier Musketeer Estate, with his medals in one hand and his marriage certificate in the other, 'for he had decided to take his mistakes with him'. At the mere hint of death I'm losing focus all over the place. My mind bunnyhops. Eventually I give up sleep and sassy Ms. Smith, and start scribbling the ideas as they come to me. I write deep into the night, promising myself just one more hour every time the long hand meets twelve, eventually falling asleep when the hadedas start making a ruckus in the orange glow outside.

Bless you Jesus!

PART II

15

LIKE DOGS, I'M SURE THEY CAN SMELL FEAR.

Something wakes me.

My eyes feel as though they have sand in them, reminding me that I haven't had enough sleep. I look down and see that I have slept clutching my pen to my heart. My notebook is at my bent knee. I feel oddly at peace with the world. I think I'm even smiling a little.

The doorbell rings. That's what must have woken me. I swear under my breath at whichever hawker is getting me out of bed at this hour but it fails to dampen my mood. I get ready to yell and shake my fist.

I look through the peephole and see a uniform. I rub my eyes.

Blue. SAPS blue. Then I see another. Their squad car is parked politely in my visitor's bay.

I feel like I've been punched in the face.

Has something happened? Has my car been stolen? The neighbour been burgled? Has my father had a heart attack?

Have they caught me buying a fake driver's license?

Did they catch me buying drugs? Those sneaky anti-crime cameras in the dodgy parts of the city can pick up number plates. It doesn't help that mine is personalised. It reads 'MERCENARY' in honour of my first novel, when now, in retrospect, I think it should read JACKASS.

I jab the speaker button.

"Hello?" I say with all the calm I can.

"Open up please sir, this is the police."

"The *police*?"

So I wasn't imagining it.

"Yes, sir, this is the police."

Oh my God, I know something is wrong. Maybe if I don't let them in they will go away.

"Well, what do you want?"

They speak amongst themselves. I hear *eish*-ing and shushing, ambush sounds, as if they're discussing how to break down the security gate so that they can slap cuffs on me and drag me to the car.

"We have some questions, Mr Harris," says one.

"Just open the gate, sir," says the other.

"Please," adds the first one.

Oh God. Good cop, bad cop. I'm about to let them in when I remember the giant mind map on the kitchen table. I run through, scrunch it up and look for somewhere to hide it. I feel panic rising and try to keep a level head. I end up dumping it in the laundry hamper in the bathroom and cover it with a towel. Out of breath, I press the buzzer to open the gate and with shaking hands I unlock and open my front door. They both stop in their tracks when they lay eyes on me. I look down and see that I'm only wearing a pair of jocks. In my fright I hadn't thought of what I had on.

"Come inside," I say. "Let me just throw on some pants."

Pants? Why did I say *pants?*

The Good Cop smiles. *Toujours la politesse.* The taller one avoids eye contact. I throw open my cupboard and reach for the first things I see: torn jeans and grubby t-shirt. I lead them to the kitchen. They decline cappuccinos. They probably hate people who drink cappuccinos. They probably despise people who sit at arty cafes and smoke Vogues while talking about literature and sipping frothy coffee drinks. They probably drink neat Ricoffy, black and scalding, or burnt, tepid filter coffee, while they find missing persons and hunt down dangerous criminals and make the world a better place.

They also decline fresh squeezed juice from my Juicerator and Francina's favourite pecan nut rusks.

The taller one is still not meeting my gaze. I look down again and see that I'm wearing an old varsity shirt that says 'Half Man, Half Horse'.

I'm sure they can tell I'm nervous. I'm fluttering around the kitchen like Albert Goldman in *Birdcage.* I plug in the cappuccino machine anyway and flick the switch. I try to calm down.

Like dogs, I'm sure they can smell fear.

"Would you like to sit down?" I ask, sure that they'll shake their heads. They don't have time to lounge around my kitchen. They've got serious cop business to attend to.

They nod and pull up a chair. I gulp and sit down with them. I read the names off their badges. Madinga and Sello. Shifty-eyed Sello. It occurs to me that I didn't ask for any kind of identification. I don't want to piss them off and it's probably too late anyway, seeing as they're sitting in my kitchen with revolvers on their hips.

"Do you mind if I … can I ask you for … some ID?" I ask, too bright by far.

They look at each other as if I've told them an old joke. Each suppressing a sigh, they reach for their cards and flash them at me, too fast for me to register anything but badly-lit photos and the same names glinting on their golden badges. The cards are back in the shadows of their pockets before I have time to blink. Seem all right. But what the fuck do I know? They may have ordered them from the same place I bought my fake driving license. I wouldn't know the difference. It's not pretty to be paranoid, but paranoid people live longer, I've read that somewhere. And now I have the distinct feeling that something bad has happened.

"Mister Harris?" Madinga asks, rather too late in the

game.

"Present." I say.

"We have some bad news for you."

I knew it! I knew it! Something horrible has happened. Cops don't just show up at your door for nothing. Madinga pronounced 'bad' like 'bed'. Bed news.

"And some questions."

"Well," I say, "can I have the good news first?"

Madinga blinks at me. Intent, Sello looks at the magnets on my refrigerator. They don't have time to lighten the mood. They prefer the Wham-Bam approach to police work.

"Mister Harris," Sello says, and my face pales in anticipation. "Evelyn Shaw was found murdered this morning."

His words take the breath from my lungs.

I realise mid-chortle that I'm chortling and stop. There are blades slicing up my brain.

"What do you mean?"

Sello takes a moment and then repeats himself. And still it takes a while for the words to make sense to me.

Eve. Dead. This morning.

When I finally grasp it I feel like the world is tumbling out of my body. I try to breathe in and out so that I don't faint on the hard shiny floor tiles, but I'm not doing such a great job. I'm dizzy. I hold onto the kitchen countertop with one hand and scratch my head with the other. Then I put my hands behind my head, elbows akimbo, and walk around the kitchen trying to get oxygen into my lungs. The pressed ceiling above me is a blur.

"*Dead?*" I say, hoping that I have heard wrong.

"Eve is *dead? Murdered?*" Hoping for anything but what these indifferent men have just told me. I know I'm pulling a strange face and I'm sorry they are here to see it.

"What happened? How do you know it was murder?" I ask.

Sello shrugs. I feel like punching him in the face.

"A car was spotted at the bottom of the river this morning by a pedestrian crossing the bridge. A beige Land Rover. We pulled it up and she was in there. We thought it was strange that … that she didn't try to get out – then we saw the lady had been killed – before she went in the river."

"What river?" I demanded.

"The Vaal," says Sello without taking his eyes off my Juicerator. I realise Sello isn't rude; he's just not good at dealing with delivering bed news.

I feel like laughing, smacking the guys on their backs and looking for a hidden camera because I can't imagine this news to be true.

That's when I experience a searing pain in my stomach. As if allergic to the lethal combination of fear and heartbreak, my spleen twists, my intestines knot, my kidneys burst. I double over. I hear the men speaking their ambush tongue again. In a jerk I stand up to run and make it to the guest toilet, just in time to heave. Afterwards it's dry and bitter in my mouth, like citrus pith, a drought-conceived lemon turned inside out. I check out my reflection and see red eyes floating in pale skin. I put my forehead against the mirror of the medicine cabinet. I sit on the edge of the bath. When I can breathe again I splash water on my face. I walk back to the kitchen and slump down on my chair. What a catastrophe, what a disaster. Someone is killed in the same way a writer has planned. Death imitating art. Meta-murder. What a cliché!

I sit with my head in my hands. It is perhaps the one time in my life that I have been truly speechless.

"We have some questions," says Madinga.

I shake my head. No one talks for a while. Eventually I get out a few stuttered words.

"I don't think I can answer any questions right now."

Laurel and Hardy look at each other again. They have a silent code. Sello takes out his notepad and lays it on the table. Then he takes a pen out of his shirt pocket and clicks it open next to his ear.

"Jesus Christ!" I explode. "Can't you people have some fucking sensitivity? I've just found out that the woman I love has been found dead, for God's sake. Can't you leave your Goddamn questions for another day?"

Sello is now looking at my glass toaster with a faraway

look in his eyes. I expect him to start whistling any second.

"I'm sorry," says Madinga, "but we will ask you now."

I bang my fist on the table. I want to roar at them and chase them from my house.

"Why? Do you think I had something to do with it? With killing Eve?" I splutter.

Madinga shakes his head. No, no, no, he is saying, no, well, maybe.

"We have no suspects yet," he says, "it is too early for that. We only ID'd her body a few hours ago. But we need to ask questions early."

I glare at him.

"It's routine," he says.

I can't argue with that. I will sit here and answer their questions like a good citizen and then show them on their way. As long as they don't ask to look around I should be okay.

"How well did you know Evelyn Shaw?"

How well did Gatsby know Daisy?

"Very well."

Madinga sees that I'm not going to be generous with my answers. Sello draws invisible squiggles on the paper in front of him, trying to make his dry ballpoint to work.

"Were you romantically involved?"

"I don't see how that's any of your business, or how that has a bearing on the investigation."

"Were you or not?" asks Madinga. As polite as he is, he's not going to be pushed around by an arty suburbian like me.

"No."

"But you said earlier that you loved her."

"I didn't mean it like that."

"How did you mean it?"

"I've known Eve for years, we were close. I loved her in that way."

Madinga's dark fingers play a piano melody on my table.

"What were you fighting about the other night?"

"The other night?"

"The night of your party, last weekend," says Sello, glad to chip in.

"Oh. It was nothing, just a few words said in a moment of anger."

"Did you push her to the floor?"

"What? No!"

"I have a witness who says you were shouting at her and then you pushed her down."

"Well, I didn't. Did you ask that person if he was drunk at the time?"

Madinga doesn't answer.

"But you admit to being angry with her."

"Yes," I say, "but friends get angry with one another. It doesn't mean that they go around stabbing each other and chucking cars off bridges on a whim. Yes, I was pissed off with her and yes, we raised our voices, but then it was over. She left the party. You can ask my domestic worker, Francina, she was here. She saw Eve leave."

"Is she around today?" asks Madinga, eyeing my smelly, crumpled shirt.

All of a sudden I'm really worried that something has happened to Francina too.

"She's missing," I blurt out. I motion to the messy state of the house.

"Well, I mean, not missing *per se*, but she hasn't come in to work this week and that's really unusual. And she's not answering her phone."

I give Sello her name, cell number and home address.

"How did you know the car went off the bridge?" asks Sello.

"Because. Because that's what you said."

"No," says Madinga, "I said the car was spotted by a pedestrian on the bridge."

158

"Well, I obviously misheard. It's a lot to take in." Fuck.

Sello makes his notes in long scrawls of vernacular.

I've had enough now. I've passed my being-polite-to-cops threshold. They stand up and Sello shakes my hand. I'm strangely touched by this.

I let them out of the front door and buzz the security gate for them.

Madinga nods a chary goodbye.

I go back to the kitchen, back to the scene of devastation. Everything I look at has Eve's face in it. I have to do something, something with my hands or I'll go mad. I turn on the Juicerator and watch the shiny blade spin. I take the biggest knife I can find in the stabbing block and grab an apple. I brutally chop it in half, then quarters, and feed it to the hungry machine. It makes short work of it – a chew, a gargle, and the apple has vanished, leaving a tot of cloudy apple juice in the jug. I feed it another apple, drawn and quartered, then a few apricots. I put in a pawpaw and a pineapple, skin and all. A peeled banana. A carrot. The jug is full now, past its 'max' marking on the side. I throw in all the kiwi fruit in the fridge. A guava quivers in the fruit bowl. The jug starts to overflow. A punnet of blueberries. I can smell the engine burning. Soon it will explode and I'll be covered in flaming engine parts and juice. I want to explode along with it.

In Chuck Palahniuk's *Diary*, an art student pours cement into a blender and switches it on. Of course it eventually, with a bit of noise and smoke, burns out, her unequivocal statement about her feelings regarding housework.

The Juicerator is shaking and overflowing.

My varsity shirt is covered in fruity offal. It looks like my organs have exploded onto my shirt: pawpaw seeds and blueberry juice. I let go of the Juicerator button and the silence hurts my ears. As if shot, I hold my fruit salad innards in and sink down onto the floor. I cry.

*

I wake up with my face glued to the kitchen floor. It's dark. My initial shock has given way to a duller kind of grief. I leave the mess I have made and go for a hot shower (Monsoon™). My mind has gone from a machine gun assault of thoughts to an unruly queue, one that I can just about control. Once clean, I set out to do what I should have done the second I saw a uniform at the door.

I retrieve my mind map with its awful dates and descriptions and creative scribblings and I tear it up into small pieces, cursing myself as I ransack my study. I cut up the photos with the kitchen scissors. I want to flush the GHB down the toilet but it has fallen off the map. I get down on my hands and knees and look for it. Breathe in floor-dust. I check the laundry basket. I shift my desk, my bookshelf, lift my couch, can't see the pills anywhere. I will look again in daylight.

I start a hungry fire in my BraaiMaster 1000 and when it's

really hot I start adding the scraps and shreds, one fistful at a time. The photos bubble and melt over the hot coals. Note-ashes levitate above the fire and catch the wind. Soon every trace I have of Eve will be gone.

When the plans have been turned to cinders I pick up my beloved Moleskine and hold it for a while. All those words! Precious, priceless words: letters and punctuation and sentences and paragraphs and pages of irreplaceable markings.

I feel like Abraham in Genesis, offering up my child to be burnt as a sacrifice. Or an island savage, keen to appease the gods, strong-arming a virgin into the liquid blaze of a volcano. Not wanting to, God knows, but knowing what has to be done.

I strip the cover off the book and throw it in, then tear the pages in half down the spine and throw those in too. Then I add extra lighter fluid and there is a woof of flames. Unable to stand there and watch it burn, I walk away.

I recheck my study for anything else that could possibly tie me to Eve's murder but think I found everything the first time round. I switch on my laptop, find my word document that I started yesterday (ten thousand really good words) and trash it. Then I empty my trash. The crumple sound-effect hurts.

The last thing I have to do is make the knife disappear. I look in the drawer of neglected kitchen utensils, but it's not there. I think I must have moved it when I was planning and writing. Caught in a thought, I could have absent-mindedly put it somewhere else. Methodically, I start going through one drawer at a time, until I know for certain it's not in any drawer then I start on the cupboards. Nothing. I start on the drawers again but this time I empty all their contents onto the floor. I switch on every light in the house. I go from room to room. After an hour of frantic searching I feel acid rising in my throat. It has disappeared: the knife is no longer in my house.

In a flash of crimson dread I remember the day I had lunch with Eve in her studio and how I went into her room and touched her things. My fingerprints must be all over the place. Jesus Christ. My stalker episode couldn't have had worse timing. My heart raps against my ribs. With shaking hands I pour myself a glass of water. I have to get rid of those damn prints. I'm sure that her place is overrun with cops at the moment but I'll have to get in somehow. Without a sip I grab my car keys and head out of the door, into the dark.

There is a police guard outside Eve's front door, as if to protect her memory because it is too late to protect her. I have to wait for almost two hours before he abandons his post for some kind of break. I move as quickly and quietly as possible and find myself standing in the lounge, gloved hands by my sides, my breath coming in short, sharp gasps.

Eve's flat is an uproar of yellow and black crime tape.

I go straight to her bedroom. The other prints can be explained but not the ones on her headboard, mirror, perfume. I start looking around to see if they have dusted for prints already but don't see any powder residue. Perhaps that's why they have the guard at the door: they haven't completed the processing of the crime scene yet. I use a bandanna I bought on the way here to wipe everything I remember touching.

The whole exercise, while peculiar, is therapeutic. Eve's room doesn't look very different from how it looked a week ago when she was still breathing. Its sameness is haunting.

When I think I am done I begin walking to the studio kitchen, but a noise at the door startles me and I jump back behind the doorframe. The door handle turns. Surely the policeman shouldn't be coming in? It's a crime scene for God's sake. Then: a woman's voice and high heels on tiles. My mind hurtles. The hair on the back of my neck stands up. I try to control my breathing. Figure out what to do. The back window is protected with burglar bars. The bathroom window is too small for escape. I hear a handbag being dropped onto the kitchen counter, and then a heavier sound, on the floor. The kettle is switched on. A sigh as a hinge yields: a cupboard door opening. Porcelain plunked on marble. The kettle clicks off and hot water streams into the mug. Another breath and then the melody of a teaspoon stirring. A snapping sound as the crime tape is ripped down. I wonder if I am imagining the moment when Eve was killed. If it is my punishment to have to relive, second by excruciating second, what happened to her last night. I sense that she is moving towards me and I dive under the bed. She turns the light on and seems to hesitate before she walks in. I'm sure she can hear my heart beating, smell the hot sweat I feel under my clothes. She walks past the bed and into the bathroom. All I can see are her feet. Elegant black shoes. She turns on the bath taps and adds foam. I don't dare risk edging closer to get a better look at her. She dims the lights, puts a match to candles. She goes back to the kitchen to fetch her tea and brings it to the bath, each time walking past the bed, so close to me I could reach out and touch her ankle.

I have no idea what to do except lie where I am and be as quiet as possible. I will stay here for days if it means not being caught under the bed of the woman I am suspected of killing. It would be impossible to explain. If I die here, under this bed, at least I will never have to put this trespassing into words.

My muddled brain tells me Eve's ghost is here: come to show me my culpability in this crime. I did, after all, imagine this over and over again, in this exact sequence. As truly shocked as I was to learn that Eve had been murdered – and I was, still am, truly, completely, exhaustively shocked – there was some kind of harrowing glint, some small flash of acquaintance with the fact, as if some tucked-away part of me knew it would happen all along.

16

The Ghost Begins Taking Off

Her Clothes

The ghost begins taking off her clothes. Heels are kicked off. A cashmere cardigan, a blouse and a pencil skirt all land next to my head. A black camisole. Wrinkled stockings, like shed snakeskin. The smell of Eve's perfume fills my nose. There is also something else familiar, but I can't think what it is. Bare-soled and naked she walks towards the bath, turns off the taps and steps in, facing away from me. It's not Eve. This woman is tall and has dark hair. What is she doing drinking Eve's tea, bathing in Eve's bath? I can't imagine a possible answer.

A pressure starts building up in my chest and I am finding it difficult to keep my breathing quiet. I wonder if it is the beginning of a panic attack and, if so, I have to get out from under here before this woman hears me. I lift myself up on my elbows and begin to inch my way out, leopard crawling with the stealth that comes with being an ex-soldier. For a moment I sense she has heard me and I freeze there on the carpet in the middle of the room, in plain view were she to turn her head. She starts moving again and I am able to slither out of there.

In the passage I almost knock over a pile of boxes that weren't there earlier, just miss tripping over a suitcase. I see the handbag and am tempted to look for ID but am spooked by voices outside. Perhaps a new shift is starting. I try to look under the front door to see if I can figure out an exit plan but I can't tell what the shadows mean.

I tiptoe towards Eve's studio, thinking there must be a way out there. The place is filled with huge windows with no burglar bars. Closer, I see why: the drop down is so high no burglar would chance trying to climb up to break in. I squint in the bad light to see if there is anything I can climb down on. The last window on the eastern side is near a tree and I consider trying to jump onto its branches but am dissuaded by my memory of a) bad luck with climbing trees and b) a particular scene in First Blood, when Rambo ends up with a branch through some part of his body and resorts to stitching it up himself.

I try the back door of the studio kitchen. It is locked, but I have extra keys on the ring Eve gave me and when I turn one of them in the lock it works. The back door leads out onto a narrow ledge used for drying washing and storing rubbish and I have to feel my way along in the dark. At the end of the row I find a metal staircase leading into the underground parking lot. From here it's plain sailing: I walk out of the pedestrian gate at the entrance and I'm home, free.

As I walk to my car, parked on the next block, I shake my head at the vast amount of trouble I have caused myself in the last few days. Any normal person would not be in this position. Then again, I have done a lot to ensure that I am not a normal person, so I guess I have to deal with the consequences. Usually I am okay with this: as long as I am fucking up my own life, I'm fine with it. But this is different.

This has gone too far.

17

AS IF ANYTHING MATTERED

Today is Eve's funeral. A relative I never knew she had called yesterday to invite me. The cremation is to happen in a grimy little place in Braamfontein (not Eve's style at all) and then there will be drinks at the unknown relative's house. Distracted, I wonder who has arranged the funeral.

The same details are listed in the newspaper obituary I hold in my hand. They ask for donations to Eve's favourite charity (the Teddy Bear Clinic) in lieu of flowers.

Fuck that, I think, Eve deserves flowers.

I arrive at the crematorium early so I can look around. I've never been to one before. I watched a funeral pyre in India once. It was colourful, poignant, fragrant, life affirming: nothing like this cave. I walk to the front and deposit the enormous bouquet I bought on my way here. It is an over-the-top arrangement of dozens of Eve's favourite papery cream-colored roses. It looks out of place in this downmarket dungeon.

The room is small and airless, with a tangible sense of

impending doom. There is a balding velvet curtain like in the movies, just not as glamorous, and wooden fold-up chairs that wouldn't take the weight of anyone over 100kg. A rugby player's grieving entourage wouldn't be welcome here. I'm not a small man so I sit down with caution, trying to not reduce the thing into matchsticks. It seems I have done enough damage.

I know about cremation. I know that Christians didn't come around to the idea until the nineteenth century. I know the furnaces are heated using gas, diesel oil or electricity. It takes about two hours, at a temperature ranging from 700 to 1,100 °C. The one I'm sitting in now is gas-operated (may as well do your bit to fight global warming on your way out) and probably gets to around 900°C. That's nine times the heat of boiling water.

I'd have thought Eve would have preferred a 'greener' burial, like having a tree planted in her honour, or something like that. But I guess she didn't have much say.

I wonder what they'll do with the ashes.

I've always thought the idea of keeping someone's ashes bizarre. I feel suffocated just thinking of being stuck in a hand-painted flea-market urn on a mantelpiece. I much prefer the poetry of graves and graveyards. If I could choose where to be buried it would be in Père Lachaise in Paris. It's not very patriotic I know, but then I'd be dead, so no matter. Imagine being buried in the same soil as Jim Morrison, Stuart Merrill, Colette! It's haunting, with its ancient trees and cobbled lanes, a grand place with a kind of rich, earthy gravitas. A place that Takes Death Seriously. They don't have gravestones as much as they have monuments to the dead, many with tended gardens, crowded with grass and roses and fat purple irises. I visited it for the first time in 1990; after escaping the monotony of school I was on the first plane to Anywhere, which turned out to be Holland. From there I spent the next two years on trains, backpacking through Europe, doing odd jobs when I needed the cash and writing all the while. I used to post my bursting journals home to Dad when they got too heavy, and he stored them in the room he always kept open for me. I discovered Père Lachaise by accident. New to the Metro (and French), I got off at the wrong stop and it was just there, like an omen. I spent hours exploring, lost in the drama of the moss-stained cherubs and slabs of marble. It is as wistful as cemeteries come: a host of cinnamon daffodils; Oscar Wilde's lipstick-coated art deco tomb and a little girl carrying a red rose, which I could only imagine was for the Little Sparrow's grave. Having *'La Vie En Rose'* play over and over in my head as I tried to find my way out. Only afterwards did I realise how much the experience affected me. I would keep seeing the winding paths, feeling the coolness of the trees, running my fingers over the names engraved on the stones. The memory burrowed inside me and now I can't go to the city of lights without paying my respects.

The ginger-haired pastor is well meaning (as some Men Of God are) and says nice things about Eve, but you can see right through his speech. He may as well be selling Chinese herbs on television. He has a paint-by-numbers template which he follows, cutting and pasting where appropriate, like Eulogies for Dummies. I imagine him going through his questionnaire with Eve's family. ("Was she kind?" Tick. "Was she religious?" Cross. "Was she beautiful?" Tick. "Was she in love?" Cross.) Then the questionnaire is fed into a machine and within seconds it spits out the funeral speech, like the novel-writing machine in Roald Dahl's imagination, called the *The Great Automatic Grammatizator.*

I find myself staring at his agitated mustard moustache for most of his one-soul-fits-all tribute. Jesus liked a bit of facial hair. In fact, I think you can go so far as to say that he was quite a fan. I, on the other hand, don't trust people with moustaches. I look around at all the strangers perching on their fragile seats. Eve never talked about her family or her past. Not a word on childhood sweethearts or leering teachers. Acting as if she was born into this world as a gorgeous twenty year old with a life all set out for her. Like someone had dreamed her up out of nowhere, or off a picture in *Hello* magazine. No one in the room looks too much like Eve. Perhaps she was adopted.

As the moustache drones on I make a note to self: to write my own funeral ceremony. Think out of the box: as in turn creative, not zombie. In some countries the dead are buried in theme-shaped coffins according to which profession they pursued while alive. So a gardener would be buried in a flower-shaped box, a priest in a cross, and a carpenter in a … well I guess a carpenter would just be buried in a regular coffin. I wonder what writers are buried in? Caskets that look like books? It would be appropriate, especially when they close the lid.

In another country they dig out their dead once a year, dress them up in their finest silks and jewels, and have a rocking party in their honour. That's more my style.

I was once sent to Mexico on a journo assignment to report on the Festival of The Dead. The piece was actually supposed to be about how different cultures experience grief and death, but I was captivated by *El Día de los Muertos* and ended up staying a week longer than I was supposed to. I found the concept of celebrating death so intriguing and after eating my first sugar skull I was hooked. The locals I interviewed believed that All Souls Day was the time when it was easiest for spirits to contact them. They would entice their deceased into visiting by laying out offerings and treats: toys for dead children and bread and bottles of tequila for adults. Also, blankets for everyone, so that they could rest after their long journey. An all-night vigil ensued, where the living ate the offerings but said they were left with hollow stomachs, because the goodness of the food had already been appropriated by the spooks. My memories of Mexico are orange. There are thousands upon thousands of marigolds strewn everywhere during the festival. They are known as the *Flor de Muerto*, Flower of the Dead, and are believed to attract the souls of the sleeping.

We left toys out for Emily. Her favourite dolls, a trike, a giant Pink Panther, a plastic tea set and some little ponies. We kept her bedroom just as she left it. The room's cheerfulness breathed cold on my neck; sometimes I would close the door.

I fight the memory of Emily's funeral. I knew this would happen. I close my eyes to keep it out, breathe deep, curl my fingers into fists.

I think of Emily's coffin and how tiny it was. Stunted, like her life. Small and white, seemingly inconsequential. White lilies. Everything else in black: a moratorium on bright colours lest they remind anyone that she was just a child.

I loosen my collar and swallow, trying to fend off the assault of the memories I know so well. Not calm, like this ceremony. Loud and wet and cold and hot. Everyone stroking me on the day I felt allergic to touch. Strangers saying how handsome I looked in my 'little suit', as if the size of my clothes saddened them, as if the clothes I was wearing mattered. As if anything mattered.

I start to feel claustrophobic. A trickle of sweat runs down my ribs.

Just before the pastor says his closing words I'm out of there, out into the new air and fresh sky. I take off my jacket, sling it over my arm and stride to my car, where I sit for a while with the aircon on full-blast, staring through the windscreen, not seeing anything.

I have a hand-drawn map of how to get to the wake, which I crumple up and throw out of the window. I don't want to go. I don't know any of these people and I'm in pain. I want to be in bed with a bottle of Glenfiddich and the curtains drawn, not eating soggy canapés and making small talk with old, fat, swollen-eyed women. But I know I can't not go, so I start my engine and pull away. The streets I drive along are dappled and pretty once I get out of Braamfontein. My GPS takes me into Orange Grove, where I narrowly miss hitting a *Homeless Talk* man running towards my car looking like Gollum. I hoot at him and show him the finger. Surely he knows that people in sports cars don't buy *The Big Issue*?

I drive past a tombstone showroom. Only in Africa. Death is such a huge business, what with the violence and AIDS. It reminds me of a main road in Lagos that stretches past the major hospital. I called it Funeral Town. There are people standing by the side of the road selling cheap coffins. They display them, looking like cardboard cut-outs. Billboards plastered on the bridge supports and perimeter walls advertising discount funerals, as if when someone you love dies your priority is finding a bargain. If that's what it looked like outside I can't imagine the chaos inside the hospital. Scamming suitcase undertakers poised to pounce, like hyenas.

It's a bustling road and people swarm around my car. There are hawkers selling avocados and peaches, wire sculptures, lighters, fake designer shades and cold Cokes. The robot is still green; maybe I'll make it through. The junker in front of me is driving so slowly it may as well be going backwards. The taxi beside me is an inch away from scratching my paintwork and the bakkie behind is so far up my arse I feel violated. Cocky, greasy, pedestrians weave their way through the traffic, touching the cars as they go. I hate it when people touch my car. The robot turns orange. I can still make it. I hoot at the car in front to accelerate but it has the opposite effect. The robot turns red and I shout and bang my steering wheel. I hate red traffic lights on these roads in particular. They may as well hand out firearms to the hijackers. I'm a sitting duck. As soon as the red light appears the hawkers hit the road in a well-practised, choreographed invasion. The *Homeless Talk* guy catches up with me and hits my roof twice – hard – to show me he's back. I feel my heart banging loud and fast, hammering away at my breastbone. The noises around me become amplified; I hear people shouting at me and cars hooting. My lungs feel like they're filling with water. I can only breathe in short, sharp breaths. I start hyperventilating. Am I having a heart attack? I hit my chest and cough hard, twice, just in case. The man is dancing for me and smiling. He knocks on my window, leaving oily knuckle marks behind. I need air but I don't want to get out of my car on this unfriendly street. My legs are unsteady.

The robot turns green, the hawkers disappear and I put my foot down.

The house is a golden oldie, probably built in the 50s. Sturdy and squat, built with red bricks, a green tin roof and plaster which is now crumbling away. The floors are polished Oregon pine throughout, the walls are varying shades of nutmeg and vanilla, and the house smells like unwashed dogs and tobacco. The original pressed ceilings and grubby walls remind me of my father's house, and that I should go and see him again. This could have been his funeral and my last memory of him would be that stuttering phone call on the night of my party.

I am shepherded through the house and out the back door into the bright heat of the midday sun. A dainty cup of tea is pressed into my hand. Oh God, I hope this isn't a dry wake. I'm still sweating from the panic attack in the car. Somehow I don't think that this tepid tea will do a good enough job of settling my jangling nerves. I dodge and sidestep to a downcast potted palm in the corner and surreptitiously empty my tea into it. Probably do the plant more good than it would me.

The garden is overgrown and parched. Tired branches, dusty leaves, desert sand. Patches of old damp blister the garden walls. The garden looks the way I feel. I abandon the empty teacup on the refreshment table. As I turn around, an old lady in a floral shift accosts me.

"Who are you?" she barks. Indigo eyes drill into my face.

"I am … I was a friend of Eve's. She designed one of my book covers. That's how we met." The way she looks at me makes me want to tell her more, but I can't think of anything else.

"How did you know Eve?" I venture.

"You're the writer, then," she says, not without distaste. She has an Afrikaans accent and speaks in a kind of undulating high pitch, rolling her r's and raising her vowels as only Afrikaans women can.

"Yes."

"Harris."

"Yes. Slade."

She wrinkles her nose.

"Have you written anything I would know?" she asks.

A cent for every time someone asked me that.

"Doubt it," I lie.

"Irma Shaw," she says, shoving her flabby hand out at me like a Nazi.

I recoil. It's cold and too soft, like toad skin. Tofu. Testicles.

"I'm Evelyn's *tannie*. Not that she knew it!"

"I'm sorry?"

"We didn't see a lot of her. She never took the time out of her ..." she clears her throat, "busy schedule. To come and *kuier*."

So much for not speaking ill of the dead.

"Yes," I nod, "she was a very hard worker. She was always working. She was a workaholic."

I know I'm rambling. I don't know where these words are coming from.

"Not even at Christmas," she sighs, fingering the gold cross on her chest. "The Holy Lord's birthday. Can you imagine? *Gena-a-a-a-ade. Haar eie familie*! Don't get me wrong; I don't speak badly of no one. It's just that, *ag* man, we missed her!"

"I never had the pleasure of speaking to Eve about her hometown," I say, "Where is it?"

As she hesitates a grey man puts a hand on her shoulder and whispers in her ear. She nods and turns to walk away, turns back, and says, "It was nice to meet you, Slade."

The sun gets hotter on my skin. Damn African summers. I decide I need to look for alcohol. There is a man in tweed bringing out clean teacups.

"Excuse me," I say with a chuckle, trying as much as possible to not look like an alcoholic, "Any chance of something stronger here?"

He looks up, smiles, but doesn't speak. Uncomfortable, I smile; typical of me to ask the only deaf/mute guy. He walks back into the house. I think I may have to leave soon. I'm not sure that I can stand here for another minute. I stare vaguely into the glum garden, planning my escape excuse. There's a gentle tap on my back and I turn around to see the smiling tweed-man. He hands me a bottle of cheap whisky and a glass of old-fashioned ice. The opaque kind, from metal ice-trays with the handle running down the centre dividing the cubes. Smooth and white, as if someone has frozen smoke inside.

I take it from him and he walks away before I get to say thanks. I don't recognise the dusty label at all but I don't care. I would drink methylated spirits right now if it was the only drink on offer. I pour a good four fingers and put the bottle on the table. Sharing is caring.

I hear a familiar voice coming from inside the house.

" … She was one of my FAVOURITE artists … "

Sifiso. I feel I could do with a friendly face.

"… Very TALENTED and also very LOVELY WOMAN …"

He strolls outside and winces at the bright sunshine. He sees me and walks over, puts his right hand in mine and his left on my back. It's very comforting. I see for the first time that he is probably a very good father to his kids.

"I'm so SORRY, Slade," he says, shaking his head. "I'm so sorry. I know how much you LOVED Eve. How CLOSE you were."

My throat constricts. I try to swallow the ache but it doesn't go away. I am overwhelmed by my gratitude to this man, for coming today, for touching me, for saying those words.

"I can't believe this has happened," I whisper to him. I reek of desperation.

"Senseless," he says and shakes his head. "It makes me wonder what KIND of COUNTRY we are living in, with all this violence. *Eish*, it's a TRAGEDY." He is still shaking his head, like a dashboard dog. "It makes me worried for my KIDS, man."

I nod. *False face must hide what false heart doth know.* Only when I am overwhelmed do I quote Shakespeare.

I wonder what Sifiso would think if he knew I had planned her murder.

I finally start to feel the warm sliding effects of the whisky. Bless you Jesus. The muscles in my back begin to unknit. Perhaps I'll introduce myself to a few more relatives and try to find out a little more about Eve. It will be my last opportunity and I need all the closure I can muster. I see Frank arrive; he stands in the doorway. Glad to see another face I recognise, I wave at him. If I had a tail it would be wagging. He flashes a look of pure menace at me. Before I know what's going on, he stalks over and punches me right in the face, smashing my nose. My glass goes flying and I hear it shattering on the slasto. I drop to the grass and hot blood shoots out of my nostrils. Beyond the black stars I hear Sifiso yelling at Frank and Frank yelling back. Frank shouts down at me "You sonofabitch! You said it was for your book! You said you weren't really going to do it!" he shoves me with his foot.

Everyone stops what they're doing to gawk at the three of us. "This is no kind of behaviour for a funeral," I can imagine the old farts saying with quivering jowls. "You'd think they'd show a little *respect.*"

"What are you TALKING about, man?" shouts Sifiso. "Have you gone CRAZY?"

The blood is shiny on the green grass. Wet, shiny rubies.

Painting the roses red.

Eve was my Queen of Hearts.

"You should be asking Slade that!"

Sifiso is impatient by nature and seems ready to punch out Frank's lights, despite being a good two feet shorter than him.

I get to my knees and hold the bridge of my nose, trying to stem the flow. It doesn't work and the front of my shirt is soon dyed red.

"You've made me an accomplice!" he yells at me, spit flying into the air.

I feel something inside me click, swivel, burst, dissolve. Something breaks, tears, starts leaking air like a bicycle puncture. Something changes inside me forever. I am damaged. Not because of Frank's words or his fist in my face, not because of Eve's tawdry funeral or mute dressed in tweed, but because this is the moment that everything makes sense and nothing makes sense. I see who I am but I don't know who that is. My mind crumples up, and I am powerless to stop it.

"An accomplice to WHAT, Frank?" yells Sifiso.

"Keep your voice down," I say to Sifiso through gritted teeth. Still in my position of surrender, I turn to Frank.

"You think I *did* it?" I ask him. "What kind of person do you think I am? You know how much I cared for her."

Frank snorts.

A dark-haired beauty arrives. She has a red lipstick smile and a tattoo on her arm that peeks out from under a silk sleeve. She adjusts her sunglasses and lights a cigarette. Despite my situation I feel drawn to her; something in her face and body language strikes me. She feels my eyes on her and looks straight at me, at my crimson shirt, and I look away.

Frank speaks in low tones now: "All I know is that she was killed exactly the same way you described it. And I find that frikkin' weird, what do you say?"

Sifiso erupts.

"What do I SAY? I say you'd better tell me what the hell's going on here before I pop a cap in someone's ass."

Okay, he didn't really say that. Sifiso is not ghetto like that. I just thought it sounded good coming from a short, angry black man.

"What do I SAY?" he really said, "I say you'd better tell me what the hell this is all about!"

*

At home I peel off my blood-soaked shirt and throw it in the bin. I have a gentle shower (Amazon Rainforest™) and watch all the brown pigment run from my body in a neat line down into the drain. I inspect my chest hair for any leftover blood and wonder briefly why we still have chest hair. I would have thought that we've evolved beyond it by now but then, remembering the day's events, my question seems to be answered.

I wash my face, gingerly, trying not to touch my swollen nose. It will scar and be misshapen. I know I should go to Dr. Olaf to have it set but I feel like I deserve this impediment, just like I deserve the pain that is everywhere in my body. I am numb already but drink Glenfiddich out of the bottle anyway. I'm hoping that I will in time click back, uncrumple, heal. I wish that fate could have taken me instead of my Eve but now I realise that I am dying too. Only Eve didn't have to suffer this torturous, slow decay.

In the mirror a purple raccoon stares back at me.

18

INDIGO SHADES

Only people who have been broken will know this feeling: that nothing matters anymore. It's when things get so bad that you resign yourself to never being happy again, to living a sham of a life. It's like having a permanent subtitle stamped on your vision: *Nothing Matters.* It's there when you close your eyes to go to sleep at night and it's there the next morning when you wake up, before you have time to think that this day will be better. It's especially apparent when you are brushing your teeth or trying to summon the energy to lift your arms to wash your hair in the shower. Apart from the subtitle there is also a kind of blurriness to the picture. Whatever the opposite is of rose-tinted glasses – maybe they are indigo shades – too dark to see through properly, making flowers and reflections look fuzzy and black.

Meaning is hidden.

You would think that *Nothing Matters* makes the pain less, because whatever is causing you the pain doesn't matter, but unfortunately it escapes this neat logic, and instead, the more life hurts, the more it doesn't matter, so the more it hurts.

19

A BAD WIZARD

Francina is still AWOL and my house is chaotic. I knew I wouldn't be able to hold it together without her. The anarchic state of the place reflects my state of mind: spiralling. I know that I should start cleaning but I'm surrounded by such dark energy that I'm finding it difficult to feed myself, never mind pick up a dustbuster.

Eve's violent death is sitting in my chest, hot and cold and heavy. With this come the mental Polaroids of the funeral: Eve's toad-skinned aunt, the mute man, warm whisky in a teacup once my glass was shattered, pain, a bag of frozen peas, and rubies on green grass. Mixed in are the foggy memories of Emily's funeral: being suffocated by the hot floral nylon dresses of well-meaning friends, the cloying sweetness of lemon cake icing, Mom, blank, looking like one of her Vermeer paintings. The smell of the over-polished timber pews. The chocolate-box picture of Em, blown up and framed for the ceremony. Dad looking like he should be the one in the coffin.

I realise that I have been standing in one spot for a very long time, staring at the state of the kitchen in some kind of zombie trance. There is just too much stuff. Too much mess. Too many memories.

I need to get out of the house. In an act of desperation I hit the tarmac in my designer running gear that I bought a year ago and have never worn except to try it on.

I stretch my calves on the grass verge and can't help feeling like an idiot. Like someone who is pretending to be a runner. While I pretend to warm up my ankles I see the little Munchkin again. Isn't that what they call the singing midgets in the Wizard of Oz? I think of how I am like the wizard. Orchestrating the show of my life only to be revealed as a fraud and a bad fraud at that.

Dorothy tells the wizard that he is a bad man, to which the wizard responds something like,"A bad wizard, but not a bad man."

I fear that I am the inverse. Or worse, that I am bad at both.

She meows at me, narrows her yellow eyes. The base of her tail shakes like a rattlesnake. I know now that she won't let me approach her, so I just keep still and try to appear non-threatening, which is relatively easy when you're wearing Polyshorts.

She meows again and minces towards me. I crouch with caution. She is within stroking reach but I resist the temptation. She blinks at me. I narrow my eyes at her. And then she is gone, tail high in the air, as if I have bored her.

I ease into the run, with Sylvia chiming in her

encouragement for every kilometre I reach. We are officially living in the future; I know this because my shoe talks to me when I run. She tells me how far I've gone, whether I'm running fast enough or not, and always congratulates me on my longest run or fastest time. If I was really dedicated I would plug it into my computer to log my runs and then I would have a graph of my performance. It's straight out of the sci-fi comics I used to read as a kid.

On the mental rim of the memories of the funerals there is something more painful. Too intense to think about. For a moment I think that I am losing the battle and that the throbbing stuff will come crashing through, but in the end I win and it recedes. It is grey, stifling, acrid. I try to push it back as far as it will go, but I can tell that it is only a matter of time before it will break free and swirl through my body. It makes me run faster. My lungs and leg muscles burn, but it feels good.

20

HER VOICE IS CHARCOAL, OR,

BLACK UMBILICAL CORD

Still broken: there is only one thing for this misery and that is to see how much more miserable I can possibly become. I decide to visit my dad.

I spend less time at Woolworth's than usual. I feel self-conscious because people are staring at my blue and broken face. Usually I enjoy the attention but today it feels like everyone can see my dirty secret. I grab a few things I know my father will like. There's no point shopping for myself – I have no appetite. And there is no Francina to cook. I stand at the shelf of tinned goods looking for sardines, thinking I'll probably have more luck looking at the pet food section.

"Hello," she says to me, as if we'd known each other all our lives. Her voice is charcoal.

"Hello," I deadpan. For once, I'm not interested. I flash my eyes at her and back at the shelf. Something tingles. Avoiding eye contact, I grab a tin of something from the shelf.

"You were at the funeral," she says.

I turn to her. It's Tattoo Girl.
Redlippedsilkshirtedinkskinned beauty. I definitely know her from somewhere.

"Yes," I say, fingering my coconut milk.

"You were bleeding," she says, and points to my nose.

"Yes," I touch it. "Yes, I was."

"Interesting thing to do at a funeral," she says.

"Bleed?" I ask.

Husky laugh. "That too, but I meant … have a fist fight."

"*Ja*," I say, "it wasn't my idea."

Her lips twist into a scarlet smile. She has the most amazing eyelashes.

"It looks sore."

"You should see the other guy."

The laugh again.

"I should be going," I say, motioning towards the junk food aisle.

"Yes," she says, and watches me walk away.

I join the queue, wait in line and pay. Only when I reach my car do I realise I have made a mistake. There was definitely something between us, some spark, maybe something more interesting than a spark. I jog back to the store to see her but she has disappeared. I check the aisles and the parking lot but she is gone.

Dad seems to be in better spirits this time. The front doorbell is still not working but I knock hard enough and he hears me.

"Good God, son," he exclaims when he sees my black eyes and purple nose. "It looks like you've gone ten rounds with Muhammed."

He means the boxer, not the prophet.

"Was it for a girl?" he asks, mischief gleaming in his eyes. The poor bastard. I think if I had nice wife and few sprogs bouncing off the walls he'd feel a lot less hopeless.

"Kind of," I say.

His ancient Dalmatian lumbers in. Domino's fat and unsteady on her old legs. Her nails scratch the floor beneath her. I stroke her head and come away with waxy brown fingers. I wash my hands under the kitchen tap with a hard cake of soap.

I slice two soft rye rolls in half and fill them with butter lettuce, tomato, sliced pickle, shaved chicken, Perinaise, a dusting of black pepper. I open a packet of kettle-fried potato crisps and shake them out onto the side of the plates. We go through the motions. Dad takes the beers out of the fridge.

"Manchester United is playing Arsenal," he announces and shuffles away in his old *stokies*.

All of a sudden I feel great comfort. The routine, the unstuck predictability of these days, my father's prickly love.

During half time he asks me if I have heard anything from Mom. It makes me think that she hasn't sent a gift for a long time and I wonder, briefly, if she is still alive. Not that it would make that much difference to us. She is not a person, not to me, not really. She is an abstract thought, a ghost, a distant memory. I can't believe he's still in love with her. There should be an emotional statute of limitations when it comes to loving someone who leaves you. After five years there should be a cutting of that black umbilical cord; a cool sharp snip and your sadness and longing should disappear.

He still keeps the photo he has of all of us above the fireplace. It was taken that summer in the Cape. I don't know how he can stand it. Inside a burnished silver frame stands a beautiful auburn-haired mother, a tall, handsome father, a cocky eight-year-old holding his sister's hand. The little sister with sun freckles and bright eyes; the prize of the family. The photo is old and faded but the vitality of the four people jumps off the page, nothing like we are now. Vast smiles and coral cheeks. I try to not think too much about it.

He catches me looking at it and I jump away, as if he'd walked in on me rifling through his medicine cabinet. At least he's taken the rest down. This mantelpiece used to be a shrine to our patchy past.

The reception on the small TV set is snowy but the game is a good one. I spend the time drinking my beer in long draughts, stroking Domino's stomach with my foot and thinking despairing thoughts. Eve was right. I don't have any meaning in my life and that's why it's so damn dismal. But where do you get meaning? I'm sure Gandhi didn't have to go looking for it. Or Charles Manson (meaning doesn't have to be right or good, it just has to be meaningful) who knew without a doubt what he was put on this planet to do and he did it, brainwashing a good few kamikazes on the way. You could be outright evil and still have meaning in your life (Hitler, Idi Amin, Verwoerd). I should have it. I am a writer, for God's sake. If anyone should have meaning it's writers and artists and leaders – people whose work affects others. Even if I don't want it, I have a certain responsibility to others because my work affects them. I don't like that idea at all. I feel that it will limit me, strangle my voice. A part of me believes that I should be able to write whatever I want to, completely unhindered by the effect it will have on the reader. Surely that is true freedom?

There is a lull in the game and I go where I really don't want to go, to the small, tucked- away room in my head I've been avoiding since the cops showed up at my house on Saturday morning. How much responsibility does a writer really have? If a writer kills someone in his story, he has to be accountable for that person. Writers can't go around willy-nilly, killing off their characters, or can they? Before, I would have said isn't that the whole point? That it's not real and so you can do whatever you want to them. But now I wonder if there are consequences. For a writer, that means controlling words, characters, action. Perhaps, *à la The Godfather*, blood really is a big expense.

Death is a great plot device. Erica Jong says that when she looks back on her eight novels, she finds that she hasn't murdered enough people. She finds breaking any of the Ten Commandments good for plotting a novel, but murder and adultery best. That authors lie about how much it hurts them to murder their characters; that, anyway, novelists love to weep.

Dad has fallen asleep in his chair, his dehydrated lips slightly parted, his wallpaper backdrop faded and peeling. I take the beer glass from his hand, set it down on the coffee table. I try to look at him without pity. That must be the worst – living with all that pity. All the kind smiles and tilted heads, the apple pies and oven-dried macaroni cheeses that still find their way to the door after all these years. I wouldn't be able to stand it. Maybe that's what he would have said at my age.

But things happen. If I don't know anything else, I know that.

I watch the sunset from the park near my house. The usual pram-pushers and dog-walkers are about. I sit cross-legged on the grass and try not to think too much. I look around at the pink clouds and the light they cast on the willows. I try to keep my mind clear, not holding onto the thoughts that come into my head. It's the most I can do at the moment: try to hold on to my sanity. I do this for about ten minutes before I give up. I wonder if I will ever feel peaceful again. And then I see her. Ink lady. The woman from Eve's funeral. She's walking down by the river. She is barefoot and has her sandals in her hand, as if she's walking on the beach. To see her twice in one day strikes me as bizarre. She must live around here. I'm not in the mood for company but I am drawn to this strange woman. I'm on my feet, dusting the grass off my trousers and halfway to her before she notices me.

"Hello again," I say.

"Hello," she smiles. She's wearing a peaked cap and sunglasses, which make her look like an undercover celebrity. She has straight white teeth. She smoothes down her black hair and it shines in the dusk.

"I'm sorry I was rude earlier."

"You weren't," she says.

She starts walking again, so I join her. We fall into a rhythm, as if we have done this before.

"I meant to ask you earlier how you knew Eve."

"Well, that's a long story," she smiles.

"In that case, let's discuss it over dinner," I say. I don't even have to think about picking up women anymore. I don't have to try: the words just tumble out of my mouth.

She stops walking, which I take as a good sign. Takes off her sunglasses to look at me. Toes the grass while she thinks about it, then looks up and says "Okay."

The soft light is in her eyes: an almost unbelievable shade of blue. I wonder if they are contacts.

"What about tomorrow night?" I ask.

"What about now?" she says.

We walk the kilometre or so until we get to the strip of restaurants and antique stores. We decide on a small Italian place that is decorated floor to ceiling with golden olive oil tins, bottles of wine with thick skins of dust, posters of *Italia*. There only eight tables in the whole place. It's my favourite place to eat. The waiter trips over himself to help us. He brings salty focaccia and a bottle of Diemersfontein. Eve doesn't want to eat, so I pour her a glass of wine that she picks up and swirls. It smells like chocolate.

"So we haven't officially introduced ourselves."

I was enjoying not knowing her name; she is perhaps the most mysterious person I have met. She puts her glass down, shakes back her mane.

"I'm Slade," I say, sticking out my hand.

"Denise," she says, shaking.

"So do you live around here? You look so familiar, but I can't quite place you."

"No, I just came up for Eve's funeral. I'm staying at her place, sorting out her stuff."

Ah. I've seen her naked.

We are serenaded by Eros Ramazotti singing 'L'Aurora' on the crackly speakers.

"I'm surprised she's never mentioned you to me. You two must have been close – I mean – if she trusted you with sorting out her things."

"It just kind of fell to me to do. We weren't that close," she says.

"Oh." There is a lull. I try to think of something else to say, but she beats me to it.

"We were sisters."

Sisters? Eve never talked about a sister.

"Let me guess," Denise says wryly, "She never mentioned a sister."

"No, she didn't," I say, "but to be honest she never talked about any of her family. The lot at the funeral could have been rent-a-crowd for all I know."

Denise's lips stutter a smile.

"When she left home, she didn't look back. She cut off her family completely."

"But Eve's not like that," I say, "Not the Eve I know. Knew."

"There were things … that happened. I don't blame her for leaving. It's a small town. Not a lot happens, but when things do, there's nowhere to hide."

"What things?"

"It's not really for me to say."

I can tell that she doesn't want to talk about it and I don't push her. Not yet.

"So you're a small-town girl?"

"Yip," she says, nodding, not offering any more details.

"Do you want to come to my place for a cappuccino?" I ask.

"Why? Are the cappuccinos here bad?"

I lean in to her. "Foul. Blinding. The worst you'll ever taste."

When she doesn't agree straight away I say, "I, on the other hand, make extraordinary cappuccinos. And I live just up the road."

It's one of my dating rules: always ask a woman in on the first date. Even if she turns you down she will know you want her.

21

Hand Touches Warm Skin

I wake up in bed knowing that something is different. I don't have a headache and my mind is clear. I don't feel like staying in bed all day or jumping in front of a bus, which is unusual. And nice.

I stretch out and my hand touches warm skin. It moans.

I open my eyes and see Denise's long dark hair splayed over the white pillow.

God.

I remember the night before with a shiver deep inside my body. The sexual equivalent of someone walking over my grave.

I look at her tattoo, close up. Leaves, curlicues and hooks. A climbing rose with no blooms. It reminds me of the thorny branches that strangle the castle in the story of Sleeping Beauty. The prince has to fight his way through his dangerous weed to wake his princess.

I smile at the irony. I'm the one who needs rescuing.

I realise that I may never see this woman again so I decide to ignore one of my most important rules and make her breakfast. For the first time in a long while I feel hungry. On the way to the kitchen I fantasize about creamy scrambled eggs, gravadlax with dill and sour cream on toasted rye.

When I see the state of the kitchen my fantasies instantly grow mould.

Where is Francina? Instead of infecting myself with some rare strain of bacteria poisoning, I decide to nip out for the breakfasts. I call ahead the order in whispers and leave a note for Denise telling her to stay where she is, and she will be rewarded. I can't believe that one night with a beautiful woman has made such a difference to my state of mind. Here I am doing a breakfast run at seven in the morning when yesterday it took me an hour and the promise of a pre-noon cocktail to get me out of bed.

I could take the easy route and say that it was the fabulous sex but I know it's not true. Denise has something I need.

A young lip-glossed waitress is standing outside the glass doors of the café with my takeaway in her hands. She looks at me with Bambi eyes and warns me that the coffees are hot. As if her warning is not enough, the text on the paper cup reads CAUTION: CONTENTS MAY BE EXTREMELY HOT. I find this a little unnecessary. Surely if someone has the linguistic capacity to order takeaway coffee they will also understand that coffee is made with boiling water?

The fresh morning air is cool on my cheeks. Everything seems brighter. I reach the house and let myself in. Balancing my swag and a smile I go straight to the bedroom where I find a stark, empty bed. Unmade. After checking the bathroom, guest loo, study, all the bedrooms, the garden, the drained pool, I realise that she has gone.

I sink down on the Chesterfield in the lounge and flick on the flat screen. Greased-up wrestlers throw each other around and break chairs on one another's heads.

I hope she doesn't regret it. I hope she didn't wake up with that one-night-stand-pure-dread feeling.

I unpack a croissant and pull it apart. Shove my fingers into its soft, warm centre, and rip it out. Swallow it down.

I didn't get her number.

I leave the coffee for a while. Couldn't bear the shame of scalding my mouth after all those warnings.

A peroxided box cut bounces a curly mop off the side of the ring. I shove the last of the croissant into my mouth and chew without tasting it.

She must feel guilty about Eve. Hell, I feel guilty about Eve. She's not dead a week and I'm boning her backwater sister. And I'd love to say that she would understand, but I doubt she would.

My curiosity about her past, their past, makes me feel itchy inside.

I empty her coffee down the drain, like an addict, and wonder if I'll ever see her again.

I decide to spend the day cleaning the kitchen. I don't

know the last time I actually did the dishes. Francina is my domestic fairy godmother. I can imagine that when I'm not looking, she swishes her *sjambok* and the dirt is magicked away. Where the hell is she? If I didn't need her so damn much I would fire her. Okay, that's not true. She knows I would never, could never. I have a tender feeling towards the old girl. Maybe this is why she has left: to teach me a lesson. To appreciate what I have. To show that there won't always be someone around to pick up the pieces. But somehow I doubt it. Francina has never been one for pontificating. She isn't answering her phone and the cops have turned up nothing. I miss her. I miss her chubby ankles resting on my kitchen table. I eat a rusk in her honour, off a side plate like she's taught me. I put on bright yellow plastic gloves that smell like vanilla and fill the sink with hot water and detergent before I remember that I have a dishwasher. I wash everything in the sink anyway, thinking that it will be cathartic. The warmth and the bubbles soothe me. I look out of the window and see that the garden is lush and filled with summer. Inca lilies, arums, cats' tails all jostle for the sun. The branches of a huge vintage pink rosebush are heavy with blooms. I feel like I went to sleep in winter and woke up now amidst all this life and pollination and colour.

I end up washing everything in sight, picking up empty bottles, sweeping up all the ash and broken glass, scrubbing the porcelain floor, shining all the brushed aluminium I can lay my hands on. After I'm finished it looks more like a scrub room in a hospital than a kitchen.

When there is nothing else to sanitise I decide to go for another jog. Get the old heart pumping again. The last run seemed to do me good. I put on the gear from two days before and head out; Sylvia's voice chimes in: "You've run one kilometre."

I try to stick to quiet roads where there aren't a lot of cars to run you over. I like the peace of a run, the way it allows me to get to that mental limbo where thoughts and ideas just flood in one after the other. Nothing practical: that all just disappears as I go into autopilot. It's one of my favourite feelings. I'm not getting there today though, I am too unfit. I do actually have to think about the distracting trivial things. Like holes in the road, and breathing. My lungs are tightly stitched leather.

In the shower afterwards (Tropical Storm™) I feel great. I feel as though Denise has opened something inside me. Like the first rupture in a hatching egg.

When I was a kid my dad took Emily and I to a farm somewhere in the North West. Those were the days when you could stop off for fresh milk and eggs. I remember tasting that milk straight from the obliging cow's udder, how warm and sweet it was. And then later, when the glass bottle had been in the fridge, how the cream formed a thick skin on the top of the milk, thicker than any cream you can buy, like soft white butter. But most of all I remember going in to the hatchery where the farmer picked up an egg that was rolling around and held it out to me in his huge calloused palm. Soon a beak was pecking its way through. I could see that the chick was struggling and I wanted the farmer to help the little bird out. I wanted to take the thing from him and break open the shell like a chocolate Easter egg. But he was patient and eventually the chick was free; a perfect little ball of lemon which, oblivious to his previous labours, hopped away to his brothers and sisters.

Maybe this painful twisting inside of me is part of some kind of genesis, and I am going to emerge as a better version of myself. It's an optimistic thought. It helps to believe in something.

Just as I am falling asleep the night after having Denise, a hovering weight settles on my chest. If she finds out about my bizarre plan to pseudo-murder Eve, she'll think I'm a psychopath and have me locked up before I could explain to her that I only did it to save my own life, and that I never meant to take anyone else's. Telling Frank was a mistake. Who knows what he has told the cops about me. God, I was an idiot to tell him. The police haven't been back to visit since Saturday but I think that they are watching me. At least I hope it's them. Every time I look out of the window or leave the house lately, I have the feeling that someone is out there, waiting, watching.

22

DIRTY DEATH METAL

I begin the annoying habit of thinking of Denise a lot of the time. It is as if I have absorbed some part of her essence. As if we are joined in some way. I try to avoid it, and the nagging non-writing feeling I have, by trying to do the things that Francina would usually do. Today I'm doing the washing as I have run out of jocks. And old Metallica and Iron Maiden shirts. It takes a while to figure out how a washing machine works but in the end it isn't so difficult. Fill the tray with a mixture of washing powder and softener (at least I think it was softener), pat it down a bit to avoid spillage, stuff the drum full of dirty Death Metal T-shirts and jack up the heat. If I am going to do the washing then I am going to do it properly! While I'm reading the paper at the kitchen table the machine jumps around a bit. I interpret that as enthusiasm and give it the thumbs-up.

An hour later when the machine stops spinning I try to wrench open the door for three full minutes before it decides to humour me. There's obviously a trick to how you do the wrenching. Not sure how to hang clothes up on a line, I throw the lot into the tumble dryer. When I retrieve them they are hot and full of static. My silk boxers end up two sizes smaller and muddy-grey but all in all, I'm pleased with my work. I hug the warm clothes to my chest. Oh! The fulfilment of an honest day's work! To be a common labourer!

The phone rings, snapping me out of my Yeats-like dream of romantic toil. Before thinking I pick it up.

"Hello?" I say. Damn it! I forgot that nowadays I'm not answering the phone.

It is quiet on the other end. Someone is there but they are not speaking.

"Hello?" I say again. Something flutters and the phone line goes dead.

Bad connection.

It rings again and now I know I shouldn't pick it up. I grab the handset.

"Hello?" I say.

Shuffling of papers. An ear-swap.

"Hello," says the person on the other side, "I'm looking for a Mister Slade Harris."

"That's me," I say, wishing I hadn't.

The voice is composed. Too composed.

"Mister Harris, good day. I'm phoning in connection with the overdue payments on your bond at 83 16th

Avenue."

"Uh-huh," I say.

"Are you aware that your payments are two months behind?" he asks, quite politely. Of course he is calm and polite. He has a job. And most likely a house. And he knows where his next pay cheque is coming from.

"No," I say, although I did have an idea. I have stopped opening the mail since Eve died, since I started feeling vulnerable. And I stopped paying bills quite a time before that. All the post goes straight from the letterbox into the rubbish bin, with minimal handling. I now know what anthrax can do to you. And letter bombs.

"Mister Harris, please be informed that we require your urgent settlement of this debt or we will be forced to begin legal proceedings."

"Yes," I say, "I understand."

"Thank you for your time," he says, and hangs up.

Yes, hang up, I think. Hang up and go home to your wife and children and domestic worker and paid-up house. So I'm a bit behind on my bond repayments. Is it really necessary to threaten legal action? I'll make the payments, I always have. I shake my fist at the composed caller: take that! Bugger.

The doorbell rings and for a second I think it is the bank with papers that say the house is no longer mine. I tiptoe to the peephole and see that it's Frank. I reasoned after what happened at the funeral I would never see him again. Maybe he has come to finish me off.

I open the front door, salute him, but hesitate to buzz the pedestrian gate.

"Hey," he says.

"Hey."

"Can I come in?"

"That depends," I say.

He looks at me.

"On whether you're here to have a beer or break my nose again."

He looks sheepish. He shouldn't. Punching me was The Right Thing To Do.

"To have a beer?" he smiles. It looks like he means it but my paranoia is hovering.

"Actually, don't come in. I don't have any … er … beers in the fridge. Let me grab my jacket and we'll walk to the pub."

"I like what you've done with the place," he jokes, gesturing to the broken window and faint graffiti.

There is a kind of neighbourhood pub just down the road. The Pint & Sausage. It's the type of place you can go to alone if your friends aren't handy. You're bound to bump into somebody you know or meet someone interesting. They serve all manner of different beers and a mean pub lunch.

The walk over is awkward, we don't say much; settled in a booth with a lager we seem to ease up.

"I've been worried about you," Frank says.

"About my nose? It's fine," I say, willing to be gracious because it's nice to sit here in this warm place with a few drops of booze in you. Besides, the swelling has gone down and the bridge isn't too skew. I touch it for good measure.

"Not about your nose," he says. There is clearly not going to be an apology.

"I've been worried because you didn't come to soccer. And then I tried to call you a few times, to see if you were okay, and you never answered."

He takes a long sip of his beer and I join him.

"I haven't been going out much. And I haven't been answering the phone."

Frank nods his slow nod.

"The thing is, I've been wrecked over Eve's death. It has completely freaked me out."

"Yeah," says Frank.

"And I've also been feeling a little … paranoid. I have this feeling that I am being monitored."

"Cops?" he asks.

"Maybe. Or someone meaning to do me harm."

Frank chortles at this.

"Like who?"

"I don't know," I say. Then he stops laughing.

"PsychoSally?" he asks. Frank is just as spooked by Sally as I am. He doesn't like to talk about her. If I mention her he changes the subject.

"Maybe," I say, "maybe she is upping her game. Or someone who blames me for Eve's death. Someone like you,"

Frank licks his lips.

"Look buddy, I was mad. When I heard that Eve had been murdered I thought it must have been you."

"It wasn't," I say, maybe too firmly. "For fuck's sake Frank, do you honestly think I'm capable of *killing* someone? Someone I ..."

"Yes?" he says.

"Well, I was fond of her," I say.

"You've killed before," he says. I can feel my face darken. I look around to make sure no one can hear our conversation. A memory taps at my skull, asking to be let in. I ignore it.

"What the fuck are you talking about?" I feel like throwing him against the wall. We stare at each other.

"Angola."

I blink, relieved.

"That's different, Frank, you know it is."

He softens.

"Yeah, I know it is."

"Being an ex-soldier doesn't mean I'm a psychopath. That I go around knocking people off. For Christ's Sake."

"Yeah," says Frank. "I'm sorry I said that. I just, well, I just thought the worst when I heard."

"Yes, well," I say, "You're not the only one."

Another draught later we're almost back to normal, but Eve's death has changed something between us. Frank seems different. On edge. I wonder if it's because he thinks I'm a murderer. Or if it's because it has been him watching me. Jesus on a skateboard, I'm paranoid. Usually we'd order dinner and drink way too much and laugh about it the next time we saw each other but, while I'd like the company tonight, Frank doesn't want to eat so we stop at a sensible number of drinks and walk back to my house, his car, without saying a word.

Then he's off, leaving me to a long night in an empty house.

23

DARK RIBBON OF RED

I have been having bizarre dreams so when the doorbell rings it in the middle of a particularly vivid one it jolts me like a defibrillator in a medical drama series. I dread the phone ringing and the doorbell jangling, it sets my heart racing. I don't want to see anyone. I want time to just sit around on my own and think. And sleep. And eat four meals of two-minute noodles in a row without washing any dishes. It rings again and I want to pull the blanket over my head and pretend I'm not home but in the end my curiosity gets the better of me.

I prowl to the peephole.

I can't see anyone out there. My persecution complex jabs me in the ribs. It might be PsychoSally. She's probably thought of a new creative way to defame me or deface my house. Probably rang the doorbell and hid behind a bush so that she could watch me admire her work. I strain my eye trying to see the impossible angle of the space behind the front pillars of the pedestrian gate. My heart has not fully recovered from the brisk awakening. Gingerly I touch the door handle and turn it. In a dream sequence of *déjà vu* I take the six steps to my newspaper, pick it up and turn around to face the house, this time expecting the worst. I don't see anything out of place. I let my shoulders relax.

"Hello stranger," comes a purr from behind me.

I jump what feels like a metre in the air.

"Christ," I say, clasping the newspaper to my chest. "You f-frightened me."

She laughs her gravel laugh.

I am frozen to the spot.

"Well," she says, swinging her hips, "are you going to invite me in?"

I've barely closed the front door when her lips are on mine. I drop the newspaper. She pushes me up against the door and pulls down my boxers and I wonder if I am still dreaming. Then I remember I read somewhere that if you ever think you may be dreaming you are, *ipso facto*, not dreaming. Then I try to stop thinking because all of a sudden my dick is in her hot mouth and it feels so fucking good and who cares if it's a dream or not. I feel like my whole body is in the dark red heat of her lips and I have to stop her before I lose it. I haul her up by the hand she has resting on my hip and, forcing her backwards, against the wall, rip open her blouse while I kiss her. She lets out a shriek of a laugh. Black clothes open up to reveal lightly sunned skin and lace. I taste her neck, just under her right ear. She is smiling but I can hear the barb of desire in her breath. I spin her around and push her skirt up over her arse. Down on my knees I lick the silk of the inside of her thigh but then can't wait any longer so I stand and find her hole with my cock and drive it into her smooth, tight pussy. My left hand is on the wall to steady us and my right is inside her bra, squeezing her hard nipple. Denise grips me, traps me, after every thrust, as if to show me that I'm not in charge. I move my hand to the tangle of her dark hair and grab it but she bats my hand away. I see her tattoo and I have a fleeting feeling of being somewhere else, somewhere in the thorny garden. Again, that feeling that I know her, that I know this body. Her moans bring me back and I let my body go. After a few final thrusts I empty myself into her, into this exquisite creature. Afterwards we crawl to bed.

Later, after she has gone, I am lying on the chaise in the sun porch reading *The Time Traveler's Wife*. I still feel a little stunned by Denise's visit, like I have been given a gift by a stranger in the street. When the doorbell rings again I waste no time in answering it, much to my detriment.

It's as if the universe had suddenly realised that nothing bad had happened to me in the last twenty-four hours so they'd better make up for lost time. It is the boys in blue: good cop, bad cop. I was feeling so buoyed by Denise's visit that morning that I was able to open the door.

"Hello, officers," I say, in a way that was not unfriendly.

"Hello Mister Harris," says the bad one, Sello.

The good one has the grace to look uncomfortable.

I buzz the gate but they don't move. It seems that today we are observing niceties.

"Would you like to come in?" I ask.

"We're here to take you down to the station," says Sello, not taking his eyes off me.

"Why?" I say, acting surprised. In fact I am a little surprised. What do they have on me? Can't they just ask me questions here?

"Can't you just ask me questions here?" I say, trying to look inviting. "This time you can have cappuccinos," I smile. I buzz the gate again.

They both look at me with a cool distance in their eyes. There is obviously no smiling allowed on duty.

"We phoned you," says Madinga, "but no answer."

"Often," adds Sello. "Maybe twenty times. We wanted you to come to the station."

"I get anxiety," I tell them. "Panic attacks. When I'm in closed spaces."

Especially in interrogation rooms and cells.

"Can we please rather just do it here?"

I think they see the genuine worry in my eyes because

they turn away from me and speak their ambush language. No one wants to be responsible for the heart attack of a paranoid post-traumatic stress claustrophobe. After a quick discussion and a shushed phone call to a superior they relent, but still refuse the cappuccinos.

We sit at the kitchen table again. My senses are on high alert and the chairs scrape against my eardrum. *Déjà vu* again, as if my reality has turned into a giant fucking hamster wheel.

"Your domestic worker," says Madinga, looking around the now clean kitchen, "she's back?"

He can't see the five unwashed noodle bowls in the sink.

I shake my head. They obviously have no news on Francina's whereabouts.

"Look," says Sello, holding his hand at his stomach and leaning back in his chair as if he has just finished a good dinner. "New evidence has come to light."

He has been watching too many episodes of *Law and Order*.

I think of that stupid Chuck Norris joke, when he introduces his legs individually as Law and Order.

"Really?" I say, "Well, that's good news, isn't it?"

Madinga looks at Sello. Both are expressionless.

"Maybe not for you," he says.

My intestines squirm and I swallow hard.

"I can't imagine what you mean," I say, trying to keep my voice even.

There is a Latin proverb that says that when one's life path is steep, try to keep one's mind even. I am way past that and just an even voice will do for now.

"What would you like to talk about first, Mister Harris? Perhaps about your last appointment with your doctor and what was discussed there? Or maybe the library titles you have borrowed? Or the fingerprints we found all over Miss Shaw's apartment?"

So they have been watching me. But before Eve's body was found? Not necessarily. They could have discovered it all afterwards. I swallow again.

"Perhaps the fingerprints are the most compelling," I say.

"We found at least six areas in Miss Shaw's flat with your fingerprints," says Madinga, "and some of your hair."

"So what?" I say, knowing I sound guilty. "We were friends. I spent time there. I was over there just the other day having lunch."

"Do you have anyone who can confirm your story?" Sello says.

I bridle at his use of the word 'story': it implies fiction.

I shake my head, more in annoyance at them than at the question.

"If that is your strongest lead I suggest you keep looking

for who really killed Eve, instead of wasting your time with me."

The men take their time in replying.

Sello steeples his fingers and leans towards me so that our faces are close. "You know what the most interesting thing about the fingerprints is, Mister Harris?"

"What?" I ask, with a touch of belligerence.

"The fact that we didn't have to call you in to take yours, to make the match."

"So you have my fingerprints on file. That's hardly interesting. We are practically living in *1984*, aren't we? If anyone should know, it should be you."

"1984?" says Madinga.

"Orwell," I say.

He blinks a few times and then writes it down.

"Never mind," I say and slump on the table.

"We have your prints on file because you have a criminal record," says Sello, "which you conveniently forgot to tell us about the last time we were here."

I harrumph.

"Why on earth would I tell you?"

"Because it may pertain to the case."

"Bullshit, pertain to the case! This case has nothing to do with me! And it certainly has nothing to do with my so-called 'criminal record', of which crime I was acquitted."

"Doesn't mean you weren't guilty," says Sello.

"It was a misunderstanding. Thai authorities aren't spectacularly fluent in English."

I wonder if they can see I'm lying.

"Moving on," says Sello, "your doctor informed us that you asked him about the technicalities of stabbing someone."

"Well," I say, "I did."

That singing bastard! So much for patient privilege. And since when did cops interview your goddamned doctor? Something feels off here. I think back to the split-second they flashed me their ID cards, not giving me enough time to study them, see if they were authentic. I squint at them, trying to work out if they really are cops.

They stare back at me with their overworked eyes.

"I'm writing a book and was doing research."

Sello leans back again.

"A book? What kind of book?"

"A novel. I *am* a novelist, you know."

"I meant, what is it about?"

I scratch my nose, still tender.

"It's about … someone who gets … stabbed."

"Ha!" says Sello. Or maybe I imagine that part.

"Like Miss Shaw?" Madinga asks.

"Miss Shaw wasn't stabbed," I say, "You said you found her drowned, in the river."

Ha! I think.

"We said we found her in the river. We never said drowned."

I know that, but I am trying to avoid falling for one of their *Law & Order* traps.

"What are you saying? That she was stabbed?"

Madinga opens up the file he brought in with him. He lays eight 12 x 9 glossy photos on the table.

I feel rising acid in my mouth and throat. Eve's blue-ivory limbs are spread before me. Her blonde hair is slicked back, brown with water and dirt. Her eyes open and milky.

One photo shows a deep slit in her chest. I blanch. I remind myself to keep breathing. I want to trace the cut with my finger. The pictures are beautiful in a raw, eerie way. They wouldn't be out of place in an *avant-garde* art exhibition. The whiteness of her water-bleached skin against the oily coffee grounds of the sandbank. The chalky lips. The vulnerability of her bare breasts, small nipples, protruding ribs. The dark ribbon of red over her heart.

I feel like I am falling away from this moment, as though I

am in danger of disconnecting with reality. Becoming unhinged.

So not only did someone kill Eve, but they seem to have followed my plan to the letter. It's impossible, I know it is. Some kind of crazy coincidence. And yet there she is in the photos, cold, bloodless marble. As I had pictured her.

Exactly as I had pictured her.

I am lying on my couch and an hour has passed. I don't remember much. There are strangers here and they are searching through everything. They are wearing strange uniforms. It is as if a UFO has descended and the aliens in hazmats are taking their information-collection duties particularly seriously. They have their scary space tools and little extraterrestrial cooler boxes and they speak in their Martian dialect. They are emptying drawers and sweeping cupboards and scraping DNA samples off everything in sight. They empty the ashes from the BraaiMaster 1000 into a plastic packet. Madinga dangles something silvershiny in front of Sello: Eve's spare keys. They are promptly confiscated. I look at my hands: my fingertips are black. Inky. How apt.

I don't remember them taking the prints, and don't understand why they would do so after saying they had them on file.

The house is a fog of white noise: I can't hear anything. I wonder what they are hoping to find, and what they will find. I don't think that anything in my house will tie me to Eve's murder but it is clear that stranger things have happened. If the person who has done this meant to frame me, then I'm damn sure there will be some evidence planted somewhere in the house that is just out of my reach.

The men swarm out in the same manner they arrived and Madinga says something to me but I don't hear him. I watch his lips move and then he is also gone, leaving the warrant on the Flokati rug next to me. The sun goes down and I am still on the couch. The darkness is comforting.

The doorbell goes again. It is really dark now and I have to feel my way to the light switch. I think it must be the aliens to take me away but then I hear her voice and I am relieved in a detached kind of way. I let Denise in and she sits on the couch with me.

"You poor baby," she says, climbs on my lap and straddles me, as if she knows just by looking at me what I have been through today. She slowly kisses my starless fingertips, my forehead, temples, cheekbones. She wraps her arms around me so that our chests are one. She feels weightless apart from where our upper bodies are joined. She pushes my face into her shoulder and strokes the back of my neck.

"How did you know?" I ask her.

"Know what?" she whispers.

"How did you know I needed you tonight?"

"I didn't," she says. "I came to say goodbye."

"No."

"I've packed up most of Eve's things and sorted out her apartment. I need to go home. Back to my life."

"No," I say again. "Don't."

She starts kissing me all over again.

"I have to," she whispers.

I don't want to be abandoned. Not again.

"I need you," I say. I have never said this to anyone before.

She is quiet as she pets and strokes me. She tilts back my face and looks into my eyes; sees my vulnerability. I have moved her. I think: this is the most honest moment I have ever had. She leans in and opens my mouth with hers. She rises a little on her knees and pushes my torso and head against the couch and I surrender to her slow, sweet kiss.

I sink.

A whispered afterthought: "Okay."

24

MY SOUL ON A SILVER PLATTER

I have unplugged my landline and only turn on my cell to listen to messages. This way I can avoid the debtors and the heavy breathers, who may or may not be the same people.

I am under attack. They want my car and my house. Francina has deserted me. People are spying on me. The police are determined to take my freedom. Sifiso wants my soul on a silver platter. In plain English, he wants my manuscript. He hasn't yet given up on me but I can feel that his prolonged tentative hope is reaching its end. I have reached the end.

I have no proof but I know that someone out there wants me dead. Sometimes I want to just offer myself to them, resign myself to their forces. They watch me. They are just waiting for the right moment before they reach out and snap me up. I am treading in someone's crosshairs. I'd rather just give up. Like a refugee who walks, unarmed and unprotected, arms lifted above his head. Let them just take my life now instead of this cat-and-mouse game, this sport. I'd rather give them a clear shot.

Sometimes I see them in the house. A head at the foot of my bed, or behind me in the mirror. Sometimes they are perched in the tree outside. When the claustrophobia gets the better of me I go for a run and I see them running, too. Or walking, or grey-bearded, rooting through rubbish bins. Denise doesn't want to leave me alone and so she stays cooped up with me. Sometimes we don't go out for days and she doesn't complain. She says she likes it. We order in groceries and I cook elaborate meals for us. I have to do something. She hardly eats a thing. I'm surprised she can actually exist on so little food. I am working my way through Ferran Adria's *El Bulli* cookbook. It takes my mind off the attack and means that I won't slowly die of scurvy, the way they want me to. It feels good to open the fridge and see that it's not empty. It's been a long time, and it makes me feel better. Sometimes I open it to make sure the food is still there. Sometimes I just open it to feel safe. Sometimes I imagine that Denise is one of Them and I hyperventilate. She knows how to calm me down. It usually involves heavy petting. She tells me that no one is after me, no one wants to kill me, but she doesn't see the faces.

I have acquired the habit of looking through the peephole to try to catch sight of whoever it is I feel is watching me. They are clever. They always look different. One day it's a black man in chinos with a rolling walk, next it's a huge Indian woman in turquoise Lycra, stopping outside my house, ostensibly to look at my roses. They've only sent the same person twice. He is tall, shinypale and always wears dark clothes: a black hoodie. He looks at me without even looking at me. When I saw him the second time I felt a cold flame zinging down my spine. I know that he has been sent to kill me. I have named him Edgar.

On a rare occasion we go out together, we find ourselves at a restaurant down the road called The Attic. It's a kind of sham-chic eatery with old-school brocade wallpaper, kitsch on the walls, and a giant pink jellyfish of a chandelier. The menu recommends a specific wine per course and they offer you *amuse-bouches* before you order. Their roast chicken is deboned, stuffed with onion and sage, and the texture of the gravy alone deserves a medal. The roast potatoes taste of lemon oil and rosemary. I have two glasses of Stormhoek Barrel 72 Semillon. Denise doesn't order a main meal but we share the hot chocolate pudding with homemade vanilla bean ice cream.

As we stand to leave, a man on the opposite side of the restaurant laughs loudly and I glance over without meaning to. He is telling a funny story. Something about him is familiar; I can't think of who he is or how I know him but I am drawn to him. I tell Denise I will meet her outside and I cross the room. He is sitting with a group of young, modish people who could be writers or artists. As soon as he sees me he shuts up and shields his face. His friends look at me, then him, then at me again, puzzled. As I realise who he is I stop in my tracks. Take off his trendy glasses, comb over his fauxhawk and swap his Mingo Lamberti shirt for tweed: it's Eve's deaf/mute relative. Except that he is clearly not deaf, or mute, nor does he have terrible fashion sense.

"Hi," I say, attempting a non-threatening smile.

He barely nods at me, hand-shield still in place.

"We met a few days ago, at Eve's funeral."

His eyes dart around, possibly for an escape route. His

friends look about nervously.

"Eve's funeral," I say more firmly, "remember?"

When he realises that I won't give up, he says, very softly, "Yes."

"You gave me the whisky," I smile.

"Yes," he says in barely a whisper. Everyone else at the table just stares.

I am so confused that I can't think of anything else to say. I turn and leave.

During the walk home I am quiet so Denise teases me. I grab her hips and push her gently against the closest wall. I kiss her to stop her from laughing. Leaves in our hair. She smells like Eve. A crisp breeze makes her shiver. I feel myself getting hard against the inside of her thigh and if I could, I would fuck her right here but common decency, for once, gets the better of me. I can sense pedestrians slowing as they pass us and I don't care. Let them look. Let them trip over the uneven walkway and shake their heads and cluck. Let them see what fire is and to hell with them if they have a problem with it. The world needs more amorous zeal, for Christ's sake. A car coasts past us and hoots, but my longing pushes everything else that isn't Denise into the soft-focus background. I don't remember the rest of the walk home but later, as soon as we're in the front door and the alarm code is punched in I'm tearing Denise's panties. God, I love her panties. Every pair she owns is the perfect balance of femininity and business. I've never known a woman who has more lingerie. Tonight: a lace-trim leopard-print bikini, low-rise, with a little bow in the front. Usually I like taking them off with my teeth, but now there is no time. I throw her onto the bed and without warning I force myself into her. She calls out and throws her head back. I hike her legs up so that they rest on my shoulders, and rub her clit with my slippery hand as I fill her with deep, rhythmical thrusts. I watch her swollen lips around my cock. I lift her further off the bed so that I can go deeper. I want to penetrate her whole body. I want to fill her up, fill every crevice, satisfy every nerve ending. I look at how her tits move as I thrust, firm bronze nipples swaying to my rhythm. I want her so much at this moment that I want to be part of her. Want to climb inside her. Slit her open from throat to triangle and crawl inside. Lay my hands on the elastic of her lungs, the smooth ivory of her ribs, the red restlessness of her heart. Then zip her up again and smooth away the evidence, leaving nothing but my scent. I am, in the words of Henry Miller, cunt-struck.

"These violent delights have violent ends."

- William Shakespeare, *Romeo & Juliet.*

25

THE COURAGE TO CRINGE

One of the messages on my phone is a man saying he is the executor of Eve's will and he wants to make an appointment to see me. I don't return his call for days until Denise makes me. She says it might help pay off my debt and then I can keep the house. She has already received a not-insubstantial lump sum. I am obviously farther down the list of beneficiaries; I'm almost surprised that I'm on the list at all. I call the man and we set up a time. I worry that it's a trap and ask Denise to come with me but she says I have to start doing these things on my own. I need to get better, she says. I need to function. I don't see the point in anything nowadays, but I go see the man anyway.

The Jaguar is dirty again. It's covered in dust and watermarks. Even the interior is starting to look grubby. I walk around it for a while, inspecting the scrapes, dimples and bald tyres. It used to be the love of my life. I could have invaded a small country for the amount of money I spent on her. I open the door and get in, then hesitate for a second before I turn the key in the ignition. I am certain it will explode and send my internal organs flying in all directions: a spleen splashing against the wall; an eyeball bouncing a few times on the driveway before rolling to a stop; a liver plopping onto the pavement. Fine needles of sweat break out all over my body. I psyche myself up. I think: if it does explode I won't even know it. My body will be in tiny pieces and nothing will matter anymore. And that gives me the courage to cringe and turn the key.

When the engine starts I laugh and I feel a bit better. I feel like an idiot, but I am alive.

It feels good to drive through the Northern suburb roads with their maple leaf canopies. I pass people traipsing to work. I switch on the sound system and press play. The XX: haven't heard this album for ages. God, I love the intro. I start nodding and tapping the steering wheel, realising that I have missed driving. It is a way to feel a small measure of control in the world. Despite the way I have treated my car in the past year, it reacts loyally to every millimetre of foot on pedal. Look, I turn the indicator on and it blinks. I brake and the car slows. I start to feel a little more normal, a little more myself. Maybe my life isn't coming to an end. Maybe it just feels like it because I am not writing. Without writing I do not exist: the longer I go on not writing, the less I will exist. I will become some ghost of myself, where people look straight through me when I ask them for the time. The man with the will is in Sandton and it only takes me ten minutes to get there. I wish that I could keep driving. Instead, I park underground and take a grimy elevator up to the second floor. I follow arrow after photocopied arrow, walking down long passages and turning corners into even longer passages. The fluorescent lights overhead expose every smudge and stain. The carpets are stiff, mean, and old air conditioners crank out stale-smelling air. The place gives me a feeling of fly-by-night operations with their tatty logos Prestik'd to the textured-glass doors. Legal offices in limbo. Paralegal Purgatory. When I reach the address I have scribbled down in my new Moleskine, I hesitate before ringing the bell. For all I know they might be waiting for me on the other side, chloroform mask and scalpels in hand, ready to steal my kidneys and leave me in bath of dirty ice. And that's if I'm lucky. If I'm not: forget the luxuries of the drugs and the ice. I ring the bell and am buzzed through.

The man with the will is dressed in a cheap suit as befitting our surroundings. He offers me coffee but I would rather stick with the cotton-mouth I have than take the risk. Who knows what kind of coffee they serve here. He begins with the pleasantries as per protocol but I zone out and just watch his receding hairline move, without hearing what he is saying. His hair matches his spaniel-coloured moustache and I find his face very distracting. What is it with these men with moustaches?

" … and so we have it ready for you," he says.

I try to focus.

"Really?" I say, hoping he might repeat himself.

"You can take it with you today if you wish, or we could store it for you if you would like to come back at a time convenient to you."

I have no idea what he is talking about and wonder how long I can play along, without him guessing I haven't heard a word he's said. He has a fat document in his hands which I surmise to be Eve's will. He lays it on the table. I think how much television and movies affect our expectations of reality. If this was an episode of *Dallas*, the whole jewel-encrusted family would be crowded in here ready to grab their share of the loot and run. But only after showing up in velvet evening gowns, watching the homemade video will, hearing what everyone else has inherited, having a false-nail catfight, and drinking neat brandy out of crystal-cut tumblers.

"I think I'll take it with me now," I say.

"Of course," he nods, "please excuse me for a moment." He stands and walks across the office to a door I hadn't noticed, and leaves the room. I try to sit still. My eyes fall on the document on his desk. I try to ignore it. Look out the window with no view. Ignore it. Look at my shoes. Ignore it.

Then all of a sudden I am standing at the desk with the will in my hands. My eyes race through it. Most of it is legal jargon which may as well be written in Mandarin, until I get to the interesting part. To one Shaw, her apartment, to another, the proceeds of the film company shares. Basically all her assets go to her family, strange because she never seemed very close to them. Maybe the idea of your death makes you feel closer to your roots. I hear the man's footsteps and I try to scan faster. Unit trusts, annuities, stocks, all divided up. And then: her twelve-million-rand life insurance beneficiary, and also the recipient of all her liquid assets totalling another four bars: not a Shaw.

The cash not left to a Shaw, not a family member, but a Fox. A Susannah Fox.

The footsteps are right at the other side of the door now and the handle turns. I drop the document and fall back into my chair. The man looks at me, I try to look bored. I don't think it's working. He's carrying a large rectangle covered in brown paper. He can just fit it under his arm. It looks like a painting: one of Eve's.

Susannah Fox. Who the hell is she? I'd known Eve for ten years and never a word about a Susannah. Whoever she is, she's now sixteen million rand richer. And since when did Eve have so much cash? I knew that her family used to be pretty wealthy but I had no idea she was … rich. Fucking rich. I knew she never worried about money. When she wasn't painting in the studio, she was always dressed in designer suits, sunglasses, diamonds. When I was making a lot of money we used to buy each other cases of champagne as gifts: we both had a penchant for Veuve Clicquot. It never occurred to me that her financial circumstances were unusual. Successful artists can be rich, just like I used to be. Just because one follows one's art, instead of becoming an accountant, doesn't necessarily mean one has to shop at PEP. Eve was, after all, a sought-after painter. But sixteen million? Then why the dingy funeral and lawyer's offices? Why the cheap wake whisky and dehydrated sausage rolls? Does her family resent her that much?

I take the mystery package from the man, shake his hand and make my way to the elevator, awkwardly manoeuvring the thing inside so that the doors don't crush it. Must be Old Money. People don't spend Old Money and that's why they keep it. Not like me: I was the worst of the *nouveau riche*. I made all the mistakes that OM like to sniff at. How was I to know I wouldn't be able to write another book? I thought I had it, the talent, the leaning towards success. I didn't know it was something that disappeared and took your life with it.

Either that, or her family were poor. Lost the family fortune. It never occurred to me before because I don't know anyone who is poor. Not personally, anyway. That would explain why Eve left them the money.

I put the car top down so that the painting can fit behind the front seats. I wedge it in so that it doesn't fly away on the way home.

When the electric garage door opens and I drive down the driveway, I see that the back door is open. Denise must be here. I hope Denise is here, I am particularly in the mood for her. I press the button to close the garage and call out to her at the open door before going in. Nothing. When I am closer, I realise that the lock has been jemmied. Cold sweat. I try not to panic, take a step inside, expecting to be clobbered over the head by a gimp with a baseball bat. My den has been ransacked. Drawers have been pulled out and emptied, books lie on the oriental carpet, some splayed out with their pages to the ceiling, as if surrendered. The wastepaper basket has been shaken out onto the floor, and my laptop is gone. I clutch my chest and have to sit down for a while. Jesus Christ. The rest of the house seems untouched: cappuccino machine, Panini Press and Juicerator remain in the kitchen, entertainment system in the lounge. The bastards could have at least tried to make it look like a burglary. I call Detective Inspector Sello who seems impatient with me.

"Don't you see?" I say, "Whoever did this is the same person who framed me for Eve's murder. They're after me! They want something from me. Come and look, the door's lock has been broken."

Sello seems distracted. Am I sure it was a break-in, he

asks.

"Of course I'm sure. The place is trashed," I say. It's clear Sello thinks my house is always trashed, which is fair. He says he'll send a team to take fingerprints when they become available, which may take up to a week. I shout, stomp around a bit and throw the phone against the wall.

I see Denise at the door with groceries in her hands. She has stopped in her tracks and is staring at the phone on the floor.

"Bloody cops," I say. "If it had been anything to strengthen their case against me, they would already be here. They would have been here before it even fucking happened."

She seems wary of me, not sure whether to come in. I walk to her and take the bags from her hands.

"Sorry," I say, setting them down on the kitchen floor and starting to unpack.

"The door is broken," she says.

"I'll fix it," I say. Fuck the cops; I'm not waiting a week before I can sleep again.

Denise is pale. I think this is the first time she believes that someone means me harm. Before, she thought I was just paranoid. I abandon the groceries and walk towards her.

"I'll fix it," I say again, pulling her body against mine. I can see that she is spooked and it makes me feel strong. I can protect her. I go to the storeroom for my toolbox and electric drill.

After the lock is fixed I add another one for good measure. It feels good to use my virgin tools. Denise inspects my work and sweeps up the sawdust from the floor. She asks about the man with the will and only then do I remember the painting in my car. I fetch it and Denise helps me unwrap it. I recognise it: one of Eve's first successes. Despite generous offers, she wouldn't sell it. She kept it in her studio, as if to remind her while she worked that she was worth something. Maybe that is why she left it to me: a reminder on the wall that if I did it once, I can do it again.

It's a picture of a man holding a basket of fruit, Tretchikoffian smoothblue skin, but the background is made up of hundreds of miniature portraits, mixed media, with tiny threads and slivers of ribbons and miniature buttons, as if some dollhouse-maker had gone crazy. Some of the people in the portraits are reading, some pulling faces, some sleeping. The detail is astonishing. I imagine Eve hunched over this canvas with the thinnest brush and a magnifying glass. If you look closely enough there are words in the fruit, disguised as shadows and texture: entourage, proliferate, strumpet. Eve loved the sounds of some words. She didn't care what they meant.

I should sell it, but know that I won't be able to. Denise thinks it's worth two hundred and fifty K, maybe more now that Eve is dead. While I still have my toolbox out, I drill space for a Rawlplug and a screw, and hang the picture in the lounge. The man's eyes follow me, like the people trapped in the paintings at my dad's house. He looks like he has something to say.

26

SEVEN LIVES LEFT

Denise wakes me by licking me. She tongues my lips, my neck, and sucks my nipples. My cock grows stiff against the groove just under her ribcage, and she moves up and down, stroking it with her soft belly. I let out a groan. As often happens when having sex with Denise, I feel like I am dying. Not that I want to die, not really, but it is usually so good that if I were to meet my end I honestly wouldn't mind.

Freud said that the goal of all life is death. *Thanatos*: the death instinct. It's supposed to be the opposite of Eros, but with Denise it feels like the same thing. Sweet, delicious cuntess Denise. She puts me deep in her mouth and I am so turned on that I have to stop myself from thrusting. I stop her before it's too late, sit up and turn her around so that she's on her hands and knees. I spread her legs, kneel between her calves and run my tongue along her cheeks, slowly, stopping only to bite. I put my whole mouth over her pussy and lick and suck her. I drag my flat tongue over her clit again and again and then plunge it into her hole. She is quivering. I feel an electric current zip through me and I have to pause for a second. Three seconds. I put two fingers inside her and reach her g-spot. I find her swollen clit with my other hand and massage it. God, she is so warm and so wet. Her moans get louder and louder. I know she wants me to move faster but I can feel how hot and alive her body is and I want to draw this out. She can't help moving her hips. Suddenly she is silent, holding her breath, and her muscles tighten around my fingers in waves. She hollers into the pillow. As my fingers are squeezed I almost come. I keep still until the contractions stop and her body relaxes, then I rake my left hand down her back and spank her ass. She breathes in gasps. She murmurs something and I ask her to repeat it.

"Fuck me," she moans, "please, fuck me."

She is so swollen I have to force my way in. I think it will crush me but then it's so smooth I am able to move. Every thrust is a rush of stars in my head. I can't feel any part of my body except for where my skin is touching hers. There's no chance of stretching this out, I have so much pressure in my body that if I don't come now, I'm sure I will have a stroke. She is bracing herself by holding the headboard. Again her body tenses up and again she shouts out while her muscles contract around me. I grab her hips and fuck her with everything I have, and my whole body erupts.

Afterwards, while spooning, her body seems lifeless and I ask her if she is all right. She turns her head and gives me a lazy smile. I notice for the first time a thread-thin silver scar running like a seam over her ribs.

"Seven lives left," she murmurs, and her eyes flutter shut again.

Despite having given up years ago, I crave a cigarette.

*

I listen to my voicemail and don't like any of the messages. The man from the bank wants to set up a meeting to see if we can consolidate my debt. He recommends debt counselling. He doesn't see there is no point: my finances are past the point of no return. I know I should sell the painting but I just can't. It's here for a reason. Denise says there's no point in having a painting but no wall to hang it on. I appreciate the irony, but I'm not selling. If I end up in a soup kitchen I'll be taking the painting with me. The second message was from my father, wanting to know how I am and when I'll be visiting. He has probably run out of whisky. Then Sifiso, wanting the usual. The most interesting message was from Detective Inspector Sello, asking if I'll come down to the station. Very polite. Too polite. I think they must be waiting with hungry handcuffs. I play Russian roulette with the messages in my brain, then acquiesce to the boys in blue. At least if they lock me up I won't have to worry about the other two.

Usually I would do anything to avoid going anywhere with bars on the windows, but I have a feeling that if I don't oblige today I will be hauled away by SAPS thugs, amongst wailing sirens and camera flashes. Also, I want to take advantage of this strange numb feeling I have, God knows I wouldn't be this calm about the situation without it. I drive to the Parkview Police Station with the top down, looking at the sky and feeling the summer wind on my cheeks. If they arrest me, who knows how long I will go without this? I have my lawyer's number on speed dial but I don't want to use it unless I have to. I don't want to be defensive. An innocent man doesn't bring his lawyer into every meeting with the authorities, does he?

I park my car on a yellow line and push open the worn, heavy entrance door. I interrupt a man stamping documents to introduce myself, and he looks confused. He yells to the other man behind the counter, who looks at me and also shakes his head. Typical, I think, only in South Africa do you practically hand yourself over to the cops only to be rebuffed by inefficient bureaucracy. It reminds me of Douglas Adams's *The Hitchhiker's Guide to the Galaxy*. Next I'll be carrying a towel over my shoulder and be tortured by being forced to listen to someone's disgracefully bad poetry. So long and thanks for all the fish.

I am busy dictating a message to the man behind the counter when I see Sello through the window. I tell the man to forget the message and head outside.

"Glad you could make it," says Sello, breathing hard. He has a light sheen on his forehead and looks a bit ruffled. Maybe he has just come from a crime scene. Despite my morbid curiosity I resist asking him about it.

"Didn't feel I had much of a choice," I say, but he has already turned and begun walking away. I catch up and he leads me around the building to a back door. It seems to be disconnected, somewhere they use only on special occasions. Rapists, serial killers, writers. I am not worried till Sello double-bolts the door from the inside. The walls are thick and the air holds a slight chill. The cold clamminess reminds me of The Old Fort on Constitutional Hill. There is no one else around and it unnerves me. We walk down a passage and turn into the first open door on the left. It is an interrogation room, empty except for two plastic chairs and a table made from an old door. There is a two-way mirror on the far wall, which tricks you into thinking the room is bigger than it really is. Sello motions for me to sit down and excuses himself. I take a chair and sit in a way that I hope makes me look relaxed, so that the people behind the mirror will say: "He *looks* innocent." There are no windows.

Sello comes back with a grubby folder in his hands. It is the same one he and Madinga brought to my house before they searched it, but it's now considerably thicker and a great deal more foxed.

"Where is Madinga?" I ask.

Sello purses his lips and his eyes move up towards the corner of the room: a classic indication of lying.

"He's busy with another case today."

He shouldn't have bothered; I am not that interested.

"Cash-in-transit heist," he adds, seemingly enjoying the small deception.

"So he is trying to catch *actual* criminals," I say.

Detective Inspector Sello ignores this and opens his folder. I start to feel the first gnawing of nerves. My underarms are wet, despite the frosty surroundings, and my stomach is tight. I hope he can't see the patches of sweat blooming from my pits. I keep my arms close to my body.

"Mister Harris," he says, "we found some disturbing things in the last few days." His face gives nothing away. I try to follow suit.

"In your house. Powder residue … an illegal drug."

God, I thought I had used all the coke in my house.

"GHB," he says, tasting all the letters.

Now I don't know whether to tell the truth or not. You shouldn't lie to cops. But wouldn't not lying be stupid?

"What is that?" I ask.

"You don't know?" he asks, knowing the answer.

"No," I say.

He is quiet for a moment. Scratches his scalp in a measured, practised way.

"Mister Harris," he says, speaking slowly. "I thought you came in to co-operate."

It's my turn to be quiet.

"Look," he says, "it doesn't matter if you admit to knowing what it is or not, or whether you have ever used it. The point is that we found some in your house."

"I'm finding it hard to see the relevance," I say. Now I can feel perspiration on my face, and I wipe my upper lip.

"The relevance is that GHB can be used as a date rape drug, like Rohypnol. Miss Shaw had it in her labs."

I laugh out loud. This has become ridiculous. It's as if someone had seen the mind map and followed it step by step. I wonder if I am dreaming. If one night after working on Eve's

Graceful Demise I went to sleep and this has just been one big, ugly dream. I pinch myself. It hurts.

So much for GHB being untraceable. I guess that's what you get from doing your research on Google instead of asking your drug dealer. Sello is watching me. I close my eyes and try not to sweat. He turns a few pages until he finds what he is looking for.

"We also found blood," he says.

"Bullshit." The word is out of my mouth before I've even thought it. "You're making this shit up."

Sello just looks at me.

"Okay," I say. "I may have had some illegal drugs in my house, but there was no blood. There was no blood because there was no fucking murder. You're trying to break me, get a confession out of me to make your job easier. Well, it won't fucking work. I was in special training in the army. I laid landmines in Angola. I was in a hellhole in Bangkok where they interviewed me with a piece of hosepipe every day for two weeks. I will not confess to something I didn't do. You can't change my mind. I am not breakable."

With his mouth closed, Sello runs his tongue over his teeth. He knows I'm lying.

27

NOT WAVING

I am sitting in my lounge, drinking merlot and looking at the blue-skinned man. The wine is a vintage Meerlust I have been saving for a special occasion. I picked up a case on some or other Cape wine route holiday. I sigh. Those were the days. I figure that if I wait till I get out of prison to drink it I would kick myself for every day of my sentence. After this bottle I have another lined up. And another.

There is something unnerving about the painting. Not only do his eyes follow me around the room, but they seem to have some knowledge of who I am and what I've done, and it makes me feel on edge. After regarding him for a while I raise my glass to him and, in a way, to Eve. I see Eve in Denise's eyes, and in the way she purses her lips to smile, but apart from that they are polar opposites. Eve was so cool and reserved and pure and Denise is mysterious, provocative, dark. Impossible to pin down. Almost as if she is Eve's shady reflection. That's why we connect: in this over-lit world, we are both shadows.

She is healing me, in a way. I catch myself thinking of her often. Wondering what my life would be like if we hadn't met.

I'm under no illusions: I know that I don't know anything about her, and that she will leave me in a beat. But when everyone else is banging down the doors she asks nothing of me. She seems to know when I need her and when I need space. As if she has had some kind of special training. I have never been in a relationship with a girl who knows how close I want her. I usually feel overwhelmed, then abandoned. Denise makes companionship an art form. An intuitive foxtrot. I wonder why she is being so good to me, a stranger. Maybe she is doing it for Eve: a final gift.

I have broken all my rules for her. I make her breakfast every morning (rye melba toast with cheddar and marmalade, black coffee, neither of which she finishes). I hold her as we fall asleep. I emptied out a bedroom drawer of mine so that she doesn't have to live out of a suitcase. She hardly takes up any space. I seem to have lost interest in other women. Sometimes, at night, when we are exhausted but too giddy to sleep, I read to her. Faulks, Gordimer, Rushdie, Niffenegger, Murakami. She purrs when I open Atwood or Mantel. She transcribes Plath and leaves the scribbled notes around the house for me to find. I discover *Contusion* hiding in the crevice of the couch, *Kindness* in the shower, *Cut* inside the fridge, *Edge* on my pillow. I whisper Ondaatjie's *The Cinnamon Peeler's Wife* into her ear. I have so little to offer, but at least I can give her that. We get lost in it, together. I keep Stevie Smith's poignant and perfect poem, *Not Waving But Drowning*, to myself. It is too true to share with anyone else. I am, have always been, the one not waving.

And, of course, the sex. It allows me to go somewhere in my head I've never been before. An intense feeling I am somewhere else. I've been trying to figure it out. Maybe it's something to do with the fact that your body is so earth-bound during sex that your mind has the freedom to explore. Sexual astral-travelling. Whatever the reason, sex with Denise is nothing short of transcendental.

"I'm going to make you start writing again," Denise announces, mid-fuck.

"You're good," I say, "but not that good."

She makes me stand near the full-length mirror in the bedroom so I can watch her give me head. She kneels in front of me, one hand on my hip, and uses her mouth and throat in a way that would make Linda Lovelace proud. After a while she lets me thrust into her mouth. I watch her body in the mirror, her black hair, her rocking tits. Naked except for her designer heels.

Maybe she is that good. Or that bad.

I go from safe in bed to being held down in the Bangkok jail cell with a shiv to my throat. It's an old dream now and I try to go through the motions without feeling the fear. Unfortunately dreams don't seem to work like that. It's always the same nightmare with slight variations. Sometimes the knife-wielder isn't Thai; sometimes the jail cell is the infested hotel room in Lagos; sometimes I survive. There is always a shiv – or something sharpened to be a knife – an enemy, and a sense of urgency. They want something from me and sometimes I figure it out in time. Tonight I am treated to the original version. A hundred and fifty kilo *Muay Thai* thug is in my face, shouting at me in words I don't understand. I want to understand: I know that if I don't give him what he wants I may as well say my prayers. But it's dripping hot, there are fifty men in a cell made for five, and I haven't had a drink of water in the last 48 hours. My left eye is swollen shut and I think he may have broken my ribs, but I stand my ground. I learnt the hard way, in the army, that you should rather cross the Great Divide than give in to the playground bully. The audience urge us on, whistling and clapping, as if this is a backstreet dogfight. Cockfight. He is hopping and shouting and spitting and I wonder how long he will be able to keep it up. He looks like he has moves but if I am clever I think I can outlast him. I am wrong. He roundhouses me, planting his foot in my mouth, and I drop. Then he is kneeling on my chest, shinysharpness to my throat. My brain and tongue are swollen and I just want to know what the fuck he wants. In the beginning I gave him my wallet, fat with US dollars. I reasoned it would buy me a few hours of safety, especially if everyone in the cell saw me do it. The man took out the notes, threw them in the air, death confetti, and started shouting again. After that I gave up trying to appease him and stood my ground, fists raised to protect my head, much to the amusement of the other men in the cell, and the guards. Then came the blows. Consistent, well-aimed kicks to my sweet spots, until I am lying there, waiting for my throat to be slit like a goat on New Year's Eve. A smaller man, a boy, is instructed to strip me, which he does, paying close attention to the buttons on my shirt. He takes everything off except my jocks. I am too distracted to be grateful. I can feel blood run down my neck where the knifepoint rests just under my skin. For the first time I wonder if I'm going to die.

Before this moment it was Another Great Story. I was thinking how I would tell people when I got home. *It was the craziest thing. All a misunderstanding. Yes, locked up! Can you* imagine? (An outraged chuckle, a sip of chardonnay) *In Bangkok! And then this Muay Thai thug starts taunting me.* It was going to be the article of my career. I wondered if I would win an award. But then the shiv slides in slightly deeper and I realise there is actually a chance of me not making it out of here. That I am going to die this silly, senseless death without the solace of knowing why. Who knows how long it will take for them to identify my body, naked and slick with dirt and blood, alert my publisher, my agent, my father.

A misunderstanding.

Ja, I guess it was. I was on assignment to write a story about underage prostitution in Thailand so instead of going and observing from a distance I looked at a menu and chose a girl – one who could speak English – and paid for a whole night with her so that I could hear her story while sitting in her damp box of a room.

I was getting some good words down when the brothel was raided and I, realising the situation and my odds, decided to run. I learnt that night that Thai whores make most of their money when they are barely in their teens and that Thai police run like quicksilver. That was unlucky, and unluckier still was being stuck in a cell with a man who had lost his twelve-year-old daughter to a violent tourist john.

Tonight I wake up before they knock me out and drag my body across the cell, depositing me in the small space between the back wall and the maggoty latrine. Tonight I wake up and I have a guardian angel silhouette bent over me, warm skin shaking me, smelling like Chanel, telling me it's only a dream.

28

CREATION OR DESTRUCTION

The cream-coloured letters started arriving about a year ago. They started off polite, even complimentary. They were delivered by hand so there were no stamps as clues. Always written in the same handwriting on the same paper. It was heavy, textured like watercolour paper, and the top centre was embossed with a decorative circle: perhaps a wheel of sorts. I always read my fan mail. My ego demands it. Also, I am always freakishly interested to see what my readers have to say about my work. Some letters are easy to ignore: the ones that say they enjoyed the book, it was okay, they would make the following changes, in fact they have also written a book, and they're sure that if my meagre offerings are published then they also have a shot. And the ones that reprimand me: for saying too little; for saying too much; for being racist/liberal/chauvinist/feminist/dishonest/too honest; for being potty-mouthed; for being a gutter-brained, debauched sex addict. Some wish me a speedy trip to hell. These never bother me, and are usually mildly entertaining. God forbid a writer mentions violence or sex. Write about life, they demand, tell the truth! But God forbid you write about the creation or destruction of it.

But some letters I have kept. Some readers say their lives have been enriched by reading my work; that it led them to some kind of pint-sized epiphany, or made them think differently about an aspect of their lives they were struggling with. Some go further – these are my favourites – and explicate some thematic concepts or symbolism that I completely missed when I was writing it. I find it interesting that a novel is a different story to each person who reads it. It's also different to the same reader, at different points in his life. As if the words are living, breathing. I've read somewhere that, *à la* Heraclitus, you can never step into the same novel twice. There is sorcery in the words.

The embossed letters started in a gentle trickle. I was flattered. I'm not exactly sure when the flattery turned to fear; probably when they began arriving every week and contained hints that the writer seemed to know private details of my life. He/she would make a passing remark about my car, the irises in my front garden, my hair that 'needed cutting'. That was the last non-stamped creamy envelope I opened.

The words in the letters were never threatening in any way, and it didn't seem that the writer wished me any harm, but those damned envelopes spooked the hell out of me. Eve laughed when I told her about them, she was sure I was overreacting. She accused me often of injecting more drama into situations than was strictly necessary, which goes without saying, I thought, taking my profession into account. She was sure it was just an ex of mine, having a laugh, or an overenthusiastic fan. Through the gap in the bedroom curtains I can see the sun is rising and the blue morning light comforts me.

I have an arm around Denise's naked waist but I am thinking of Eve.

29

I Am Missing A Hand

I feel as though I am coming back to life, but it is a different life. I feel as if I have stopped chasing whatever it was that I was chasing. Not because I found what I was looking for but because I have given up. I see with absolute clarity that life is, ultimately, pointless, and this knowledge makes me feel like I am drowning. Not fighting the current that takes my warmth and my air but instead, letting it pull me down.

I no longer feel the need to travel, to find people's secrets, to risk my safety. Day to day is dull. I don't know why Denise stays. Without writing I am a shell. Gwendolyn MacEwan said that authors have the Jekyll hand and the Hyde hand. The idea is that a writer has one hand for their mundane existence, like walking the dog, jerking off, or flipping a pancake, and the other for creating. In my case it's about creating havoc. The inseparable twins: Havoc and Harmony. I am missing a hand.

30

NIGHTS ARE QUICK

I begin to worry about Denise. How my psychological vacuum is affecting her. She hardly eats, hardly goes out. Has she always worn this much black? I wonder if she has contracted my emptiness. When we are together we are still alone. Is this love?

We don't talk about it. I spend time in my den, trying to get words on paper, giving up, then drinking enough whisky to fell a small elephant and generally wallowing in my existential angst. She disappears into the garden. I have stopped cooking. Even grocery stores seem out of bounds to me now. When I think I am being overtly paranoid I look at the rock that was thrown through my front window. I keep it in the lounge near the jagged window frame. It's a warning. 'Stay on your toes,' it breathes, 'there are people who mean you harm.'

I want to write to Denise, tell her she is crisp and honeyed but that makes me think of apples and fruit-juicers and Eve. I want to type words about the corrugated silk on the inside of her body but my fingers just hover, impotent, above the keyboard, thinking of the pink pills, the mind map, the porcelain knife. I want to scribble that without her, I wouldn't get out of bed in the mornings, wouldn't eat, wouldn't shower. The days are everlasting but the nights are quick. She wraps me up in her molten body till I fall through the floor.

31

RED ISLANDS ON HER NECK

I find myself outside in the weak morning sunshine. I sip coffee and walk barefoot on the cool dewdamp grass, looking at how the plants have swelled and multiplied. Yellow arums, peach incas, and lavender grown wild and spindly. Their proliferation makes me feel shrunken. I hear the dog barking next door and, as I turn to look in the direction of the noise, I see movement behind the wall. I duck behind a shrub. I think it was the dog, but one can never be too safe. I inch my head around the leaves to get a better look and that is when I see her: Munchkin is back. She slithers easily through the drainage holes at the bottom of the wall and rattles her wiry tail at me. I wonder to whom she belongs, if anyone. She has me well trained and I crouch down and rub my fingers together to beckon her towards me. This time she comes. She drags her body along my knee, then chin-cheeks my outstretched hand. Her purr is too loud for her delicate build.

"Denise," I call softly to the house, "come and look."

When I don't hear her coming, I call a little louder but this spooks the cat and she dashes back through the wall. Shinyblacklightning. Denise comes to the door.

"Did you call me?" she asks, "what is it?"

I stand up and dust my hands off. Pick up my cold cup of coffee.

"Nothing," I say.

After checking the peephole for Edgar and his cunning associates, I slip out to the letterbox to get my newspaper. The post goes straight into my wastepaper basket. I delete all the messages on my phone. After the obligatory few hours in the den, scratching a hole in my notebook, I give up and read instead. I have always found it difficult to find enough time to read all the books I want, all the books that would help me become the writer I was meant to be. The writing usually takes over, but not now. Now I read at least a book a day. I am finally demolishing the swaying pillars of books I have piled up in my house. When I bought this place I thought I'd turn one of the rooms into a library but I never got around to it. They lie around the house in great toppling stacks, impatient to be read. Truthfully, I like that they invade every room in the house; it seems right, somehow.

Denise wakes me up with her tongue in my mouth. The den is dark and I can hardly make her out. I must have dozed off. She kisses the scar on my cheek, then pulls up my shirt and eats my nipples. I don't know how long I have been hard. I put my hands on her head but she shakes them off. She straddles me on the chesterfield, lowering herself onto me. She is not wearing panties. I gasp at the suddenness of her hot crush. She rides me in slow arcs and I dream I am in a new bright place. She gets me to the top and just before she lets me slide down the other side, she raises herself off me, turns around, lifts up her skirt to show me what she's got. I grab her butt cheeks; try to pull her towards me. I want to taste her, but she resists. Something buzzes through my body and I can't take it; I wrestle her to the floor, pinning her down. She resists, breathing fast, like an animal, and tries to bite me. I hold down both her wrists with my left hand, and use my right to slip myself into her. Then I put my fingers around her neck, as if to strangle her, and she groans. I can feel her excitement grow as I apply more pressure. Her breathing is laboured. I start to move inside her. This is good. So good. I can write about this.

More weight on her throat and her back arches. I can feel her pulse in my palm. My body is electric with power; I build up and up until my mind dissolves and I fly out of my body for a sublime second. Denise stops resisting and I think she has come too until I get back to myself, and her, and see she is not moving.

I shake her still shoulders. I try to make out her face in the dark.

"Denise!" I yell. "Denise!"

Oh my God, oh fuck. Jesus Christ. I turn on the lamp near her head.

Her face is bloodless. Red islands on her neck.

A mental flash of light: Eve.

Eve, dead. Blue and leached of all goodness. Flash, flash, flash, till I can't see what is in front of me.

"Eve!" I cry.

And then her chest is moving and I hear her breathing. I touch her chest and feel her strong heart racing. A laugh bubbles up from her; she takes my hand and kisses my fingers.

"Jesus H. Christ," I say, taking my hand back and running it through my hair. She laughs again but there is sadness in her eyes.

"Are you okay?" I ask, touching her neck. She nods and pulls me down so that we are lying together. I am extra gentle with her as I rub her back, kiss her spine. I wait for her to go to sleep before I carry her to bed.

32

KISS THE BRUISES

I am in the garden, shirtless, reading, when the doorbell rings. I watch to see if Denise will answer it but she doesn't. She has a habit of disappearing without telling me where she's going or when she'll be back. I put down the novel and approach the door with caution. It is a teenager in a suit. I swing open the door in what I hope is a menacing manner. It has the desired effect and the youngster takes a step back, as if he has just realised he has stumbled upon the (half-naked) village madman.

"You a bible basher?" I ask. "Jesus Freak?" He shakes his head.

"Jehovah's Witness?" Headshake.

"Hare Krishna?"

"No, sir," he says. He doesn't look like a Hare Krishna.

"What are you selling?" I ask, eyeing his fake leather hand-me-down briefcase.

He opens his mouth but says nothing.

"Vacuum cleaners? Stain pens? Avocados? Lawn dressing?"

"Uh," he says.

"Well, I don't have any money. So you may as well move on. Mrs Fritz next door seems like a nice old lady."

"I know," he says.

This catches me off guard.

"You know Mrs Fritz?" I ask.

"No," he says, looking at the ground, "I know you don't have ... any money."

"What?" I bark.

"I'm from United Bank," he says, digging for a business card in his shirt pocket.

"You're from my bank?" I say, not without incredulity.

"Yes, sir, Mister Harris. I have paperwork for you to sign."

"Who sent you?"

"The bank, sir."

"Not Edgar?"

"Er ... no."

I consider him for a full minute before buzzing open the gate. I find a wrinkled shirt slung over my gentleman's valet, sniff it, and throw it on.

In the kitchen the kid opens his briefcase and sheaths the table in legalese. He has a giant pen uncapped and offers it to me. I cross my arms.

"Shouldn't you be in school?" I ask.

He smiles a tired smile.

"Are you going to tell me what this is about?"

"Oh," he says, confused, fingering his forehead. "I assumed you had been advised."

I give him a hard look.

"But," he says, searching for words, "but you got three letters."

"*Ja*," I say, "I get a lot of letters, what's your point?"

"The letters from the bank sir," he says. "Three letters."

"Are you going to tell me what the hell is going on?" I demand.

"F-foreclosure," he whispers.

"What?" I wind my watch.

"You have failed to make your last six payments. And we've had no communication from you."

I shoot up and the chair falls behind me.

"We tried to contact you on various occasions. We offered you payment plans and debt counselling. Quite frankly we did everything we could."

"The bank is repossessing my house and they send a punk kid to break the news? How old are you, anyway?"

He clears his throat.

"Thirty."

I kick the kid to the curb. The house seems different now that it's not mine. I touch the cool walls; admire the pressed ceilings. Wonder what the fuck I'm going to do.

They say that you should not measure your worth by the things you own but what else do I have left? What will happen to my ShowerLux™? How will Francina find me if she comes back? How will I stay safe without these walls around me? The blue-skinned man watches me pace. I curse the bank with every bad word I know in every language I know. Bloodsuckers! Bloodsucking mothertruckers! When the money was rolling in, the managers were tripping over themselves to give me crappy free desk pads and take me out to lunch, now I have nothing and they send a ten-year-old to break the bad news in his breastmilkbreak.

Denise gets home and I tumble into her. I kiss the bruises on her neck.

I call Sifiso to ask for another advance on the royalties for the book I have not yet written.

"Look, Harris," he sighs, "I've been meaning to call a meeting."

"Yes?" I say, still hopeful.

"They're pulling the PLUG. They're tired of waiting."

"What?"

"I did everything I could."

"They can't pull the plug," I say, almost amused. "It's a three book deal. They've already practically paid me for the first one."

"Yes, they'll be needing that advance money back," Sifiso says. He is almost whispering. I have never heard him this quiet.

My mind somersaults.

"They're being rash. I have the book in me, I just need to get it down on paper."

Sifiso sighs. "That's what we told them this time LAST year."

"I can do it," I insist, knowing that I can't.

Sifiso is quiet.

"Look, Harris, you're going through a dry patch. It happens to EVERYONE. I'm sure that something will come to you, but Starling & Co. won't wait any longer. Their lawyer will contact you to agree on how you'll pay them back."

I laugh. And then I am angry.

"Those unclefuckers!" I shout, "We had a contract!"

"They held up their side of the contract for a year longer than legally required."

"Whose fucking side are you on?"

"I'm on yours, Harris, but you haven't given me anything to WORK with. Nothing, not a SCRAP!"

"Well, fuck you!"

"I understand that you're angry …"

"You understand fuck-all, you lousy fuck. You're fired!"

I chuck the phone against the wall and it springs apart. Fucking editors. Fucking publishing houses. Fucking banks taking my house away. Fucking phones that break every time you throw them. The rage builds up so quickly that I am no longer in control of my actions. I kick a pile of books in a clumsy stumble and then push over the bookshelf next to it. It lands on its side with a crash. Dull thuds of books and spinning of ornaments on the floor. I pick up the fruit bowl and smash it. Send the kitchen bin flying with my foot. Then the pictures in my brain fade to white.

I come to, minutes later, surrounded by destruction. Blindviolence. The place is trashed and I don't remember much of what I have done. I limp through the house; broken bits stick to the bottom of my shoes. When I get to the lounge I fall to the floor. Eve's painting. It has a hole ripped through it: the blue-skinned man is decapitated. I cradle it awkwardly in my arms. I stroke his face. A thought hits me hard in the stomach: I have nothing. I am alone and I have nothing.

I zone out for a while and when I come back to my body, I

am still bent double and stroking the painting, as if to soothe it. The paint near the tear is flaking off like skin and there is a muted colour underneath. I start to peel off the top layer and it reveals shapes, textures, more colours. Leaves. It's a photo-realistic painting of people in a garden. I get a knife and scrape the paint off the canvas in the areas where the paint won't peel. I unearth strelitzias, ivy, bougainvillea, jacaranda in bloom. A scorched lawn. A family. Conservative-looking parents: father choking in a dark suit, mother in a floral sack, with icy eyes staring into the camera through horn-rimmed glasses. Both gripping the shoulder of a blonde-haired little girl as if to prevent her from running away. I turn the canvas around and tear off what is left of the brittle brown backing. There is a photo wedged in the wooden frame, the one the artist used to paint from. It's faded: the trees have turned blue. The pencil scribble on the back says 'Shaws, October 1979: Miles, Nicolette, Evelyn (10)'. I flip the photo around again and look carefully. It's washed out and grainy. I recognise her cheekbones and her lips, the way she sticks her chin out. It's Eve. She painted over her family portrait. I sit there for a while and think.

Denise doesn't come home.

PART III

33

A LIFE IN THE SKY

I feel as though I am standing on a ledge on the outside of a high-rise building. The Ponte Tower, perhaps. Enough people have fallen to their death from its soulless windows to make it some kind of macabre landmark. So I am on the fortieth floor and the rubber at the bottom of my leather slip-on brogues is the only contact I have with the earth. My body sways in uneasy arcs and I feel the wind lifting my hair. Below the cars and people are in a hot swarm as if today is their last. Above is all oxygen-blue sky and near silence. It is understandable that a man in this position would take the easy way out and opt for a life in the sky instead of down there. But first the man has to be brave enough to be devoured by the earth. Brave enough to bend his knees and lift his soles in a childish hop, or merely step off, stiff-legged, into oblivion. I feel the pull. I feel the earth calling in its husky *sotto voce*. But I am not a brave man.

It's a kind of psychological vertigo. I feel myself being drawn in by the darkness: age, defeat, despair, the black hole that is my life, the inescapable feeling of loss that I have carried around in my pocket since I was eight. But there is something else too, some power that is holding me back, doesn't let me stumble, doesn't let me jump. An invisible harness. If I believed in God I would be tempted to say that it is His mischief.

I decide I won't jump.

Not today.

34

NIGHT OF THE LONG KNIVES

When Denise doesn't show up in her own family portrait (or for breakfast the next day), I give in to the hungry paranoia and look through her handbag. She has the usual feminine trinkets: a half-empty pack of tissues, a rattling tin of mints, cinnamonwax lipstick and a spare, slightly scuffed tampon. I also find her wallet, a sleek rectangular mockadile rectangle with a large silver clasp but, in it, only cash. The paranoia coldpaws the skin on the back of my neck. I rationalise: not everyone has a credit card. Not everyone has a driving license. Not everyone carries their ID around like it's 1984. And anyway she must have a second wallet, a second handbag which she has with her now or how would she get around? I wonder fleetingly if she has left me and so check the drawers for her clothes, which all seem to be there, tousled and softsable. As I am fingering her things I feel something hard and cold. Small metal symbols on a circle. I extract them and see that they are three keys attached to a silver apple key ring. Eve's house keys.

The doorbell rings and without looking I know it's the cops. They have come to handcuff me and push my head down into their shrieking blue and white car. I grab the tote bag out of my cupboard. It is pre-packed with a few changes of clothes, essential toiletries, condoms (force of habit) and my Moleskine. I packed it days ago when I began to suspect that my life was about to take an unusual turn. It reminds me of the bag my mother kept in the latter months of her pregnancy with Emily. She would sit with it on her bed and unpack it once a week, shaking out the clothes and receiving blanket and smoothing them down, only to refold and pack them again. Dad used to shake his head and make vague cuckoo gestures. She's at it again, he would say with an elbow in my ribs. I wondered if that meant she did it for me, too.

I reach under the bed for my emergency wad of cash. The envelope isn't as thick as I remember it but it's all I have, so I toss it in before zipping up. I can't take my car because A) it no longer belongs to me, and B) the cops will be camped outside the front of the house where the garage is. The doorbell goes again. I consider leaving a note for Denise but I have no idea what to say. I take the keys instead.

The boundary walls in Johannesburg are notoriously high and usually barbed or electrified but there is a chink in my neighbour's barricade I think I can slip through. I sling the tote over my back like a backpack and launch myself up into a tree. If I can climb along the branch we share, I should be able to make it over the deadly palisade fence without losing my manhood. Crouching there, holding on with hot fingers, I wonder what the hell I am doing. I should definitely climb back down and hand myself over. Be responsible. Be an adult. Face whatever consequences there may be. Instead I scuttle and jump and land on happy groundcover. When I stand up, I'm in the neighbour's garden and I hear a growl.

The dog isn't that scary. I mean, it's not one of those Dobermans like Higgins has in *Magnum P.I.*, the ones that look like the Devil's dogs. And I am sure this particular dog's growl can be interpreted as 'Oi, have we met?' rather than 'I'm going to tear you limb from limb', but one can never be sure. He looks like a giant whippet. I don't know what they are called, perhaps a greyhound? I hope he doesn't recognise my voice from all the times I've yelled at him to shut up. I don't know much about dogs but I know that greyhounds are fast, so I need to outsmart him because there is no way I will be able to outrun him. I look him in the eyes and try to act firm but friendly. I take a few slow steps in the direction of the west wall. He barks, once, twice, like Lassie reporting a girl child fallen down a forgotten well.

"Gravy," comes a sweet female voice from heaven, and then a beckoning whistle. "Gray-vee, c'mere boy." Another friendly whistle. Gravy doesn't take his eyes off me but rears back and lifts his snout in the air and barks again. I take a few more steps away. I motion wildly for him to go toward the voice. He is not fooled – until there is clanging of metal food bowls – then he is gone in a wag of a tail.

I am able to climb over the west wall too, thanks to a giant compost cube; from there I jump down onto the grassy pavement where I am free and clear. As soon as my feet touch land I run in the opposite direction to my house and the visitors. My heart is pumping, my muscles are singing and I feel good. Thank God I have been running in the last few days. It takes five minutes to get to a main road where I point upwards with my right index finger to signal a taxi to take me into town. A red kombi in particularly bad nick comes barrelling past but then slams on the brakes so hard the cars behind him have to squeal to stop. I hop in and the passengers shuffle aside to make space for me.

I am heavy-breathed and sweaty but the taxi is overcrowded, so I guess there is no chance of a window seat. There is kwaito on the sound system which more or less blankets the noise of the angry hooting outside and once I pay and sit back, the rest of the passengers seem to get over the novelty of having a white man in the car and start talking again. We lurch forward, nudge our way back into the lane in small jumps and we're off. Various parts of the interior are stuck together with Prestik and masking tape. The rear-view mirror is barely hanging onto the ceiling of the car, weighed down by purple fuzzy dice, a hula girl and some prayer beads. The driver eyes me, suspicious, and I look away.

When we reach town I have to ask a few people how to catch the next ride: I don't know the hand signal or where I should go. Someone outside the Chicken Licken on Bree Street directs me to a huge taxi rank I never knew existed and find my way pretty easily from there. Strangers smile. They must think I am a lost (or brave) tourist and they flash their gums at me. I wonder how they would react if I was driving my air-conditioned Jag XKR around here, instead of sweating through my shirt, trying to find the way out. To reach the rank I pass market stalls which deserve to feature in *Visi* magazine: beautifully arranged bowls of colour with green Granny Smiths, vibrant *naartjies* and bruised guavas. A few meters on, the panorama of food becomes nightmarish: tables of sheeps' heads, some skinned with bursting eyeballs, others still in their wool, matted with blood. There are men without their shirts on, bloodslick on blackskin, with *pangas* in their raised hands. There are women squatting on beer crates, hunched over and stirring aluminium pots over small fires. *Skaapkop*. Sheep's head. I smell the guavas and the milky-eyed *skop*. Flies buzz in the hot air.

When I reach the taxi rank it is easy to find the right car. The stereotypical taxi driver is aggressive, disrespectful and violent and most times I wouldn't want to be caught in a dark alley with one, but today there is a sense of levity with whistling and comradely shouting back and forth. I wonder if there is an important soccer match today. I have to wait for the minibus to fill up with passengers before we head off and this takes about half an hour. I spend the time trying to plan what to do next but I don't come up with anything promising and instead walk around reading bumper stickers. I jot the best ones in my Moleskine:

This Taxi Stops Anywhere.

Thank God I Was Born Black.

If Women Were Good, God Would Have One.

All Whites Are Racists.

Don't Rush Me, I'm On Time.

Three Missed Calls.

Wasted Time Never Returns.

When Days Are Dark Friends Are Few.

When the driver deems the taxi suffiently overcrowded we're off. Apart from ploughing through the occasional red light, he is a good driver.

*

When I arrive at the house and ring the doorbell everything looks the same but I feel I have been away for years. I see him stomp up to the frosted glass and I wait while he shuffles keys, then opens the door. He squints at me, blinks, adjusts his glasses.

"Slade?" he frowns.

"Hi Dad," I say. "I need a favour."

My father pours me half a glass of beer from an open quart of Amstel. He slaps my back as he gives it to me, as if to say that it will sort me out.

We stand, awkward, in the kitchen.

"You fixed the doorbell," I say. He presses his lips together.

"I had to. Some *tsotsi* tried to break in and made a mess of the damn gate. Had to re-wire the whole thing."

All of a sudden my mind is clear of my own predicament.

"What? When did this happen? Are you okay?"

He unbuttons his shirt to reveal a continent of purple on his chest.

"Bugger smashed my chest in with a knobkerrie."

I look at his liver-spotted hands holding open his shirt, the fabric trembling, the blood under his skin.

"Fucking savages," I seethe. "You need to get out of this house. It's too big for you. And the neighbourhood has gone to shit."

He shakes his head. His pale eyes are moist.

"What more will it take? Next they will be in here slitting your throat with a bread knife!"

"Good God," he says, taking a sip of his beer. "This isn't Rhodesia, son."

"Zimbabwe, Dad."

"No, I meant Rhodesia. Night of the Long Knives, or something like that. Besides, there's nothing of any value here to steal."

I won't argue with that.

"Have the cops been round?" I ask.

He buttons his shirt and picks up his beer.

"Yes, they took their time but when they arrived they took fingerprints. And the bloke filling out the report could read and write so I was pleasantly surprised."

"No," I say, "I mean, looking for me."

"What?"

"The cops. Have they called?"

"Er …"

"Look Dad, I'm in some trouble."

He looks at me long, as if he didn't hear, then snaps into real time.

"Anything you need," he says. He doesn't ask what kind of trouble, he doesn't round on me like I do him. He just looks at me and waits to hear what help I need.

"There has been a misunderstanding," I say. "The police think I've done something and they want to arrest me. But I'm worried that if they do, they'll stop looking for the person who actually did it. So I need to find that person."

He frowns. "They can't arrest you without evidence. Without a warrant."

"There is plenty of evidence. Unfortunately it all seems to point to me."

He looks into my eyes and something touches his face, as if he wants to tell me something, but then it clears.

"I need to get out of the city. Can I borrow the Merc?"

Dad has a Mercedes Benz from the 1950s that used to embarrass the hell out of me when I was a kid but it's so old now, it's cool. He keeps it as a spare car. Dad's never been good at getting rid of things.

"Of course," he says and leaves the room. When he gets back he hands the keys to me with a slight tremor, along with a wad of cash. I protest but he doesn't say anything. He just presses the cash into my hands.

"I'll pay you back," I say. I move as if to leave but he puts a finger in the air as though he's just remembered something. He opens his ancient fridge and retrieves a Cornish pasty still in its wax paper.

"I was saving it for dinner," he smiles, handing it to me.

He walks me out to the car where he opens a padlock on the inside of the garage door. The door is one of those ancient ones with two long, heavy weights on either side, like metal punching bags. I shoulder my way in and try to do most of the work. As it gains momentum and gives way the light pours in and the world is lost in bronze dust particles and the scurrying things that live in abandoned places. We say goodbye. My father reminds me not to step on his footbrake too hard and I nod. I shake his hand and he pats me on the back. I climb in, praying to no one in particular, and it starts first time. I reverse into the street and Dad salutes me before he closes the garage door. I open the cubby hole to throw my things in when I see his wallet. I whisperswear and pull back into the drive. I try to open the garage door but it's already locked so I go around to the front entrance. His spare house keys are on the car keys so I let myself in and call out to him. Wallet in hand I bound up the front steps. He is standing in the entrance hall with his rounded back to me, holding the phone up to his ear. No wonder he didn't hear me. I'm about to call him again when I hear him say, "Yes, he's just left. Yes, in the Merc. LDR 504 GP. Out of the city. No. No, he didn't say."

I place his wallet on a nearby chair and back soundlessly away.

35

HERE BE DRAGONS,

OR,

ELBOW BACON

As I speed away from my crumbling family home, I try to imagine who it was he was talking to, but I decide I don't want to think about it. I'm feeling pretty fragile to be honest, pretty fucking down-in-the-mouth and I don't want to think of anything that will further retard my emotional state. I get on the highway, not knowing where I am going. I feel like pulling in to the closest bar and downing a few fingers of whisky but know if I do that I may as well drive straight to the cop shop and show them my wrists.

I have no idea who is behind this … this thing my life has become. This person who sends me letters and watches me from dark corners is interred so far in my head that I have begun to turn on myself. I have no idea where to even start looking. I drive for a long time before I have a vague idea. The thing that I have in common with this nebulous antagonist is, obviously, Eve. So if I start with Eve, start at the beginning, maybe I will find my way to this person. The problem with this idea is that I know virtually nothing about Eve's past. If only I could trust Denise. Why would she never talk about Eve? Why would neither of them talk about growing up? I'm a writer, for God's sake, not a private investigator. I get off the highway somewhere in Houghton and park the car on the shoulder of the road while I pull out my phone. The screen is cracked but it still seems to work. I Google Eve's name but it is too wide a search, she has been in the media consistently for her art and there seem to be hundreds of entries on her latest exhibition alone. I Google 'Denise Shaw' but none of them is my Denise. Resisting the urge to throw the phone out of the window, I try to breathe and to focus. There is no air-con in the Merc and my skin is sticking to the cracked leather upholstery. I try to think of any clue she has ever possibly given me but I draw a blank. How could I have known her for so long, loved her, when I didn't even know who she was or where she came from? And then, not learning from mistakes, go on to do the exact same thing to her shadowsister?

I pull the photo of her family out of my pocket and search it for clues. It could be a picture of any (white) family in South Africa in the 70s: overdressed, overexposed. Probably taken after a Sunday Lunch. The mother with sticks for fingers and too many gold rings. Eve squirming under the gaze of the camera. Even the intimacy of a family portrait was too much for her. Despite the feigned formality of the occasion she is dressed like a boy, in shorts and a t-shirt. There is a kind of logo or insignia on the shirt but it's small and the picture isn't sharp. I need one of those programmes in CSI where they take a blurry photo from a hundred years ago and miraculously zoom in and sharpen it up to high res. It's circular, with text on the circumference and some kind of graphic on the inside, but that's all I can make out. I lean back into the car seat, close my eyes and think of Eve: I see her in her studio, bent over some finicky project, face and arms covered in paint and wallpaper glue, looking up at me as I tease her, her mouth showing one big, beautiful grin. The room darkens and Denise now stands where Eve was working. She is wearing Eve's splattered work shirt but has nothing on underneath, and the paint is scarlet. She begins to lift the shirt over her ...

A car driving past me hoots, making me jump. Asshole. I study the photo again and try to make out the words in the logo on Eve's shirt. Aurohine, Automin, Aoruhin, like characters in a Tolkein novel. I jab them all into my keypad but the results look like gobbledegook, or Czechoslovakian. Eventually a variation I try—Auramine—picks up some promising results. On the www it tells me that Auramine O is a fluorescent dye also known as Basic Yellow 2, but on the South African pages AuruMine is a name of a mining operation in Nigel. Gold. Au. Aurum in Latin. Gold Mine.

Half an hour later I have left civilization behind me and am heading east towards the hillbillies. There is a roadblock just outside of Jo'burg and when I see the blue lights I start to sweat. I have the urge to run my car over the centre island and start a high-speed chase on the wrong side of the highway. End my life in a blaze of glory. Instead I swallow a lot and try to look normal. I don't want to avoid looking at them because I'm sure that's what criminals do, nor do I want to look too directly at them. Nothing screams guilt more than looking someone straight in the eyes. I make sure that I'm wearing my safety belt. The fake driver's license burns a hole in my wallet. The cars around me slow down to a virtual stop at the officers' command and I can just feel that they are going to pull me over. The music on the radio is shouting at me so I turn it off. I am a few meters away from a busty policewoman who is bursting out of her uniform and has wet black marbles for eyes. She blinks at me, looks too long. She holds out her hand. She has recognised me and is going to pull me over. I look left and right for an escape route but am boxed in by cars on all sides. I think of jettisoning the car and running but I wouldn't stand a chance with all these uniforms and walkie-talkies about. Just as I lose my hearing to the blood in my ears, the policewoman shunts her arm at the car behind me, signalling it to park. Bless you, Jesus. The breeze rushes in the window as I accelerate, away from the spinning lights. Maybe my luck is turning, after all.

Within ten minutes I am far enough away from the cops to feel hopped up. I can see how Bonnie and Clyde became addicted to being on the run. The frisson of the open road; the rushing knowledge that one has just dodged a bullet. The tinny banjo tune from *Deliverance* strums my brain. High-rise steel and glass gives way to crumbling concrete and bad paint jobs. Trees morph into pylons. The smell of city grit gives way to the rotten vegetable smell of abandoned fields. The land becomes flat and I drive past a glass factory and commercial cold storage. A fine dust covers the car. I eat the pasty.

When I reach what I guess is halfway, before the first toll road, I pull into a quiet service station and fill up. In the convenience store I find cheap orange razors, nail scissors, black hair dye, a Hawaiian shirt flocked with flamingos and a pair of cheap Ray-Ban knockoffs. Instead of using the public toilets I walk around the back of the building and find the staff amenities. I lock myself in and begin cutting my hair. I mix the dye and massage it in. The plastic gloves are too damn tight and they split as I am working, leaving me with black welts on my hands and mechanic's fingernails that look like they have been slammed in the door. While the dye is in I shave off my beard, find a bottle of bleach in the supplies cupboard and try to clean my hands with it. It's soapy and feels good, the way it stings my skin. I wash out the dye, using my T-shirt as a towel, then put all the used things back into the plastic bag and dump it. When I get to the car I take off the license plates and chuck them in the boot.

I drive through Boksburg, Brakpan, Springs and, just when I think I'm going to fall off the edge of the world (Here Be Dragons!) I see the sign, a huge green mining wheel: *Nigel Welcomes You.* Not very auspicious, I agree.

I have hollow hope that there is a pleasant place to stay. I head slowly to the main road on the lookout for promises of accommodation but end up collecting hostile stares instead. The locals here don't like strangers. Especially strangers like me prowling around in old junkers looking (I can imagine) like evangelists, molesters, or crack dealers. I pass giant peaks of fine yellow sand, mining dust melted by the rain, like wax mountains. Eventually I roll on down to what seems to be the popular part of town. There is a butcher, a bottle store and a steakhouse, with a church on every block. What more does a small town need? I will stick to the bottle store for my brand of entertainment. In general I am not anti-religion, just anti-stupidity. I drive past a shop called 'Tombstoneland' and it reminds me of the gravestone showroom I saw on the way to Eve's wake, a hundred years ago. A minute ago. Am I the only one who finds this bizarre? You would think that with my preoccupation with death, I would delight in bright yellow signs on shop windows promising marked-down caskets, but I don't. If it was my coffin then perhaps I would be interested, enough even to venture inside and run my fingers over the cheap finishes and Chinese satin but, as they stand, they remind me of what I have lost, and I drive on.

I park, remembering not to stamp on the footbrake too hard. I buy a half-jack of cheap whisky and slip it into my pocket. The sun is on its way out and the dusk leaches the colour out of the street scene. My life in black and white. The red light of the steakhouse sign flickers on; I stumble into the darkness. The restaurant is all heavy beams and brick arches and makes me think of a hobbitwarren wine cellar, complete with flagstone floor and dusty fake grapes for décor. Walls made out of bottle bottoms and huge black metal light fittings straight out of *Braveheart*. There is a chalkboard illustrated with exotic sounding happy-hour cocktails: cheap thrills for locals. I approach the bar over which a giant Jagermeister bottle hangs and order a pint of Windhoek draught. A coaster with an illustration of a Yorkie is put in front of me. It is number sixteen in a series of fifty. I flip though the rest of the pile of thoroughbred coasters until I find a less gay dog. Halfway through I find a Rottweiler which I purloin. A cosmo would work, or a strawberry daiquiri, but it would just feel wrong to drink a pint off a Yorkie.

Large beer in hand I find a table and I order a fillet, bloody, with rough-cut chips. When the waiter brings me a steak knife and condiments I ask him if he knows of a good place to stay the night. He gives me a baleful look.

"Upstairs," he says, pointing to the suspended barrels

obscuring the ceiling.

"There's a place to stay … upstairs?" I say, over-enunciating, thinking he has misunderstood the question.

"Yes," he says, as if I am slow, and walks away.

I have visions of a *Texas Chainsaw Massacre* scene where naïve tourists are promised rooms above a steakhouse only to be chopped up in the middle of the night and end up on the locals' plates the next day. Roast thigh. Deep-fried finger chips. Elbow bacon. I remember watching a documentary about the making of the film, where they said they didn't have a big enough budget for fake flesh and blood so they used the real thing. They showed the scene where the girl with the long bare legs is running from the chainsaw-wielding maniac and she trips and slides on all these small, sharp bones that cut up her knees. They were real chicken bones. And they shot in Texas, in summer, and as the shoot progressed all the meat started going off, so some of the scenes where the characters are retching and crying didn't require much acting at all. A man dressed as a chef limps up to my table with the food, so I gulp down my beer and order another one. He nods and lurches away. I poke the rare red meat with my fork and wonder if I should have ordered vegetarian.

After I pay the bill I head up the narrow stairs to the hotel. There is a no one at the reception desk so I move towards ringing the bell and as I touch the metal, someone behind me speaks and I jump.

"Good God," I say, trying to recover my composure.

It is the waiter, *sans* apron. He moves to behind the desk.

"Would you like a room, sir?" he asks, as if I hadn't already told him that downstairs.

"Er," I say, "yes, please." I smile, as if to show him I see the humour in the situation but he doesn't smile back, and hands me a key.

"Number 3," he says, motioning vaguely to his left, "straight down the passage."

He moves away from the desk, puts his apron back on and walks downstairs.

The room is a shock of bad taste, small and stuffy. There are gimcrack prints framed on the wall: kitsch paintings of an Italian landscape complete with generous fountain, some kind of snow palace I can't place (Russia?) and, of course, the old Eiffel Tower, all splendidly mounted in chipped, gold-painted wood. I open the bathroom door and am shocked when I see a man with black hair. I run my hand through it. I can't believe how different I look. I step closer to the spotted mirror to inspect my face. My eye sockets are no longer purple and my nose has healed with a slight bump in the bridge. The old scar on my cheek is almost invisible. I grimace and check my teeth. I can't even tell which are mine anymore. I shake my head sadly at the shower; it's a crude rusty rose stuck onto a pipe. The floor of cracked tile hides behind an antiseptic-green shower curtain. A shower curtain! I switch off the light before I gag. I close and bolt the main door, then turn to the opposite side of the room and slide the window upwards and open. My stomach is a cement mixer of dread and indigestion; I feel the acid in my throat. Looking out onto the dark street I wonder how long I have before the cops catch up with me. I wonder if tonight is going to be my last night of freedom and I have chosen to spend it here, in this blazing hellhole. For all I know this could be a wild goose chase. The only clue I have is a twenty-year-old photo of a child's shirt that may or may not contain the word Aurumine. The breeze is good but my paranoia gets the better of me, so I close the window again and lock it. I lie on the bed, on top of the houndstooth bedspread, and watch the ceiling fan chop the air. I open my half-jack and drink straight from the bottle. It may be my last, but at least it's an adventure.

36

BLACK GLITTER

I wake up with a start. There is someone in my bed. I freeze. I feel the extra weight on the mattress; I can smell there is someone in the room. Who would be able to get in? The creepy waiter would have keys. But it isn't him. The body is smooth and it has long hair. It is so dark that I can't see my hand in front of my face, but I know the black glitter is Denise. I don't understand how she found me, or how she got into the room, but I am half asleep and dreaming so I don't think too much about it. Neither of us speaks: there is nothing to say. She is stroking me, and when she gets on top, her body comforts my core in a meditation of deep motion. She takes her time and I stay in the trance until I can't hold on anymore. As I come I wake up and there is enough light in the room to see that I am in bed alone.

37

THE GOLDEN GIRL,

OR,

AN OLD SECRETARY TRICK

I chew through an awful fried breakfast at the steakhouse while I plan the day. The obvious thing to do would be to go to the schools in the area and try to access Eve's records. Her parents weren't at her funeral, so I guess they must be dead or otherwise lost, but there may be other clues. I can't help thinking that I am being an idiot. How will this amateur sleuthing help the insane situation I am in? Why would anything in Eve's childhood be an answer to who is responsible for framing me? So I am an idiot, but I have no other leads. I can't bear to go to jail, and I can't sit around in fear and loathing. What I wouldn't do to be in Vegas instead of this backwater town.

Without finishing my bacon I throw some cash on the table and duck out. The light is whitebright outside and, fresh out of the hobbitwarren, it takes me a while to adjust. I get into my father's car and start cruising, my new, cheap sunglasses feeling strange on my skin. You'd expect the houses to be quaint here, but they're squat and ugly and I feel I have gone back in time to when this country wasn't a nice place to be. No wonder Eve and Denise hightailed it out of here and didn't look back. I expected a gold mining town to be a bit glam, a bit bling. The way you can tell that Jo'burg was built on gold: everyone is obsessed with materialism, fast cars and diamonds. Cape Town is a lot more down-to-earth: they were given the mountain and the sea. Bald and boring Nigel looks like it was given short shrift.

I drive past church after church. At the hotel reception this morning there was a list of Nigel's 'attractions' pinned to a mutilated cork board: six out of the ten were Afrikaans churches, and the rest were the Spar, the local butchery, the steakhouse and a bird sanctuary. I relax back into the seat and turn on the radio. It feels good to be in a place where no one knows me, knows I'm wanted by the police, knows I'm wanted by people who mean me harm. To these people I am just an ordinary man, driving an ordinary car, on an ordinary day. Out of the corner of my eye I see a sign that says 'Ferryvale'. There is something distantly familiar about the name. I roll to a stop and try to think where I may have heard or seen it before. The car behind me, a grey Datsun, slows down too. I think the driver is going to offer me help or directions but instead, he picks up speed again and roars past me and out of sight, covering my car in the fine white dust that seems to suffocate everything in this place.

I start the car again and enter Ferryvale, sure there is a reason I am drawn to the name. An image shimmers in a far corner of my mind, too far for me to make out what it is. The area seems a little more upmarket than I have seen so far, but not by much. Soon I am driving past the much-lauded bird sanctuary. It looks like they have filled up old mine shafts with water and reeds and called it a sanctuary. Still, it provides a pleasant break in the hot powder that makes up the rest of the scenery. A good place to dump dead bodies. My writing hand itches.

Soon enough I drive past a school called, imaginatively, Ferryvale High. It is fenced, unsettling with razor wire. It must be first break on a school day because the place is squirming with white limbs sticking out of teal uniforms. I consider staying in the car until the bell rings but anyone who sees a man in a day-old Hawaiian shirt hovering here will surely call the police. It's steaming. I get out of the car and am thankful for the cheap breeze on my back and neck. I walk through the front gate and over the peanut-brittle walkway, into the building. I jump as the bell rings, right next to my ear, which sends my heart dashing. I didn't realise I was so on edge. An overweight woman peers at me, adjusts her glasses, licks her coral lips. I walk towards her. I can tell immediately that she is not married and has no close friends because she is wearing a vast turquoise blouse that can only be described as a disaster, and clearly no one has told her. I remember then that I am wearing flamingos, so I guess I am not in the best position to judge. She looks me up and down, as if she knows I am a fornicator, wear old Metallica T-shirts to bed, or both, and doesn't approve, either. She peels her lips off her horse's teeth in an attempt at a smile and greets me with an Afrikaans accent. I put on my best face.

"I was wondering if you could help me," I say, in my Polite Voice. "I'm doing some research for a friend of mine." The desk fan against the wall slowly rotates to face me, causing all the papers on the wall to flutter.

"What can I do … to help you?" she asks, breathless. I'm guessing it's because of her size, not my good looks or sense of style.

"If you could allow me access to previous class lists from the early 1990s I would appreciate it. I assume you have a … system," I say, and look in the direction of the dinosaur PC.

She shakes her head. "We haven't archived that far back."

I wait for her to offer another solution but she just stands there and looks at me.

"Right," I say. The papers pinned to the wall are whispering again.

"Do you have the lists as hard copies then, in a file, in the library perhaps?"

Again she shakes her head.

"Old yearbooks? School magazines?"

She narrows her eyes at this. She does everything unhurriedly. It's irritating. She takes a few steps towards the phone and punches the keys with the back of a pencil. An old secretary trick, so that you don't ruin your nails, but her nails are short and square. Maybe she learnt it from a movie, or maybe she has given up wearing nice clothes and having nice nails. Maybe someone broke her heart. After chatting in what sounds like baby-Afrikaans she hangs up and says that I can go to the library and look at the old school magazines. She tells me the way, I thank her and I walk away. She calls after me: "I can't promise you'll find what you're looking for."

Story of my life, I think, without turning around.

The library is cool and neat, apart from the wall-to-wall bald blue carpet. The librarian is expecting me and shows me to a seat and a pile of books. She is ancient and tiny, a pocket granny. She's very talkative for a librarian, and for someone without any of her real teeth, but when I ignore her she doesn't seem to take it personally. I start whipping through the books, starting with 1993 and going backwards. Eve wasn't in matric in '93 or '92, but a photo in the 1990 magazine catches my eye. Standard seven class, it says, above a messy collage of athletics, science projects and fun days, and right in the middle is Eve, smiling shyly at the camera. Bingo. I check the subsequent editions again but she has disappeared. I page to the standard seven class list and there's her name: Evelyn Shaw. I check all the other classes but there is no Denise Shaw. I take the magazine up to the librarian.

"How long have you worked here?" I ask.

She seems thrilled at the prospect of a conversation.

"It's coming up for thirty years," she says, fingering the gold chain around her neck. I guess she had limited career opportunities.

"Is there any chance," I say, "that you remember the Shaw girls? They were here in the early nineties."

"I've seen thousands of children here," she clucks. She smells like baby powder.

"The Shaw girls," I repeat, "Evelyn and Denise." She closes

311

her eyes and breathes through her nose. I show her the picture of Eve in the magazine. When she shakes her head at it, I pull out the family photo I have.

"Oh!" she exclaims and gives a little jump. "The Shaws! Of course I remember them ... Mister Shaw was the most famous man in town." Then she drops her voice: "More famous than the mayor."

"So you remember the girls? Eve and Denise?"

She looks confused. I'm sure her memory is not what it used be, being a century old, and all.

"I remember the daughter. She was called the golden girl. They were a prominent family. Mister Shaw was the manager at AuruMine."

Yes, I think. Aurumine and the Golden Girl. I jot it down in my Moleskine.

"She has – had – a sister, Denise," I prompt.

"No," she says, "That girl was an only child. That's what made it so hard, you know."

"Made what so hard?"

"Pardon me?" she says.

"You said that's what made it so hard. Made what so hard?"

"I'm sure I don't know what you're talking about," she says, pulling on her chain.

"The Shaw family," I say, "What happened to them?"

"I don't know any Shaws," she mutters. "I've seen thousands of children here."

I can see she is agitated but I need an answer. I jab at the photo with my finger. "Mister Shaw," I say, "More famous than the mayor?"

She cowers, bewildered, and I realise I have raised my voice. I take a step back. She shakes her head, mumbles something to herself, has tears in her eyes. I walk back to the table and rip out the pages I need, put them in my pocket, and stalk out.

Out of the school buildings I see the grey Datsun parked under a pine tree a little way down the road. I get into my car and slam the door. I take out my phone and Google 'Aurumine, Shaw'. Nothing. A knock on the window makes me almost shit myself. It is the turquoise receptionist. I wind the stubborn thing down.

"I took the liberty," she drawls, "of calling someone about you."

Fuck. It's always the quiet ones you have to beware of.

"Who did you call?"

She rests her fat forearms on the car door as she leans in.

"Mrs X," she whispers, then gives me the benefit of her horsey smile.

I feel I am in a particularly bad episode of an outdated local soap opera.

"Mrs X." I sigh. Of course.

"She said that she would see you."

"Nice of her," I say. "Who is she?"

The woman hands me an address scribbled on the back of a photocopied work sheet. Geometry.

"She likes to be known as The Oracle."

You have to be kidding me.

"But we *sommer* call her the Town Gossip behind her back."

I look at the crouching car in my rear-view mirror and put my foot down.

The address is in the suburb of Sub-Nigel, which makes me think there is a whole parallel-universe version of this town: deeper, darker, stickier. Sub-Nigel. Sub-human. Creatures which have chosen to inhabit the other side of the tracks and perhaps only come out at night. I drive past houses with pre-cast front walls that wouldn't keep anyone out, some shaped like picket fences, some like mining wheels and painted pink or aquamarine. Houses with their fronts falling off, watermarks on their walls like muddy waterfalls, rusted steel roofs and peeling concrete planters holding on to their long-ago perished plants. Sunsleeping dogs, broken down playsets and feral-looking barefoot kids who stop playing to look at me as I cruise past.

I use the GPS on my phone to find my way. When I arrive at the address I see the house I have been looking for since I arrived. It is the size of a mansion and looks like it was designed and decorated by someone whose wealth is indirectly proportional to his or her good taste. On top of the high walls, on watch and ready to swoop, are statues of eagles, painted gold. The walls themselves are embellished with every pre-cast detail you can imagine, and then some. There are concrete ties and bows and bowls of grapes. I ring the bell and as the giant black gates swing open I see a water feature on the front lawn the size of the Trevi fountain. I can't help smiling.

A tall black gentleman with high cheekbones walks out to greet me. I stick out my hand.

"Mister X, I presume?"

The man smirks and leads me inside. It turns out he's the butler. He purses his lips at the shirt I'm wearing, then hands me a jacket off the coat rail. It's the right size. The interior décor is as deliciously hideous as the exterior. Italian renaissance meets Parisian whorehouse. The walls are covered top-to-bottom in maroon brocade damask wallpaper. The pattern is broken up only by the over-lit Roman statues and mirrors framed in golden waves. If Francina ever won the Lotto this is how she would decorate her house. The butler (A butler, really? In Sub-Nigel? I couldn't believe my luck) escorts me down a long passage. I try to walk slowly so that I can peek into the adjoining rooms but he will have none of it and I have to hurry to keep up with him. I have the distinct feeling that I am a hare hurrying down the rabbit hole. There are paintings of toy dogs on the wall and the carpet pile is so lush it seems as though I'm tripping. Eventually the dark passage brightens and the butler disappears. I pick up my pace and get to the spot where I saw him last: there is a velvet-curtained entrance to a drawing room. I duck inside.

"Mister Harris," booms the voice that is Mrs X.

"How did you know my name?" I ask.

"She knows … everything," purrs a small man to my left whom I hadn't noticed.

"I prefer not to reveal my sources," she booms, "I'm sure you understand."

The butler motions to a chair with his white glove and I nod at him and sit.

I look around the room, as it glitters and glints and shines at me. Mrs X adjusts her feather boa.

"Why have you requested an audience with me?" she asks, showing me her little teeth. It occurs to me that she thinks she is the queen. The queen of Sub-Nigel is, after all, still a queen.

"I need information," I say. The little man nods furiously. The Pomeranian next to my chair yaps at me. Was he there before? He looks like a Chihuahua fresh out of a tumble dryer.

"I need to know about a family that lived around here twenty years ago. The Shaws. The father was the mine manager at …"

"Yes, Mister Harris," she says, "the Shaw family."

The dog yaps.

"He comes from royal blood," she breathes.

"Mister Shaw?" I say.

"Ha!" she laughs. "Ha! Ha!"

The little man laughs. "Ha! Ha!"

She puts a taloned hand on the shimmering lamé of her jelly breasts, then fondles her pearl necklace. She dresses the way she decorates.

"Dasher." She says.

"Sorry?"

"Dasher, the dog."

"Ah."

I look down at the dog.

"What do you want to know about the Shaw family, Mister Harris?"

I sit forward on my chair.

"I want to know what happened to them. Why they disappeared."

"No one disappears," she says, taking a drag of a cigarette I never saw her light. "They always go somewhere."

"I'd like to know what happened to them and where they went."

Dasher barks and we stare at each other.

"That, Mister Harris, is a seedy story of which I desire to reveal no part. Ask me something else. Like who will assassinate Obama, or what you had this morning for the breakfast you couldn't finish."

"I need to know about the Shaws. Someone is trying to kill me."

"Yes," she sighs, "I saw The Mark."

Oh God, here comes the mumbo jumbo. She wants me to ask what mark. There is an uncomfortable silence.

"What mark?" shouts the little man.

She's going to say: The Mark of Death.

"The Mark of Death," she says, and Dasher begins to growl.

38

PIGEON

This is a David Lynch movie and I have stepped right into it. All I am missing is a giant and a midget who talks backwards. I decide to play along.

"I know I am marked," I say, "and I need to find who is behind it."

The butler arrives with a tray of Piña Coladas and cashew nuts.

"She has passed," Mrs. X hisses. "The Shaw girl."

"Yes," I say. Mr X throws his drink back and I follow suit.

She strokes her chin.

"I am a good Christian woman, Mister Harris, and I don't partake in gossip mongering."

"How much?" I sigh.

"Five thousand, for starters," she sighs, "I usually charge more but I know you don't have it."

"Five THOUSAND?" I splutter. "Rand?"

"For starters."

"For a shred of information that may or not help me?"

"It will help you," she says.

"It's extortion."

"I prefer the word 'donation'. Do you think," she says wildly gesticulating, "that this lifestyle comes cheap?"

She looks around, as if for something to eat. I look at Mr X who is scrunching up his eyes and upper lip in a smile. The butler reappears with a tray of dirty Martinis and a bowl of pretzels.

"Okay," I say, "I don't have it on me. Can I come back later?"

"Come for dinner. Entrées will be served at five. We're having pigeon."

Dasher pants and paws his pillow.

"Dasher likes pigeon," twinkles Mr X.

The butler shows me out. I start to shake off the jacket but he insists I keep it, saying it's mine.

I attempt to race to the hotel to get the money, but Sub-Nigel will have none of it. There seems to be some kind of signal interference and the map on my phone confounds me further. Despite taking different turns I end up going past the same pylon again and again. The road names are like something out of *Alice in Wonderland*: Right Way; Left Avenue; This Way; Ring Road; Wrong Boulevard. I haven't felt this frustrated behind a wheel since I 'borrowed' Dad's car when I was fourteen and then couldn't find my way home. I'm in the same car now. Karma is a bloody bastard. I look at my watch: it's already 16:45. My reflection in the rear view mirror is shiny. Eventually I see a road that looks different and I take it. It is windy and seems to go in circles but soon I see houses I remember from the journey in.

"Bless you, Jesus," I mutter, not without sincerity.

I screech to a halt outside the hotel and run up the stairs. The envelope is where I left it, wrapped in a plastic packet and stuck to the underside of the cistern lid. It's an old cliché but seems marginally safer than under the bed. I empty my wallet out on the dresser – the money my father gave me – and count out the notes with shaking hands. All together it comes to five thousand, four hundred Rand. I put the four hundred back into my wallet. If I pay Mrs X what she wants I won't have enough to pay for this room or for petrol for the trip home. I imagine being marooned in Sub-Nigel for the rest of my life. Then I imagine being dead, and shove the envelope into my jacket pocket. I throw my toiletries into my bag, stealing the mean bar of complimentary hand soap in the process and giving the shower one last glance of malcontent before slamming the door behind me. I leave the door key at the empty reception desk. In seconds I am outside and I throw my bag in the car, then jump in.

The sun is still high in the sky but my watch says 17:02. I drive as fast as I can to Mrs X's house, this time only making a few wrong turns. I panic a little while finding my way.

What if there is no Mrs X, no house and no Pomeranian? The whole experience felt like a dream and I wonder if, cracked by desperation, I have just made it up.

I am elated when I park outside the manor house at 17:14. So much so that when the gates sweep open, I see a new charm in the concrete relief bowls of grapes. The cherub pissing water makes me want to sing. I bound out of the car and through the gates that close behind me, tapping my rib to make sure I still have the envelope of cash. I approach the oversized front door and lift the lion's head of a knocker but before it has the chance to make contact, the door is opened by the cheekboned butler.

"Mister Harris," he says, with a distinct Nigerian accent which makes me take an involuntary step back. If anything I expected him to be Kenyan, or at the very least, Mozambiquan. Did he have an accent before?

"Hi," I shout, "sorry I'm late."

"It's not a problem. I have a message for you from Mrs X."

"Oh? She can't tell me herself over the … pigeon?"

"The pigeon is no longer on the menu," he says.

I nod. I understand. Not everyone likes pigeon. Unless he's trying to tell me something. Is *the pigeon is no longer on the menu* a code for something? It sounds like it. I try to think of an appropriate response.

"What is on the menu?" I venture.

"Nothing, sir, the dinner has been called off."

Now that could mean anything.

"Are you saying that the deal is off?"

"No, Mister Harris, only that dinner is off. If you hand me that envelope in your pocket the deal is still very much on."

My mouth is dry and swallowing is difficult. It goes against every instinct in my body to hand over a fat envelope of cash to a Nigerian. These are people who kidnap tourists, scam grannies by email and keep hyenas as pets. I hand it over.

"Thank you," he nods, and begins to close the door. I jam my foot in.

"I need to see Mrs X!"

"There is no need for that."

He is looking decidedly more Nigerian the longer I stand here.

"Look," I say, giving him the most threatening face I can muster, "I need to see her. She has the information I need."

"Mrs X has gone on holiday."

"Holiday?" I cough.

"Aspen. She is fond of skiing."

"But you said … the deal is on."

"You have everything you need Mister Harris."

I laugh.

"Beautiful. That's just fucking beautiful. So, you wait to tell me that *after* I handed over the cash."

He motions almost imperceptibly towards the inner pocket of his jacket.

I hesitate, feel mine, then pull out a letter with gold wax insignia. Sealed with an X.

"Have a pleasant evening further," smiles the butler and closes the door.

39

The Sun Sinks

The fountain is fizzing and the late afternoon sun lends a peculiar glitter to the birds of prey, making them look ready to pounce.

I shake my head. Aspen, for God's sake. I picture Mrs X dangling on a ski lift, sipping *Moët* in a golden winter suit, making kissy noises at Dasher, poking his ear-muffed head out of her trembling handbag. As I leave the property an uneasy feeling stirs. The one I should be used to by now. The one that tells me someone is watching me.

There is a man standing by the Merc. I lift a hand to shield my eyes from the setting sun and blink at him. It is Edgar. We both freeze, then he turns and runs. Without thinking I take off and follow him. Anger propels me forward and I gain on him but I'm unfit and he is a fast fucker and after a few hundred meters, he turns a corner and is gone.

I lose my temper, dig my phone out of my jeans pocket and hurl it onto the tarred gravel.

"FU-U-U-U-UCK!" I scream with what little breath I

have left. How the fuck? How did they know? Panting, I goose-step back to the Merc and kick the tyre.

"Fucking FUCK!" I scream. The shoes on the people around me are stuck to the pavement. Fucking tracking system on the car. Fucking smartphone GPS. I jump on it. Then I stick my hand under the car arbitrarily looking for some kind of wire I can pull out but come up with nothing but a greasy hand. I want to throttle someone; preferably Edgar. The people who are stuck to the pavement start walking again, slowly, keeping a wide berth. No wonder they don't like strangers. It is clear that before I do anything else I have to get the tracker off the car. Only in South Africa would a clapped-out car like this be fitted with a tracking system. Fucking insurance companies, fucking criminals. The sun sinks.

Being a kind of outlaw myself, I wonder who would agree to remove the system from the car. There is a township nearby called Duduza. Call me a racist but I reckon that's my best chance. I get in the car and before I do anything else I uncap a new bottle of whisky I don't remember buying and have a good long *sluk*. I start driving and after taking the first few turns, I see the grey Datsun parked on a grass verge, behind a Privet hedge. There is a shouty laugh in my head, *à la* Mrs X: Ha! Haha! as I jump out and let down all four of Edgar's tyres. As I drive away I think, well, at least I hope they were Edgar's tyres.

It should be a ten-minute drive to the township, but without GPS it takes me half an hour and when I get there it's dark. I see people frowning at me when I cross the boundary. Despite it being 2011 South Africans are still vaguely surprised when they see a white person in a township. Ironic, because it is quite possible it is one of the safest places one can be, because when you are so obviously out of place you are protected by your very conspicuousness. Except in Soweto, I guess, where there are so many whites nowadays I'm sure the tourists feel scammed.

Duduza, despite its name, has a brutal past. The black people who lived in Charterston were forced to 'resettle' here because their close proximity to the white town of Nigel made the government feel uncomfortable. The same government named it: a Zulu word, meaning comfort. I remember seeing Duduza in the news in the 80s as violence flared up – boycotts and marches – one in particular ending in what was supposedly the first mob necklacing in the country.

I drive on the sandy braille roads set between the shacks that hover on the edges, squatting on the red soil. There is the large heart of Duduza, which has tarred roads, schools, pretty gardens and streetlights, and then there is the overspill in every direction, a sprawling informal settlement. My money is on the shack dwellers for what I have come for, so I keep to the dark, smoke-choked radius, dodging drunken pedestrians and street dogs with glowing green headlights for eyes. I weave slowly ahead, hoping to see someone dodgy-looking. A young teenager with a torn shirt flags me down and I roll down my stubborn window.

"*Heita* brother," I say.

"*Dagga*?" he offers. "*Tik*?"

He is thin and his skin is ash-dry.

"I need someone to help me with my car."

"Blow job?" he blinks. I cough in shock, and shake my head.

"I need help with this car. I'll give you money if you show me where to go."

He looks worried and glances side to side. Probably thinks I'm a pervert, or a cop. But at the mention of money he opens the door anyway. Poor bastard.

As he climbs in, I can see how nervous he is. He slaps the dashboard and smiles. "Nice car!" he says. The stink of poverty fills the cramped space. His anxiety makes him animated: he motions with his hands and grunts to show me the way. We drive deeper into the darkness. I look over at him every now and then, trying to gauge how truly fucked I am. He has scars on his cheeks.

"This house," he says, "here!"

It looks just like every other shack we have passed. There are lots of people milling around. I take a deep breath. When driving in here I thought the best possible outcome would be to do this job quickly and cheaply and then get the hell out. Now I'm hoping that I don't get knifed. We get out of the car and I lock it, then on second thoughts I open it again and grab my bag, slinging it over my shoulder. We walk towards the house and before we go in the young man puts his hand on my chest to stop me. He motions for me to wait outside. I look around. People are glancing at me, some chuckling. The smoke in the air makes my eyes burn. I look down and try to stay out of trouble. I feel like a prat in this dinner jacket.

Thank God I don't have the Jaguar. Despite my circumstances I can't help feeling this is an experience I'd like to write about. The feverish energy in the smoggy air, the young tattered boy. Between this and the taxi rank in downtown Jo'burg, which feels like years ago, I've really got some good material. I'm glad I have travelled all over the world for the sake of my writing but realise, now, I have largely ignored the dirtygritty beauty of my own country. Perhaps things do happen for a reason. Perhaps after this disaster of a year I really will have some good stuff in my pen.

The youngster comes out, trailing a handsome man behind him. He doesn't look anything like a criminal. He walks right past me and up to the car, sizing it up.

"Hi," I say, offering a hand. The man lifts his chin at me.

"You want to sell?" he asks.

"No," I say, "I need ..."

"It's a good car, easy to sell. But not a lot of money."

"No, I want to keep the car," I say, "It's my father's car. I need to keep it to get home."

He looks annoyed and whacks the kid hard on the back of his head, shouting at him in ambush language.

"Stop!" I shout. "I'll pay you." I take out my wallet and shake it at him. "I'll pay you to take out the tracking system."

"Tracker?" he says.

"Yes, take the tracker out, and I'll pay you."

"Five hundred," he says.

"So you can do it?" I ask.

"Five hundred," he confirms.

I look in my wallet. I only have four hundred and change. Plus I need to put petrol in the tank to get back to Jo'burg. And I need to pay the kid.

"I only have two hundred," I say, "Can you do it for two hundred?"

He clicks his tongue at me and says something I can only guess is not complimentary.

"Please," I say, grabbing him forearm.

"Nice watch," he says. It takes a moment before I register what he has said. I look down at the wristwatch Eve gave me. Worth thousands, but that's not why it's my most precious possession. I close my eyes, sigh, undo the clasp and hand it over. He puts it on straight away and admires it, flashing his teeth at me.

"I'll give you the rest when you're finished," I say. While he fetches his tools I slip the kid R100. He hops. The man gets to work on the car. The youngster hovers and learns. The man switches on his miner's headlamp and starts inside the car, near the dash, then hoists the Merc up with a jack in jerky motions so that he can get underneath. I back away, looking for somewhere to sit for a few minutes. I have another long sip of whisky and sit with my head in my hands.

Out of nowhere time freezes in a big white flash. Then

there is red and yellow – only then does the shattering blast strike me deaf. I am on the stony ground and there is no air. I can't feel my arms or legs and for a terrifying second I think they have been blown off until I lift my leaden skull to check and they all seem to be there. My hearing trickles back but the screams I hear are dull. I roll my numb torso over and get a mouthful of sand. My brain has short-circuited from the shock. Finally I stagger to my feet where I feel the heat in the air. I am almost knocked over by people running past me. Some stay behind: wailing. Others are singed and sleeping. The car turns from a hot orange bloom into a black, smoking shell. I walk away.

40

BIRDSONG

I walk for hours until a car picks me up. They speak urgent Afrikaans to me, pointing to my bleeding ears and blackened face. Their voices are muffled. They want to take me to the hospital. They want to take me to the police station. I say no and try to get out of the car but they peel my hands away. They want to take me home to clean me up. I don't have a home, I want to tell them, but my mouth isn't working. I lose consciousness.

I wake up in a strange house. I am lying in a child's bed, my feet hang over the edge. The walls are pink and there are fairies and decrepit stuffed toys. I can't possibly imagine where I am. I close my eyes again. The memories come to me in startled flashes. The man wearing my watch. The young kid in the torn shirt. The blinding crunch of the bomb blast. Tears burn my eyes and leak down my temples, staining the pillow. I can't help wishing I had been in the car. At this stage, death would be sweet oblivion. My body convulses and everything hurts, then I am again dragged away by sleep.

I wake up to birdsong. It's difficult to move but I manage

to swing my heavy body out of the miniature bed and try to open the bedroom door but it's locked from the outside. The *Deliverance* song banjos my brain. Taking fright I rattle the doorknob and shout. Perfect, I think, to be kidnapped by the Deliverance Gang. What's next? Hallways of chicken bones?

The door is unlocked by a woman I don't recognise.

"Sorry for that," she blushes, "we just locked it for safety." She hands me a tray of breakfast food and leaves. Fried polony and margarine on white toast isn't my thing but I can't remember when last I ate and I inhale the plate in minutes. The coffee is instant and over-sugared but it is one of the best cups I've ever had. When I'm finished I take the tray into the kitchen. Everyone stops what they are doing to stare at me, including two cereal-mouthed, saucer-eyed children at the breakfast table. I look down to make sure I'm wearing clothes. My limbs are blackened so I guess my face is too, apart from the lines the tears left. One of the men gives me a threadbare towel and shows me where I can shower and, afterwards, on the way out, points me in the direction of the bus station. He tries to give me cash, some pink fifties, but I refuse, showing him my wallet.

I'm astonished at their hospitality. This would never happen in Jo'burg. The criminal climate just doesn't allow for it. As I limp towards the station my breath is shallow. I wonder if I have broken a rib. Perhaps there is something to be said for backwater towns after all.

Once I am on the bus destined for home I feel safe, cocooned. I wait for the pylons to turn back into trees before I take out the letter from Mrs X and hold it in my hand for a while before opening it. It's a little bent and marked and the gold wax is cracked. I think: This had better be good.

Goldfields Manor

49 The Straight

Sub-Nigel

Dear Mister Slade Harris

Mr X and I apologise for our hasty departure. We had some *urgent* business to attend to. Okay, that's a lie. We're off on a shopping jaunt in Aspen and thought we'd practice our alpine skiing while we're here. Mr X was taken by a sudden fancy for fake snow and so we had no choice but to leave immediately. I *am* sorry that you will not get to taste Cook's pigeon but the universe obviously has its reasons and *who are we to quarrel* with the stars?! Dasher is most disappointed. He took a liking to you, of course, but it is his dismay at missing the pigeon dinner I am referring to. These Royal Dogs are very sensitive! Perhaps the next time you have The Mark Of Death you can pop by and we can try to accommodate you once again.

Butler is packing my clothes as I write, the sweet man. I don't know what Mr X and I would do without him and Cook. And Gardener, of course! And Maid. But now let's stop with the idle chatter and address the reason why you came to see me today and *why you are reading this letter*!

Here's the thing: you wanted to know what the Shaw

family attempted to hide from this town twenty years ago. But you should know by now, Mister Harris, that no one hides *anything* from Mrs X. Oh sweet! Dasher is barking like a rabid dog. He must know it is to you that I am writing. Okay Dasher darling, calm down, Mommy needs to finish this letter so that we can jump in the chopper! Now settle down and here, have a treat. Good boy

The truth is that the Shaws caused an absolute scandal here back in the 90s. It is a sad story and this is how it goes: Dasher! You naughty thing! You've just laddered mama's stockings! Butler! Butler! Where were you, I've been calling you for centuries! I need new stockings. Yes. I don't care, just get them! Yes, I'll have another Buck's Fizz, thank you. Dasher knows that Mama needs her medicine.

Miles Shaw was the mining manager at AuruMine here in Sub-Nigel. It's closed now but when he was running the show – and believe me he was a man that was large and in charge! – it simply churned out a fortune of wealth. It made the town rich and so Miles became a bit of a local hero, despite being English. He had a trophy wife, a real *poppie*, a little stick insect who used to be weighed down by all the gold Miles used to give her. Oh God, what would I do without Buck's Fizz? Bottoms Up!

They tried for years to fall pregnant, and then one day Miles announced that they were going to have a daughter the *whole town* was behind them! And that daughter was born healthy and beautiful and kept growing more and more beautiful and she was the poster child for Nigel. So you can understand that when what happened, happened, it was shame on a drastic scale! I take it that you knew this daughter and so you will know what it was that caused the uproar. But what you won't know is Miles was so outraged, so disappointed, so shocked – he was English, but had the moral values of an Afrikaner! – he banished Eve from town. She was only fifteen when he kicked her out with nothing but the dress on her back. We never heard from her again. And of course the other family *was disgraced*! After that Miles slunk into a deep depression and within the year, he had gassed himself in his home garage. All because of an illicit *love affair*! Can you *imagine*?!

So that is what you wanted to know, Mister Harris, I hope I have helped you in your quest. What the tragedy of the Shaw family has to do with you I can only imagine. I wish you good luck but I must also *warn you* that you are in grave danger. *Nothing is what it seems*, Mister Harris. If you can just manage to stay alive for the next few days you will outlive the shadow that is upon you. Now I must run, the chopper is here and Dasher seems determined to choke on a fur ball.

Ciao!!

Mrs X

PS. You mentioned a Denise Shaw, sister to Evelyn? She doesn't exist. At least not in this particular universe! Toodle doo, darling.

41

PUPPET MASTER

I arrive at the Sandton Bus Depot at dusk and catch a taxi to Rosebank, to Eve's flat. The ride there is rough, the driver malefic, but I am becoming accustomed to this new dangerous way. My plan is to ransack the place and not leave till I find what I am looking for. At the block of flats a strong feeling of *déjà vu* hits me in the chest. I stumble but keep going. In my backpack jingle Eve's keys, the ones I lifted from Denise, so I let myself in. The crime tape has been taken down, half-heartedly, as if the person responsible didn't see the point. I drink water in hungry gulps straight from the kitchen tap. I look for food in the refrigerator but it is a dark empty cave.

Eve's bedroom is exactly how I remember it from the last time I was here, except that there are some sealed boxes on the floor. Her essence is still here. I can feel her energy, smell her. I pick up a few things on her dressing table. A hairbrush, a half-moon of face powder. Her perfume is gone. I slide open the drawer. It is a mess of alien things: bracelets, lipstick and clips. No gold – Eve never wore gold. I recognise one pair of earrings and pick them up: black chandeliers. They remind me of a day I spent with her a few years ago, before I began to worry if I would ever be able to think of another story. We joined some of her friends at the Johannesburg Country Club for a picnic and fireworks display. We were a motley crew: writers, artists, directors, bankers. There was a great deal of champagne and we all got on pretty well. Fair weather friends: none of those people bothered to come to her funeral.

I put them back, close the drawer and prowl towards her studio. I think I hear something outside and I freeze. I wait for a few minutes, ears trained, before I carry on. Her studio has not yet been packed up. The unfinished canvases sit patiently on their easels, frozen in time. Paint brushes wait in their jars of turpentine and the walls, still layered with overlapping pieces of paper: quotes, rough sketches, photographs, look like the scales on a dead fish. I start studying them as if they hold some kind of clue to what happened to her, to what is happening to me. For a long time there is nothing. I scan every page, standing and crouching and standing again. Every now and then I see something I think means something: a bridge, a mountain that could be a mine, a woman who could be Mrs X, a man who could be Edgar, if I knew what Edgar looked like. She had been working on some kind of puppet-themed project. At first I thought they were dolls, but now I see the spider webs shooting out of their arms and heads. Almost invisible, the fine threads hold the dolls in various poses, ready for commands. There are scribbled doodles of marionettes and photocopies of all kinds of puppets through the ages. In the corner there is a plaster cast of a tall, long-eared rabbit with jointed paws and legs. With so many puppets, I think, this could be an abstract illustration of my life. Always playing at puppet master: realising now that I was never in charge. And even if I was, for a short time, that every puppet master has his puppet master. That people play with other peoples' lives but in the end the universe has the final say. I am seized by a reckless feeling. I hope that whoever is trying to kill me will just show up tonight. I won't run away. I need to know what this whole thing has been about; I need to understand, even if it ends in my death. It's not as though I have a life to go back to, anyway. I have lost my world.

I continue scanning the wall. Every now and then an illustration makes me stop and I have to step closer so that I can take in its delicate lines. I look at a photo and automatically move on. There is a tingling and an urge to go back. A bell. A nagging. I look at it again. A photo of two young girls, arms over each other's shoulders, their school blazers hunched up around their necks in the easy embrace. Sisters, maybe twins. The crest on the uniforms: Ferryvale. I tear the picture off the wall. The girl on the right is blonde, petite, and lifts her chin up to the camera as she grins. Eve. The other girl is sable, curvaceous, with a dark twinkle in her eyes. Denise? I flip the photo over, but there is no inscription. I swing my bag off my back and poke around for the stolen school magazine pages. I search the thumbnail portraits of Eve's class for this girl-version of Denise, and I find her. Except that her name isn't Denise or Shaw. It's Susannah. I must be wrong. I look again, holding the picture to the page. It's the same girl. Susannah Fox. Susannah Fox. The name is familiar. Why would she lie about her name, about being Eve's sister? Why would she be the one packing boxes? In some spare corner of my mind I see her name in print. I see it on a piece of paper, A4, white, on a desk. In Eve's will. Eve left her everything.

"Slade," comes a voice from behind and an electric current runs through me.

42

A CONVERSATION WITH A HOLOGRAM

I spin around, cry out. The studio has grown dark and at first, I think it's Eve, but then she walks forward into a shaft of light and I see Denise. Susannah. The woman who had sixteen million reasons to kill Eve and anyone else who stood in the way.

"Susannah," I whisper into the dark.

"You can call me that," she says.

"Why did you say your name was Denise?"

"I never did. That's the name you chose."

I shout out an ugly laugh.

"That's the name I chose," I splutter.

"Yes," she says, stepping closer.

"But now you're Susannah," I say.

"Yes," she says, "if you like."

"I found this photo of you, and this one. Your name is Susannah."

"Okay," she says.

"And Eve was an only child," I say. Denise nods.

"Why did you pretend to be her sister? What was the point? Why didn't you just take the money and run?"

She looks at me as if I should know the answer.

"I didn't know about the money," she says, then shakes her head and corrects herself. "I knew about the money but not about the will. Not about the life insurance."

We keep quiet for a while.

"No one suspects you. No one even knows you …"

"No one even knows I exist," she says. Her words echo in my head. No one even knows she exists. She is close now. If I reach out I will be able to touch her. Heat creeps up my body in a smooth, liquid motion, as if I am being filled up with boiling water. There is anger in every muscle, organ, cell.

"How could you?" I demand.

"I didn't," she says.

"You may as well tell me the truth. I'm going to die tonight, aren't I?"

"Are you?" Jesus, it's like having a conversation with a hologram.

"I'm surprised you didn't do it sooner," I say, "You had so many opportunities."

We had been so intimate, I feel sick with it. Sick with the blood-red intimacy.

"I didn't kill Eve," she says again.

"Why would I believe that?"

"Because I was in love with her," she whispers.

"What?" I say. I am confused, knocked off balance.

"I've always been in love with her."

"What?"

"We've been … lovers …since school."

"If that were true I would know," I say. "Eve and I were close."

"We kept it secret. Telling the truth caused a lot of pain."

"What do you mean?"

"We were fifteen when we told our parents. My dad beat me so badly I had to be hospitalised. You've seen my scar," she says, touching her chest. "One of the broken ribs punctured my lung. Eve's parents didn't touch her, wouldn't touch her, wouldn't look at her, just threw her out. Her father's reputation was ruined."

I search her eyes but I can't read them.

"She moved to Jo'burg. She used to write to me but if my dad found a letter from her he would lay into me. It was worth the risk, just to hear from her, but when I told her she stopped. That's been the pattern of our relationship our whole lives: bad things happen when we are together, but we can't be apart. Because we love each other, we want to protect each other, so we stay away. But sometimes we can't help it, and then we have to deal with the consequences. The last time we were together is the last time I saw her alive."

"I don't understand. What consequences? Do you mean because you are gay?"

"No, being gay has nothing to do with it. Being in love with Eve didn't make me gay any more than being with you didn't make me straight. Love isn't held back by gender. The consequences I am talking about run deeper than that. We were never meant to be together. We were star-cross'd."

"Romeo and Juliet," I murmur. Their fate was sealed the moment they locked eyes on each other. In the end, their actions were inconsequential because their destinies were already in the stars.

"You didn't kill her?"

She is close now, our bodies are touching. She takes my hand.

"How could I?" she breathes into me. "Killing Eve would be like killing myself."

This makes sense. In my mind they are becoming the same person. Yes, I think, you are Eve's shadow.

She pulls my head down and forces her lips onto mine. I hesitate. I try to think. Slowly, slowly, she draws me out. Her mouth is safe and familiar. I feel the wall come up from behind me and touch my back. I don't remember taking off my clothes but we are skin-on-skin. I feel weak and we sink down onto the spattered sheets. She senses my weakness and takes control, manoeuvring so that the whole length of her body is on top of mine. Then I am inside her and she rocks up and down, up and down until I am hypnotised. There is weight on my wrists. I open my eyes but it's dark. I feel her fingernails – she is holding me, pinning me down. She is a Black Widow spider. Up and down, the smoothest breast-skin, breast-silk, her nipples graze my chest. I start to feel the build, coming from somewhere far away. A spark, a low flame.

She whispers something into my ear but it seems so far away that I can't hear what she is saying. The flame creeps nearer.

"What?" I say, my voice is a growl.

"I said, 'So now you can stop the act'."

"What are you talking about?"

She leans right in, her lips touch my ear.

"I know."

The flame is a fire. As she continues to rock I feel all the blood I have go to my cock.

"What do you know?" I groan. There is a rushing in my ears.

"I know your secrets. I know what you are."

"Tell me."

Oh God, the trail of fire is coming at me fast.

"I know it was you."

Must have misheard. Paranoid. She doesn't stop rocking.

"I know you killed Eve," she says.

My eyes fly open. Here eyes bite into mine. I try to shake her off but she is holding me down, her hands full of new power.

"Don't be ridiculous," I say. "I had no reason to."

"You had the oldest reason in the book: you loved her and you couldn't have her. You thought, if I can't have her, then I will have her story. You sacrificed her for your writing."

"No," I say. No. "I wouldn't. Couldn't."

She is heavy, she is squeezing me. I feel dizzy. Flashes of light on my brain. Pictures in fast forward. I see my violently scribbled notes, the mind map, the knife in my study. I see myself sneaking into Eve's apartment in black gloves and balaclava.

No.

I see Eve's bloodless face, the savage red ribbon on her chest.

"No," I say, "The police think I did it because I planned to do it. But it was only a plan. A concept. An experience, for a … story."

"The police think you did it, because you did it."

I try again to buck her but her strength is Amazonian.

"Just like you did it before."

My spine turns to ice.

I retreat as far as I can into my mind. Into the space where I am allowed to hide things. A safe corner of denial. I want her to kill me. I would rather die than listen to this. I wish I could die. God, I wish I could just stop existing. I wish I had never existed.

"I didn't do it before," I murmur, more to myself than to her.

"Why do you think your mother left you?" she snarls.

I am slipping into a hungry pool of darkness. I try to think of something else, but the cold blackness is swallowing me whole: toes, ankles, calves. Knees, thighs …

"She left us because she couldn't stand it any more. She couldn't stand our … mortality."

"After Emily." she says. Anger shoots back into my body, makes me stronger, and we struggle.

"How did you know about Emily?" I shout into her. She is my secret. My haunting. "How did you know?"

I am filled with a sudden power and I am able to throw her

off and stand up. She comes at me but I manage to swing her into the wall and she hits her head with a *thunk*. She is still for a second, then she stumbles for me again and we are two shadows wrestling in the dark. I kick her legs out from under her and as she falls, I pounce on top of her. Swift, stealthy, like a killer. Like I have done this before.

"It was an accident!" I shout into her. I don't want to hear another word erupting from her mouth. My hands are around her throat and I am squeezing as hard as I can. She is making sounds I don't want to hear, so I press harder. "It was an accident!" I shout over and over, shaking her, causing her head to bounce on the concrete floor, until at last, at last, at last she is quiet.

"The descent into hell is easy."

- Virgil

43

ROLLING AND WAILING

Now that she is quiet I can let go. Now we don't have to fight. Now we can just go our separate ways and never look back.

"Now you are quiet," I say, touching her cheek. It is cold. My knees are locked. How long have I been sitting over her like this? I must be heavy. It must be hurting her. I climb off, taking her hand.

"Get up now," I say. "It's time to go."

I sway her gently. I shake her shoulder. It's time to go home. God, how I want to go home.

I lift my hand to stroke her hair and as I do, I know she is dead.

When I come out of it I am still beside her, rocking and moaning. I remember this feeling from when I was eight. On the riverbank. Coming to, rolling and wailing, wondering where I had been in my head and not glad to be back. I look at her black outline. I need to get rid of her body. I stand up, switch on a lamp. Start looking around. I need to get rid of it but I don't know how. No more bodies in rivers.

44

STILL SKIN

I find some flammable liquid in the studio. I am numb so I can't tell what it is, but I know it will burn. I soak Denise's clothes and then cover her body with them. Susannah'sclothes. Susannah's body. Pour it in her hair. Empty it onto her. Drops bounce off her still skin.

There is a thought that keeps knocking, but I try to keep the door closed. It starts like this … *if I am capable of murdering Denise* … and then I shut it out. It comes back over and over again. *If I am capable of murder* … and with it comes flashbacks of Eve's ivory face, Emily's marble body. The thoughts slow me down until I am still and I put my head in my hands and bellow as loudly as I can to drown them out.

I find more bottles and douse the rest of the place. I paint the wall with it. The white paper flutters and turns translucent. After the studio is done I move into her bedroom and soak everything in there too. The taped-up cardboard boxes; the near-empty cupboards; the curtains; the pillows. I hear sirens in the distance. They know I am here: they have tracked me down. I start looking for a lighter, or matches. I attack the kitchen drawers, hauling everything out and dumping it on the floor. My fingerprints are everywhere. Nothing in the kitchen, nothing in the passage cupboard. Back in the studio I pillage the drawers. Blindly I loot and sack and strip until I see something I recognise. Not a lighter, but a sheet of cream-coloured paper. My body wants to keep searching for fire but this thing stops me. I pull it out, feel it between my fingers. My senses are coming back. It is thick, textured. I take it towards the lamplight. The top centre is embossed with decorative circle: a bit like a wheel.

45

HEADFIRST INTO BLACK DEW

I am lost, but then I hear the siren again and that wakes me up, tells me I am in this place with a job to do. I crumple up the letterhead and add it to what will be the bonfire. I almost give up on the lighter but then I think: incense and candlelit baths. I walk to the bathroom and find a box of matches in the first cupboard I open. There are only a few in the box but they will do. I reach around to make sure that I have my bag on my back. The fumes are making me unsteady on my feet. I hear the wailing of the police car as if it is in the next room. I pour the last of the fuel down the entrance hall and up to the front door. I stumble around, my fingers are thick. I drop the matches, pick them up again. There are bright lights blocking out my vision. I need to get to fresh air or I will pass out. I don't even bother to turn the handle, I just kick it open. Once outside I take a few clear breaths to make the stars recede. I see parts of the floor, parts of bricks on the wall. I put an arm out to steady myself. The siren arrives downstairs. The car brakes with a scream and crunch and the siren quits half-shriek. Doors open and boots hit gravel. Terse words are exchanged. It will take them less than a minute to get up here. I peer through the stars into the matchbox. I grab one but drop it on the floor. Another one. Then I take two and hold them steady against the flint-side and as it sparks, the wind is knocked out of me and I am pitched forward, teeth-to-tiles. The matchbox skitters across the floor. I forget about breathing and start crawling towards the box, but Edgar gets there first and picks them up in a neat collect. He glances backwards at me, white grimace in black hood, and takes off. Next thing I know I am up on my feet and chasing him. He darts down the narrow emergency steps and I follow. As we descend I can hear the cops ricocheting off the main stairway, in the opposite direction. Despite the assault, despite the blurred vision and bubbling lungs, I keep on going. We hit the basement floor and run through the parking lot. Edgar bounces off a station wagon, bounds up some concrete planters, rushes through a garden and out of the pedestrian gate. He is fast and putting extra distance between us. He is hard to spot in his dark clothes, and he runs like a pro. Trust me to get the athlete stalker. We corner the block, hitting a straight road and he picks up speed. I can feel my legs disappearing under me. I am just about to stop running when he makes a sound: a yelp. He has tripped over something, some sweet thing, and sprawls headfirst into black dew.

He ploughs into the lawn on all fours and scrambles to get up. I reach him just as he manages to lift his knees off the ground and I land a clumsy drop kick into the washboard of his stomach. He lets out a howl like a wounded animal and I kick him again, this time in the ribs. He tries to get away, clawing at the ground and trying to get a footing but the grass is slippery and I have my foot on his back. He doesn't fight back. Acid loathing makes me kick him once more: a heavy jump on his spine and he is flattened. I grab his shoulder to roll him over and rip off his black hood so that I can see his face. I recoil at the sight: shiny pale plastic glinting in the streetlight. A mask. I dig my fingers underneath it and peel it off. The face I see topples me. He may as well have punched me in the face. I let go of him with an exclamation.

"There are some things you learn best in calm,

and some in storm."

- *Willa Cather*

46

His Strings Cut

We sit on the pavement in identical postures. We have both had the wind knocked out of us and need to stay close to the ground.

"Frank," I say.

"I can explain," he says, his breathing heavy, one hand up in defence, the other on his ribs.

I want to laugh. He says it sincerely, as if an explanation could make a whisper of a difference in this situation. As if it could undo terrible things. If only words could.

"You've been trying to kill me," I pant.

"I've been … helping you," he says, spitting out blood.

The bastard.

"Helping me?" I shout.

"Guarding you," he grimaces. His eyes glow. "You can't see that now, but you will."

I wind my arm back and punch him in the face as hard as I can. There is a simultaneous crack, as my knuckle breaks his nose and breaks itself in the process. He is KO'd, sprawled like a dummy on the ground, his strings cut, blood pumping out of his nose. I shake my hand out. I see figures in the distance, running. I bolt, leaving Frank to bleed.

47

Skinless

They're persistent, I'll give them that. I hurdle over a low wall and land on the soft ground on the other side. My bad ankle twinges. I hear their hurried footfall just metres away. I remember trying to outrun the cops in Bangkok and hope that this time I will have better luck. I charge down to the *spruit* where I am whipped by willow branches and splash in, wading thigh-deep in the murk to get across then up the oily hill on the other side. They have torches but not dogs. I look for a way to get into one of the properties on the other side but the walls are all so high and the electric fence lines glimmer hostile in the moonlight. All I can do is keep running, even though I can feel them gaining on me. Eventually there is a wormhole: a house under construction has a sharp, square hole in their temporary entrance of ramshackle tin. I drop my bag and push my body through, tearing my clothes and scraping off a good layer of skin as I go. Once inside I find my way through the maze of walls and punch-outs for windows, making the wrong turn twice before finding the exit. Blinking in the dark, trying to see where to go next, I hear a whistle. Involuntarily I look in the direction of the noise and something behind me knocks me out.

I come to in the police van, handcuffed and lying across the backseat. It smells like petrol and sweat. They are speaking their ambush language, boasting about their catch. Every now and then the radio crackles to life but they ignore it. The back of my head is blazing from where they hit me, and my broken knuckle is throbbing. I feel a sense of downward resignation and traitorous relief. I won't die tonight, I think. I have escaped. Other thoughts are hammering but I try to hold on to this one for the feeling it gives me, but then it is gone, and so am I.

I come to again and my vision is crossed with lines. I am lying on top of a grey mattress in a grey jail cell. I recognise the walls from my previous visit. Is the main block of cells full up? Why am I always relegated to this spare building? I sit up too fast and my head fills with sparks so I sit still for a long time until I feel that I can stand up. My ankle is stiff and swollen and it hurts to breathe. Panic fills my chest. I limp to the bars, rattle them and shout for someone. I do this over and over but no one comes, so after a long while of shouting and trying to catch my breath I lie down again, to try to forget where I am.

When I open my eyes, Sello is standing outside the cell.

"Detective," I say, swinging my legs off the bed to sit up.

"Hello, Mister Harris," he replies, more polite than usual.

I touch the lump on the back of my head. It has stopped bleeding.

"Was it really necessary for your boys to pistol-whip me?"

"Apparently so."

"Seems like a violent way to deal with someone you know isn't the murderer."

"On the contrary," Sello says, shifty-eyed.

On the contrary? I think they must have switched *Law and Order* for old reruns of Sherlock Holmes mysteries.

"We have found all the evidence we need."

"I can explain that," I say. Sello shakes his head. "The time for stories is over."

"Do I get a phone call?" I ask.

"If you wish," he says, "I advise you to call your lawyer."

He unlocks the door with a clang that resonates through my body, and walks me down an abraded linoleum corridor to a pay phone.

Still cuffed, I pick up the receiver and balance it between my ear and shoulder. The machine wants money before I dial and I don't have any. Sello fishes in his pockets and slips a shiny R5 coin into the slit. I nod my thanks and dial my father's number.

It rings for a full minute before he answers. He sounds distracted, annoyed.

"Dad!" I can't help the emotion that pushes the word out of my mouth and down into the receiver.

"Slade?" There is feeling in his voice too, as if he never

expected to hear from me again. I stumble, not sure what to say.

"God, Dad, I don't know where to start."

"Do you need help?" he says.

"Yes," I say, "Yes, I need help."

Both of our voices are unsteady.

"What can I do?"

"Can you come down to the police station? I've been arrested."

"Arrested?"

"Never mind that, I just need to talk to you. I need to tell you something."

"I'll be there in half an hour."

On the way back to the cell I ask Sello if I can have a shower and some clean clothes. Anything to avoid the darkcloudconfines of the cell. He slams the door shut. It is obvious there is no other way to close cell doors.

"No," he says. "This isn't a hotel."

I think he still holds the offer of cappuccinos against me. We are on his turf now and he wants to make it clear there will be no cappuccinos. Back in the cell I feel I am disappearing in all the grey. My mind is blank: grey. I lower myself onto the mattress, play steeple with my fingers, and wait.

When my father arrives they let him into my cell. He smells like shaving cream. We hug for the first time in as long as I can remember. Like two bears with sore heads. When we pull away, his eyes are shining. I offer him the seat of the bed opposite mine and we sit. It is a small cell and our knees are almost touching. We are quiet for a while.

"I need to tell you something," I say. My voice is not to be trusted.

He shakes his head. Tries to talk, then gives up and shakes it again.

"It's about Emily," I say.

"No," he says, clearing his throat. "You don't need to tell me … anything."

"That day … by the river," I start.

"I know you blame yourself, son."

He called me son.

"But it wasn't your fault. It was an accident. Everyone knew that … except you."

My face is wet.

"And look what it did to you."

Am I an empty shell because of that day? That precarious minute?

"You've been punishing yourself ever since. Pushing everyone away, trying to get yourself killed. Angola, Nigeria,

Thailand. And now you've finally committed a crime that vindicates your punishments. You're like a goddamned Kafka character. You're stuck in your own twisted novel like a fly in amber."

I blink at him, wanting him to say more and therefore postponing the words that will have to leave my mouth.

"Your mother couldn't stand it," he says, "She couldn't stand your mortality. She told me that when you were born it was like some part of her was cut open, never to heal. Every bruise you had hurt her, every scratch. It was like walking around without skin."

I have heard this a hundred times. Every time I asked where Mom had gone in the year after she left, I heard this speech. Skinless. She couldn't stand it, he always said. But I knew it was because she couldn't stand me. Couldn't stand the memory of that day, of what I had done.

"That's not the reason she left," I whisper, head in hands.

"Of course it is. She told me so. She was so … depressed. She'd go days without changing her clothes, or washing her hair. She wouldn't talk. Do you remember that? It got to the stage that I didn't know if she would … survive … her grief. There were warning signs. Extra bottles of pills, Minora blades in the bathroom, sitting in her running car in the middle of the night. That's why I let her go. She wouldn't have survived the life she had with us, with me."

"That day," I stammer, "At the river. I pushed her under."

Dad looks at me, not understanding what I am saying. "I pushed Emily under and Mom saw it happen."

48

A Monument To Lost Causes,

Revisited.

It was my idea to swim. I knew that we weren't allowed to, that it was dangerous. At first Emily said no, she didn't want to get into trouble. But I jumped in, told her how cool it was and called her a chickenshit. She always hated that. She sat on the bank for a while with pinched lips and watched me while I did tricks for her: backward roll, dead man floating, walking handstand. She crept closer and closer, edging down onto the slippery rocks until, splashless and without a ripple, she was in the water. We laughed at how the cold water made her breathe too fast. Her summer dress floated around her body like a giant lampshade and we giggled at that, too. I tried to teach her how to backward roll but she got a nose full of water the first time and didn't want to try again. I was always trying to teach her things. She was my baby sister. Then I thought of a new game. We could go to the deeper part, just a few metres away, and dive down for jewels. Whoever got the most jewels would win. We were pirates on a dangerous mission – going to the deeper part would mean that we were just in view of the family holiday house – and if we got caught we'd get a really good thrashing, or not be allowed to go to the beach the next day, or both.

Emily dived down first. I thought I'd give her a head start, her being small, and a girl. I watched her wild underwater kicking as she tried to reach the bottom. She stayed down a bit longer than I thought she would and, just as I was about to worry, her head popped out of the water, grinning and gasping, a stone clasped in her hand. It was a good game and we played for a while, piling up our treasures until the time that Emily didn't come up. I thought she was playing a joke so pretended not to worry for a while but then it seemed too long, so I went under with open eyes trying to spot her ballooning white dress in the browncloudy water.

I saw her right away, swept a small distance way from me, struggling against some unseen thing, some watery ghost. I swam towards her with every muscle pumping and when I reached her, I went under to find what was holding her down. She was fighting hard for air and managed a lungful every now and then but her head stayed mostly underwater. I went under again and again to see what it was and I flailed around her in the hope of somehow detaching her.

Only then, when the desperation hit, did I think of calling for help. I broke the water and yelled with all my might. I screamed and shouted, but the dry world was still and quiet. Em was slowing down now, not kicking as vigorously as before.

I screamed for help again then ducked under. That time I saw her dress was caught on something: a root or branch, a sharp black arm pulling her under. I grabbed it with both hands, trying to break it, but without being able to touch the river bottom my arms were powerless. I tried to unhook

Emily's dress but she was pulling too hard in the opposite direction. I came up again, gasping for air, with not enough breath in me to yell. The only thing left to do was to push her under and at the same time, unhook her dress. She was pedalling in slow motion then, as if asleep, but when I tried to push her down, further into the water, she woke up and thrashed around, kicking me and scratching my cheek. She was almost low down enough; I could feel the material give somewhat with my right hand. I pushed her harder, deeper, and the dress was released.

A feeling, a golden feeling came over me. Emily would be okay. I brought her to the surface and looked up in triumph. A small white face stared back at me from the faraway house then disappeared into a run. That's when I noticed that Emily wasn't breathing. I floated her in my arms, not sure what to do, when there was a yell and a blast of water in my face.

A man I'd never seen before snatched my sister out of my arms and handed her upwards to another man standing on the bank, who laid her on the grass and began beating her chest and breathing into her small blue lips.

The man in the water was as big as a giant. He lifted me with one arm and carried me out of the water. On land, he placed his vast hand on my shoulder as we watched, then he swapped positions with the other man. On land, my heart was sprinting, my legs were riverweed. Eventually they stopped beating her and kissing her. The giant picked her up in her sticky white dress and cradled her in his arms.

I looked up at him, the man like a tree, the image forever burnt into my mind: a Monument. An animal noise made us look over to the other side of the river, where the houses were, and the white face came racing toward us. Mom. Gasping, shaking, all four of us dripped.

We waited for the screams in silence and dread.

49

The Memory of Water

"She saw you?" he asks. He is as grey as the room.

I nod. It has been a difficult secret to keep, and at last I am free of it.

"She could only have imagined the worst," I say.

He sits back. "Yes," he says, taking a while to grasp the implications.

"Dad, she left because she couldn't live with what she saw that day. She couldn't live with a murderer for a son."

Dad is shaking his head again. "What a waste," he mutters with clenched teeth, "What a goddamn shame. Why didn't you *tell* us?"

"What could I say? At first I didn't want to get into trouble, I couldn't imagine being responsible for such a loss, such heartbreak. Then later – I felt like a murderer – I did whatever I could to pretend it never happened. She would be alive today if it weren't for me."

We are both crying openly now. He reaches into his top pocket for a crumpled tissue.

"I loved Emily, Dad. I loved her. I would never have hurt her."

"Yes," he nods, and blows his nose. "I know that. We all loved her. Perhaps too much. She made us … skinless."

An avalanche of relief: I have confessed. I have confessed. I sob. I say that I am lost.

After a long pause, he says, "Sometimes getting lost is part of finding your way."

When it is over we stand and call the guard. My father hugs me once more but he is shaking and it leaves me feeling empty. The cell is locked and I am on my own. It astounds me that after such a revelation the building is still standing, the cell is exactly how it was before. A shift has taken place in me; you'd expect the tornado in my head to have affected the landscape too. You'd expect roofs to be lifted, walls smashed, pets missing. But instead here I am in a little cell, looking at my hands, awaiting my fate.

The feeling comes at me full-force, with no warning tease. I stand up and my body – exhausted, bruised, dried out – is filled with hot-blooded purpose. It's the fingertingle. The zone. The feeling that if I don't write now, if I don't put these words on paper then they – and I – will be lost forever. I shout for the guard and he tortures me with his lazy sway.

"Pen!" I shout, "Please! Pen and paper!"

He looks worried.

"They said you would ask for that," he says. "I don't know."

"What don't you know? You don't need to know anything, just bring me something to write with. I will pay you! I will give you anything you want!"

"I don't know how they knew. They told me to tell them when you were ready."

Despite my delirious state, this sounds ominous.

"Who is 'they'?" I ask. And then I understand.

"I'll confess," I promise, "I will write everything down. Whatever it takes, I will do it. Just bring the pen."

"You are ready," he says, and leaves.

While I wait, I think of what I am going to write. Words, before so aloof, now tumble down on me. The floodgate is opening and I brace myself. Of course, I will write about this adventure of mine. This insane, nonsensical exploit my life has become. I will write about everything that has happened to me since I became blocked a year ago, about what it has taken to unblock me. And this time, I will write the real story: I will finally write about Emily. Not in the way I used to write about other people, using and discarding them, but a different kind of writing, with truth and integrity. The confession I owe to her and the world. The unwritten, unreadable diary I carry: The Memory of Water.

But how does it end? Sitting in a cell being bathed in a glorious revelation is not satisfying enough. Besides, I am raw from the encounter with my father. I need a better ending: the story demands it. I'm going to have to wait and see; but for now, as far as I can imagine, there could be three different endings. The first one involves the protagonist being sentenced to life in jail. He is made to wear orange overalls and eat out of his hat, buying the guards Mister Delivery KFC so that he can keep his small luxuries: a pen, a book, a toothbrush. And his cappuccino machine. He would peel potatoes and lift weights and watch *Days Of Our Lives* during the day and scribble all night. He would write on smuggled-in paper and when that ran out, tissues, toilet paper, and chickenwinggreasy serviettes. Like Nelson Mandela. Okay, nothing like Nelson Mandela, apart from, well, illicit writing in prison. Life would be a heady mix of trying to stay alive despite the rusted jerry-built shivs, the guns, the rapists, the gold-toothed guards and the gangs. Christ, imagine the material; imagine the murderers I could meet, the things I could write about. It almost makes me want to go until reality hits and I realise that I'll probably end up in some maximum-security inferno. I probably won't survive the first lights-out. The second ending is a little more optimistic. My lawyer develops magical powers of persuasion overnight and somehow wins my case for me, pro-bono. I am acquitted and set free among an insane media frenzy. My back issues start selling again and so Starling & Co. decide to renew my contract, enabling me to buy back my house. I spend the days creating brilliant new novels, having long showers and eating paninis.

But it's too easy and karma isn't that forgiving. Something will have to give and I guess it will be the most important thing. My writer's block will return and I will never be able to write again. That will be my punishment. I will have this crazy story to tell and I just won't be able to get the words down. I have used so many people; it makes sense that the fruit of that abuse is toxic, even though my intentions weren't.

In the beginning of my writing career my motives were pure enough: to tell the truth. Writing is above all, telling the truth. But it's not sustainable if you don't live truthfully, which I haven't done since I was eight years old. And now that it's too late I know what Eve said that night was true: that my writing is a gift and if I misuse it, it will – and did – abandon me.

I feel I have turned a corner now. I understand that the universe wants more out of a person than I have been offering. It is time to live a more authentic writing life.

The third ending. I can hear voices through the swing-doors, down the corridor, low and muffled. I want to tell someone about my epiphany. Anyone will do at this stage, even Sello. Their muted voices grow louder as they near. I stand up and try to look through the bars but the angle is wrong, so I pace for a while and sit down again. I wonder if they will bring me a pen. I perch on the end of the bed and play imaginary piano on my knees. And I wait.

50

WAKING UP WITHOUT YOUR LEGS

Sometimes, things in life happen which shock you on such a fundamental level, you know for sure that you will never be the same person again. They don't happen often, and perhaps some people don't ever experience it. It's like being hit by a car you didn't see coming, despite looking both ways before stepping off the pavement. Like waking up without your legs, or being turned to dust after being caught by an early dawn.

The first time it happened to me was that summer in Pringle Bay when I held my sleeping sister in my arms. And now it happens again. My heart stops beating, the hair on the back of my neck stands up, and the air turns to clear jelly. The double doors swing open and in she strides.

"True friends stab you in the front."

- Oscar Wilde

51

THE ULTIMATE BETRAYAL

At first I think, Oh Fuck, I have finally snapped the delicate and trembling cord that was connecting me to sanity. And it's about fucking time. I've had just about enough of the sane life. It was too hard and it never made sense.

I try to stand but find my legs no longer belong to me.

"Hello Slade," she says.

I am numb, deaf and dumb. The jelly holds me in place.

"Eve?"

"Hi," she says, as if it's the most natural thing in the world to be raised from the dead. She takes a key out of her pocket and opens the cell door. I know I should be happy to see her, or at the very least, relieved. But seeing her walk in here has spun the world in the opposite direction, leaving my brain behind. Her movements are measured, fluid, confident. She has been planning this for a long time. When I realise that I may not be mad and this may in fact be happening, I gag.

She walks towards me, takes my hand, hoists me up and

leads me out of the cell, down the corridor and into a large room where people are waiting for me. In the nervous crowd stand a tear-stained version of my father, an astounded Sifiso, a broken-nosed Frank. The room is whirling. I also see other faces I recognise. The executor of Eve's will, the boy from the bank, the detectives in plain clothes: Sello and Madinga. The deaf-mute cousin who almost gave the game away. Everyone manages to look grim and hopeful at the same time.

"Surprise party?" I joke. I address Sello grimly: "You shouldn't have."

"I know I went too far," starts Eve. "It started off as an idea, a small project, a benevolent hoax ..."

"A betrayal," I say. "The ultimate betrayal."

"No," she shakes her head. "Not a betrayal. A gift."

I spit out bitter laughter.

"A gift? I almost died!"

"You were dead already," she says, "We brought you back to life."

"I thought you were dead for Christ's sake!" I am shouting and my voice bounces off the spinning walls. "Do you know what that did to me? Do you have any idea? And to make me think that I played a part in it? Heartless, hateful ..."

"You did play a part in it," Eve says, "the most important part. It was your plan."

"What?"

"It was your plan, your mind map, on the kitchen table. I saw it a few days after our fight at your party – I had gone to apologise – and that's when I had the big idea. You planned to kill me in theory; all we did is continue the story. We followed it to see where it would go, to give you an authentic experience."

I turn on the others, casting venom at my father and Frank.

"And you!" I shout, "You traitors! You cold-blooded traitors!"

"No one was against you Slade, the whole time everyone was with you, helping you, taking care of you."

"Frank! Helping me? He was trying to kill me! And Dad … spying on me."

Eve is calm. "We lost you once and your father let us know where you were and which car to find you in. He was helping us to look out for you. You became more and more … unpredictable. Frank has been acting as your bodyguard since the day of the 'murder'. He made sure that you didn't do anything too dangerous."

I think of Edgar, AKA Frank, knocking the box of matches out of my hand. I am quiet for a while.

"When you started battling to write I wondered if a small mystery might coax you into a new story, so I wrote you a few letters. When that didn't work, I spray-painted your wall. Threw a rock through your front window. That didn't work either, so I gave up, until I saw your plan. It was perfect."

"You all stood around and let me lose everything."

"You lost nothing," she says. "It was all part of the setup. I thought you must feel as though you have lost everything to realise how much you really had. Everything is exactly as it was before we started. You have your house, your car ..."

"Your contract with Starling," pipes Sifiso.

"Everything is as it was before?" I say, "Nothing is as it was before."

"Well then," smiles Eve, "We have accomplished what we set out to do."

"Which was what, exactly?"

"Whether you see it now or not, we have given you your life back."

"You could have fucking fooled me."

"You needed something ... devastating ... to get you writing again. You were desperate, you told me so. You thought you were finished. I decided to show you that you weren't. I gave you what you were begging for."

"It wasn't for you to do."

"And who else would do it? If we hadn't done this, where would you be?"

"I would be safe, at home, drinking whisky, instead of standing here with twenty years taken off my life."

"Your reaction is understandable; we expected you to feel

this way. We planned everything to the last detail. But that wasn't enough ... you kept on surprising us."

"I dare say I return your sentiment."

I am angry but I start to relax into the thought that I no longer have to fear for my life. More importantly, Eve is alive. The relief is heady.

"You really had us on our toes. We had a full team working on the project 24/7. We had actors, mostly, and some guys from the film production house to help with make-up and photos and props, like crime tape."

"Your funeral," I say.

"It was the best we could do at such short notice. It was practically rent-a-crowd. I was there, watching you through the curtain. Out of vanity, I guess. Although I noticed that you didn't cry."

"I was too busy having panic attacks," I say. "The crying came before that, and after."

"We felt like we were in control of the situation until you took off. That made us concerned. It was easy to manage while you were at home but when you left, there were so many ... variables ...so many things that could go wrong."

"And clearly went wrong," I say.

"And you went to *Nigel* of all places?"

"That's where you pointed me to," I say. She doesn't understand. "The logo on your T-shirt, when you were a little girl, in the family photo."

"Yes," she smiles, "of course. But then something happened when you were there."

"Yes," I say.

"You had a kind of … episode."

"I guess you could call it that."

"You stayed in your room for three days with a case of whisky. You wouldn't eat or talk. We were going to abort the mission, call in a shrink, when you deserted your father's car and just started walking through the town in the middle of the night."

"What?"

"That's when we got those locals to pick you up, give you bed for the night and some food."

"That's not what happened," I say. "I had to meet Mrs X. I went to Sub-Nigel. I almost got blown to pieces in that fucking explosion of yours in Duduza. Your special effects were astounding, realistic."

"Explosion?" she blinks, "Mrs X?" She catches herself, half-chuckles. "Do you think those things happened?"

"Of course they fucking well happened. I almost got my head blown off."

"Slade," she smiles, but her eyes are worried. "There is no such place as Sub-Nigel. It's the name of an abandoned mine. You must have seen a sign for it somewhere in town."

"The explosion was real." I say.

"No," says Eve, "there was no explosion."

I look down at my wrist and my watch stares back at me. I blink and touch it, to make sure it's there.

"An episode?" I say.

Frank talks: "You just lay in bed, man, for days. Watching the ceiling fan. I thought you were one beer short of a six-pack. I was worried. I told Eve to call it off."

I think of Mrs X, the outrageous décor, the pigeon, the Pomeranian. I pull her letter from out of my jacket pocket. Instead of the heavy stock and gold wax I remember, it is a cheap letterhead from the hotel: blank.

"You did what you do best, Slade," she says, "You retreated into your imagination."

I get flashes: plastic grapes, and toy dogs on coasters at the steakhouse bar; Dasher; Mrs X's wall. A cocktail menu, dirty martinis, Buck's Fizz. At the hotel: Paris, snow, and a fountain, framed in gold.

"This thing you did," I say to her, "this experiment, hurt people."

She shakes her head. "No one was hurt. Except Frank, a little."

Frank shrugs and touches his nose. "You owed me, buddy."

"What about Denise?" The blood rushes to my head. "That was also engineered, right? She's okay?" I look around the crowd, desperate to see her face. "Where is she? I don't see her here."

Eve frowns, and looks uncertain.

"Who is Denise?"

52

BACKWATER BEAUTY

"Oh, for God's sake, you're fucking unbelievable. You know who I mean. Susannah. Susannah Fox, or whatever the hell her name really is."

"Er …" says Eve, "I really don't know who you mean."

"Your sister. Or, at least, she said she was your sister. At the funeral."

"We hired actors for the funeral, no one was told to play the part of my sister. I never had a sister."

"I know!" I say.

"Susannah Fox," she says, "was a made-up name for my fake will. It was a red herring."

"No," I say, "Denise was real. She lived with me. We were together after you died. She helped me through it."

Frank is shaking his head and I want to punch him again.

"No one entered or left your house for the whole week after Eve's funeral," he says.

"Don't be ridiculous," I say. "I'm mind-fucked enough now, stop playing around. I thought I'd fucking killed her. Do you know what that does to someone?"

The room stares at me. Silence. Frank clears his throat.

"Did anyone else see her, speak to her?" Eve asks, looking around. Everyone stares blank-faced.

I rack my brain. She never seemed to be around for introductions. She wasn't around for much. She never ate anything. She had no ID.

Frank steps forward. "She doesn't exist, man. I have been following you every second and you haven't killed anyone."

"Have you checked your apartment?" I ask Eve. "Her body is there."

"We checked it," she says, "full of thinners and turpentine. No body. Certainly no dead body."

"If I'm so deranged, then how do I know this is happening? How do I know I'm not lying somewhere, catatonic, dreaming all this up?"

"This is happening," says Eve, touching my arm, looking into my eyes. "This is happening."

I look around the room.

"What about Francina?" I say, "Was she in on this too?"

Eve shakes her head.

"I tried everything to get her to co-operate but she refused.

Said it wasn't right. She wouldn't even give us your house key." She pulls silver out of her pocket and jingles my spare keys at me. "Luckily I had my own."

"What did you do with her?"

"Don't say it like that," she says, "don't say it like I am some kind of Godfather who makes people disappear."

"What did you do with her?"

"I sent her on a paid holiday. I told her she could choose her destination. She flew back from Mauritius yesterday."

I take a deep breath.

"It was never meant to get so complicated," she says.

"Famous last words."

"I'm sorry. It spun out of control. It was a risk I took. I just thought, like you have often told me, that if you don't risk anything, you risk everything."

"Yes," I say. "Although I didn't quite mean for you to risk my life."

She touches me again, I flinch. She bites a nail.

"I went too far."

I take a breath, and look long and hard at Eve. Magic woman, witch, porcelain doll, back-from-the-dead. Stolen mantle of Master Puppeteer.

The real Backwater Beauty.

"Thank you for saving my life," I say, "but I never want to see you again.

"Writing is not life,

but I think that sometimes it can be a way back to life."

– *Stephen King*

53

MORE TO LIFE

My father runs to catch up with me as a leave the police station.

"Slade," he calls, and I ignore him, keep walking. He catches my arm. "Let me drive you home."

I acquiesce. I don't have a choice.

In the car, he says, "I take responsibility for the part I played in this. But I didn't realise the extent of it. All Eve asked me to do was call her if you ever showed up, which I did. I knew you two were friends. She said it was to protect you. All the rest of it was nonsense."

That may be the understatement of the year, but I take his point.

"But what happened between me and you today, that was real."

I look at him; familiar hands gripping the steering wheel, flushed face concentrating on the road.

I realise in that moment that there is more to life than writing.

"Yes," I say, "That was real."

He drops me off outside my house and tosses me the house keys. It's strange to be back. To be in such a familiar place, feeling so different. So altered. On the outside, everything looks almost the way I left it. The window has been replaced, the front wall bright with a fresh coat of paint. Again I am surprised that the roof is not missing, the walls are not knocked down. But inside: inside it has been Francinarised. I stand open-armed, breathing in the smell of furniture polish and bleach. There is a visitor on the couch, someone who took the liberty of moving in while I was away. Munchkin looks at me, bored, stretches, and goes back to sleep. I walk through to the kitchen. The place is spotless and shiny. The huge refrigerator is well-stocked and restored to its previous magnificence. There is a flower garland on the kitchen table, and a note written in Francina's spidery scrawl. "Bless You, Mister Harris."

I put the garland around my neck and glide through to my den. Everything is in its place. I take a new Moleskine off the bookshelf, sit down, and uncap my pen. I open the book up on the first blank page and I start writing.

54

INSIDE OUT

And then of course there could be a fourth ending. A real ending. How wonderful it would have been, how neat, if Eve were miraculously alive again and she loved me – enough to wreck my life, teach me meaning. To have the troops rallying around me, to have been willing to turn my life upside-down, like a game, like a too-clever film. In fact, I may well have seen the device used in a movie a long time ago, and it resurfaced while I was having my 'episode'. It's an ending only a smug writer could come up with. Too-tidy, contrived. Desperate: down to the repainted front wall, the cat, the flower garland. It would have been good for the old Slade, the pre-fucked, pre-confession, pre-jail Slade, but it won't do for me now. I feel different, turned inside out. A neat ending will no longer do.

"Can I get more paper?" I ask the guard. I have used up the SAP issue notepad they gave me earlier – hours (days?) ago. Once he snorts and obliges I take a breath and begin again. The real ending isn't as pretty and it's the last thing I will ever write.

55

INVISIBLE LEASH

I hear the ghost's high heels clacking towards me and I don't look up until they stop outside my cell. I look up just enough to see a beautiful pair of shoes. Denise. The guard makes a show of taking out the keys and opening the heavy metal door. She strides in, bloodlipsticksmile.

"I thought you were a ghost," I say, putting down my pen. "I thought you didn't exist, that I had made you up."

She runs a slow finger through my hair.

"You did make me up," she says, "in a way."

I shake my head. I want to dash my head against the bed frame, crack my skull, let the demons out.

"I strangled you. You stopped breathing."

"No, I didn't stop breathing. It was a game we played. Don't you remember that?"

"I remember trying to make you stop talking, squeezing too hard."

"If that were true," she says, "I wouldn't be here right

now."

"Are you here?" I ask.

"What do you think?"

"Honestly, I'm not sure."

"That's good enough, for now."

We sit and look at each other for a long while.

"You still don't recognise me, do you?" she smiles.

I rub my eyes, stare at her. I see a flashing of faces. A dark corner. A kitchen knife. She takes off her black wig and shakes out her red hair. Peels off her eyelashes.

The world cracks open. "It can't be," I say with my heart beating out of my chest.

She wipes off her red lipstick, leaving a messy, stained mouth. Blood-grin.

"Oh, it is. Have I changed that much? Or it is because you hardly ever actually looked at me when we were dating? All I've had done is a nose job."

She pauses a while, her cheeks colour. "And my lips. I had my lips done. And my boobs. But that's all. You still could have recognised me, for God's sake."

My cheek and mouth muscles go slack. The temperature in the room drops.

"It can't be," I say. "You were supposed to be the red

herring."

Her blue irises flare.

"Fuck you," she says. No one can quite deliver that line like PsychoSally.

I look at the concrete floor, trying to piece the last few days together. Another pair of shoes arrives: tan loafers, wet grass.

"Hey buddy," says Frank. Kicked-puppy eyes.

"You got to Frank," I say.

"I didn't *get to* Frank, I've always *had* Frank. That stupid soccer club of yours was my ticket in." She rests a hand on her hip. "You weren't at all suspicious? He's no soccer player. He's built like a prop for God's sake. I had to pay him double when he actually had to play."

Frank dumb-shrugs.

"And if that didn't tip you off, you should have been suspicious when someone actually made friends with you. I mean, it's a pretty rare occurrence, taking your personality into account."

"Well I actually …" begins Frank, before he is shoved by PsychoSally.

"Oh, shut the fuck up," she snaps, trying to blink away her irritation. "None of it matters anymore. You're going to get what you deserve and I am going to watch it happen."

I look at her, with her dark wig in her hand and coloured

contact lenses, her blonde eyelashes, cracked tattoo, fading spray-tan, and I try to see Denise, but she is gone. The venom in Sally's face has wiped out any trace of the woman I have been living with. There is cold water where my organs used to be.

"What did you do?" I ask.

"Nothing you didn't think of. When you told Frank your plan to murder Eve I couldn't believe my luck. You handed me the blueprint to your undoing. All I had to do was follow the plan. I admired your boldness. I would never have done it if it weren't for your … writing project."

"You killed Eve? Dumped her body?"

Sally laughs. "Don't be ridiculous. I'm a lady," she slaps Frank on the shoulder, "I paid this schmuck to do it."

"You're a hit man?" I ask Frank.

"Well, I prefer …"

"Shut up Frank!" she shrills.

"So you murder Eve to frame me. What about all the orchestrated details? Why would you do that? The actor at the funeral? The dodgy lawyer?"

"None of that was staged. That actor is some kind of schizo. Or crackhead. He pretends to be a new character every time I see him. Some kind of *avante-garde* acting experiment. He used to work for Eve's film studio. What can I say? That woman surrounded herself with fuck-ups. The lawyer was genuine, though. Hence the dodginess."

"Sub-Nigel?"

"I think you know the answer to that."

I dream of ripping open my shirt to reveal a wire over my nipple, or pressing 'stop' on the recorder I had been secretly stashing under my pillow, but I have neither.

"The look on your face," Sally says leaning over to kiss me, "has made it all worthwhile." Her lips are as cold as I remember.

"Come," she barks as Frank and he follows on an invisible leash. As they get to the door of the cell Sello appears.

"Mrs Ellis," he says. Sally stiffens. Sello grabs her wrists and motions at Madinga to handcuff Frank. "You have just given us ... everything ... we were waiting for."

I jump up.

Sally starts swearing, calling him a cocksucker over and over again, struggling with her new metal bracelets. Frank doesn't look surprised at all.

I can't believe this is happening. At a loss as to what to do, I put my hands on the back of my head.

"You were the wire!" I say to Sello, "you were taped to my chest hair!"

He ignores me and speaks ambush language to Madinga. I don't mind. The room spins and I have to sit down again.

After a while he turns his attention to me.

"I'm sorry we had to keep you in the dark," he says, "it was the only way to draw her out. We've been monitoring her since the vandalism episode. You aren't the only one she was threatening. You were in no danger; we had people watching you 24/7."

"How …?"

"We had people following you, and the room bugged."

I am out of words. I just nod.

He motions to my scribbled notes.

"Collect your papers. Your father is here to pick you up. He has been co-operating with us."

I remember the traitorous phone call I overheard.

"Says you will be living with him for a while … until your next book is finished."

I crumple up all the papers with their inky scratches and words and dump them into the bin. I walk out of the cell, out of the building, into the brisk air and weak light of dusk.

That, I think, will be a very long time.

ACKNOWLEDGMENTS

Thanks go to my editor, Jayne Southern, and my
proofreaders Keith & Gill Thiele.

Thank you to the following authors and publishing houses
for their generous permission to quote their
material in this work:

Neil Gaiman; The Willa Cather Foundation; Stephen
King's 'On Writing' by Pocket Books, and Peter Godwin's
'When A Crocodile Eats the Sun' by publishers Little,
Brown and Company.

ALSO BY JT LAWRENCE

The Memory of Water (2011)

Why You Were Taken (2015)

The Underachieving Ovary (2016)

Grey Magic (2016)

How We Found You (2017)

ABOUT THE AUTHOR

JT Lawrence is an author, playwright
& bookdealer. She lives in Parkhurst, Johannesburg,
in a house with a red front door.

STAY IN TOUCH

If you'd like to be notified of giveaways
& new releases, sign up for JT Lawrence's mailing list
via Facebook or on her author platform at
www.jt-lawrence.com

www.ingramcontent.com/pod-product-compliance
Lightning Source LLC
Chambersburg PA
CBHW021123260626
47169CB00005B/1426